About the Author

Angela Gould grew up on a vineyard in Australia, where the scenery fuelled her imagination. She now lives in the UK with her husband and two children. Working initially as a nurse, she later obtained postgraduate qualifications in economics and law. Although she is very busy, like all wives and mothers, the lockdowns provided time for her to produce her first novel, *The Good Suburb*.

The Good Suburb

Dear Jonathan

Angela Gould

The Good Suburb

*Thank you for your
friendly nature when
visiting,*

Angela Gould

Olympia Publishers
London

www.olympiapublishers.com
OLYMPIA PAPERBACK EDITION

A CIP catalogue record for this title is
available from the British Library.

ISBN: 978-1-80074-915-3

First Published in 2025

Olympia Publishers
Tallis House
2 Tallis Street
London
EC4Y 0AB

Printed in Great Britain

Dedication

I dedicate this book to Thomas and Charlie.

Acknowledgements

Thank you to my parents for their encouragement.

CHAPTER 1

The Dead Body

'What the hell,' Andrea says as she tries to do her first school drop-off in a new country, as there are police blocking the entrance. Her twin thirteen year old girls, Sophie and Alice, are in the back seat. They are excited at the prospect of not having to go to school and that maybe they could spend the day at the shopping mall instead.

'Coooool,' says Sophie.

'No school today!' says Alice.

'Ma'am, you can't park here,' a policeman announces.

Andrea tries to find out what is happening, but the policeman just wants her to move her car. He explains that a text message went out this morning to all the mums, telling them not to drop their kids off. But Andrea didn't receive any text message because she's new to the school.

For the police to be interested, it must be something serious, Andrea thinks. She wanted to move to the US to live in a lovely crime-free suburb in Philadelphia. It's not working out well so far.

'Please turn the car around, ma'am. We're waiting for the coroner,' he orders.

'Coroner!' Andrea knows there must be a dead body inside.

The policeman realises he's just given away some information without thinking.

'Then there's a...?' she mouths the word *body* so her daughters can't hear.

'We're trying to work here,' he says pensively.

'Okay. Okay.' Andrea turns the car around. She thought she had come to a safe place. A place far away from her job in MI5 in London. She had heard of suburbs in America where people feel safe enough to leave their front door unlocked when they go out.

Andrea was '*only an Analyst*' at MI5, as she would tell close relatives. Employees are not allowed to tell friends that they work at MI5. But she knew some things, no real details though. She analysed data and looked for patterns. Relatives thought she knew more than she actually did, about terrorism and other things. The only people who know anything in the intelligence industry were the agents.

Andrea had heard about the peaceful suburbs in the States from her in-laws. No crime. Seems hard to believe. Spring Town had the best statistics, no murders or kidnappings, no drug arrests, and good schools. *What could go wrong? she thought.*

Greg, her husband, wanted to return home to the States. He had grown up in Blaxland Village a few miles away. His parents were elderly, so he wanted to be close by. Andrea's parents were still quite young. She felt she could leave them in London where they could enjoy the theatre and the restaurants. They had plenty of money to retire with. Now, driving home, she begins to doubt her decision. *Has she done the right thing?* she wonders. *People can carry guns in this country.*

'Was this a mad decision?' she says out loud.

'Probably,' Sophie says, thinking it's mad to make children go to school so soon after arriving in a new country.

'Can we go to the mall?' Sophie asks with a fake American accent.

'Yeeeeeah, the maaaaaallll!' says Alice. The girls laugh at their attempts to speak like an American teenager.

'No. I think we'll go home, and you guys can study,' Andrea orders. That lead to groans, huffs and puffs from the teenagers.

The girls are a handful at the best of times. Alice and Sophie are very clever and have unusual habits, like entering neighbours' houses without an invitation, spying on them and moving objects around.

They also like gadgets, computers, weapons and target shooting.

Andrea calls her husband to tell him what's happened as they drive home. She is keen to get to work as she had decided to take a job that was low-risk when leaving the *security business*. As she called it. The man she bought the house from asked her if she needed a job, so it seemed to fall into her lap, a job in real estate. She needed a job, and she thought what was the worst thing that could go wrong? It seems anyone can get a job showing people around houses. They just hand over the keys and you're away. She couldn't tell them about her time in MI5. But instead, said she worked as a researcher and her colleague provided a reference on fake headed paper. Apparently, this happens all the time.

After a ten-minute drive, Andrea and the twins pull up in front of their new house. It takes her breath away again, like the first time she saw it. It is a big, white, colonial looking house with a lot of French doors wrapping around the lower floor. Shutters painted pale yellow and trees full of pink flowers. Andrea goes straight to the letter box to see if the redirection of her post from London has started working.

'Make me a cup of tea, girls,' she yells out as if the morning's drama is already forgotten.

'Yes, Mother,' the girls relay simultaneously, in posh English accents.

She watches as their hair flies about as they run up the front steps. They are both blonde and so Andrea's still not sure if she collected the right pair of twins at the hospital. She and Greg are both brunette. Reaching into the post box, there are some wooden blocks on top of the letters. She pulls them out to find that they are children's building blocks. There are many. She had found one a few days before. It said, 'I for Ice Cream'. She just thought a kid had put it there for a joke. But this time, there are many more.

'What is this?' Andrea says out loud. She wonders if they are a present or a joke. She looks around to see if anyone's watching her. An elderly lady across the road waves at her and comes over.

'Hi there,' the old lady yells while crossing the road to greet Andrea.

Andrea waves back at her.

'Hi, I'm Muriel. You must be the new neighbours,' she says.

'Yes. Hello. I'm Andrea and my husband is Greg, and the girls are…'

'Sophie and Alice,' Muriel interrupts. 'Yes, they have introduced themselves already. They seem like very nice young ladies.'

'Oh! You're the only one who has called them that,' Andrea jokes.

Muriel gives Andrea a puzzled look. Andrea realises she has said something inappropriate.

She corrects it by saying, 'Yes, they are well behaved with *other* people.'

'Children can be hard work at times,' Muriel says, as if she has also been a mother.

'Yes. Do you live here alone?' Andrea says directly.

Muriel gives her another odd look as if Andrea had been rude to ask.

'I'm a widow.'

14

'Oh. Sorry. Well, nice to meet you properly. Why don't you come over for afternoon tea one day?' Andrea says, without meaning it.

'Oh yes, that would be nice.'

'Yes. I have to get in now...' Andrea tries to get away.

'Are you working?'

'Pardon.' Andrea is irritated that she can't get away from Muriel.

'I mean are you in during the day?' Muriel insists.

'No. I'm working,' Andrea informs.

'Oh.' Muriel seems disappointed.

'I'll tell you all about it when we have tea.' Andrea keeps walking backwards towards her house as if to show Muriel that she doesn't want to talk now.

'Okay then, I'll wait to—'

'Sorry. I've had a stressful morning so I'm just going to...'.

'Yes. I heard about the school...'

'Did you?' Andrea seems puzzled that Muriel would know so quickly.

'Yes, I heard. Hopefully it's just an accident or something.'

'I must go in and set the girls some schoolwork to do.'

'Yes, nice to meet you,' Muriel says loudly.

'Yes. You too.' She escapes.

Andrea goes inside and then remembers the toy blocks. She runs out and sees Muriel walking back across the road. She grabs the blocks. There are several of them falling onto the lawn as she can't carry all of them and the post. She pulls her jumper out in front of her and throws them into it like some sort of pouch. She turns around to see if the neighbours are watching her and only sees a man walk past wearing a hoodie, smoking. He doesn't look like a neighbour, but he looks up and stares at her as he walks past. Andrea walks into the kitchen and the girls look at her struggling with her new acquisition.

'What do you have there, mother dearest?' Sophie asks.

'Well, I think someone thinks we have small children living here and they want to give us some toys... in the post box.'

'That's weird,' says Alice.

'They could have just put them on the porch though,' says Alice.

'Or knocked on the door like normal neighbours,' Andrea comments, irritated.

'Maybe they're not normal,' Sophie suggests.

'Maybe we'll find a finger in the post box tomorrow,' Alice jests.

'And a horse's head in Mum's bed,' Sophie laughs.

'Girls!' Andrea's fed up with them now. After a failed attempt to get rid of them for the day, they are now at home irritating her. The whole family has been together since they moved to the US and Andrea thought she would get some rest from them. But someone had to go and drop dead to ruin Andrea's respite.

'And a bunny boiling in the kitchen.' More humour from Alice.

'GIRLS!' Andrea yells.

'Sorry, mother,' they chant together.

Andrea reads out the letters on each block. 'Okay. So, we have... P for Pool, S for Sweets, B for Bike, M for Maze.'

'Riveting,' Sophie says sarcastically.

'I also have I for ice cream from the other day,' says Andrea.

'It doesn't make a word, or an acronym, does it?' suggests Alice.

'Or a name?' says Sophie.

'Let's see… PSBMI… makes…' Andrea is frustrated. It's a weird thing to do to place blocks in someone's letterbox. Andrea instinctively searches for a pattern in the letters as it's what she was trained for when working for MI5.

'Oh well. Probably just some random toddler roaming around in a nappy with nothing better to do,' suggests Sophie.

'Yeah. He may have escaped his horrid mother and has a backpack full of milk bottles and pureed food,' laughs Alice.

'Okay. Get your books out. You already have a lot of catching up to do,' demands Andrea.

'No. We don't,' Sophie says defiantly.

'The UK system is *far* more advanced,' Alice professes.

'You've changed your subjects,' Andrea interrupts. 'You're at a different school. It's a different system here. If you want to be known as the posh lazy girls, go ahead. But the teachers won't like you.' Andrea says all of this while pointing her finger at them both then walks out of the kitchen to call Greg again.

'Chaaarming,' Sophie mutters.

'It's rude to point,' Alice says, knowing that Andrea can't hear her.

'Probably the menopause,' Sophie suggests.

Time flew by and before she knew it, Andrea had to rush to do a house viewing with her first clients. Greg came home to mind the girls and Andrea left to go to work. They exchanged looks in the hallway and the girls ran upstairs to study.

The house she was showing was a lovely pastel grey cottage just on the edge of town. Andrea arrived there early to spray some perfume and open the windows. The house was well decorated and homely. She could easily sell this house. *It would sell itself*, she thought.

She showed the potential buyers around, room by room, and

with each room they smiled at each other, then smiled at her. She then gave the couple some space to have a look on their own. Andrea waited outside on the front lawn and made a call to the office to check her schedule for tomorrow. Her online diary was still not up and running but the day seemed to be getting better after the eventful morning. A dead body and a nosey neighbour had put her on edge.

Suddenly, just as she is disconnecting her call, she hears a scream from the house. As she rushes up the path to the front door, the couple ran out, straight past her.

'What is it?' Andrea tries to stop them to talk.

'It's haunted!' they yell as they run to their car and speed off like they are being chased by zombies.

'Haunted! What the fuck?' Andrea says out loud.

She stands there stunned for what seems like forever. She looks at the house. She looks at her phone. Andrea doesn't know whether to walk into the house or call the police. But curiosity gets the better of her and she takes a cautious step inside the front door.

'Helllooo. Is anyone there? You have just frightened off my buyers. Are you squatting? House sitting?' she asks.

She hears a noise like someone is moving around in the loft. She runs out back to the front lawn and calls her boss, Caroline.

'Hello,' answers Caroline.

'I have a weird one for you. Mr and Mrs Cooper have just bolted out of number 54 Cambridge Street, yelling that there is a ghost in the house.'

'Oh,' Caroline replies without any surprise.

'Yes.'

'They just flew out. Oh well.' Caroline sighs. 'Don't worry, honey. They seemed a bit weird. I bet they'll come back with a low offer, claiming that they need the extra cash for an exorcism,'

Caroline jests.

Andrea laughs nervously. 'Are they all weird in Spring Town?' she asks seriously.

'Pretty much,' Caroline reassures.

That evening, the family are all snuggled up on the only sofa they have, watching TV. More furniture should arrive from the UK in a few weeks.

'Put the news on. I have a text from the school saying that the police want more time to investigate. So, no school tomorrow,' Andrea says.

'Yipppeeeeeee!' the girls yell and start dancing around.

Greg changes the channel to the news.

'*A twenty-four-year-old man was arrested in New York today for planning to blow up a bank. He was a previous employee and was disgruntled when he was fired for stealing money,*' the news reporter reads.

'Get a job, loser!' Sophie remarks.

Andrea looks at Sophie disapprovingly.

'*And now for local news. A school was closed today in Spring Town because a body was discovered by the janitor in the early hours of this morning. The body has been identified as a teacher at the local school and her relatives have been notified. She was found floating in the swimming pool at eight pm. Her husband said she went missing last night but did not call the police.*'

'Jesus!' sighs Andrea.

'I knew it!' says Sophie.

'You don't get that many police cars at a school for nothing,' says Alice.

'*The police are treating the death as suspicious so if anyone has any information, please contact the Spring Town Police*'

Station.'

'So, it's *not* an accident,' Andrea says to Greg.

He shrugs his shoulders.

'This gives me the creeps. I think we should put the girls into another school until the killer is caught,' Andrea suggests.

'Let's wait and see.' Greg tries to calm her down.

'Wait! For what?' Andrea demands.

'Well, they may arrest someone. Let's give it a few days. I doubt the school will reopen this week.' Greg tries to calm Andrea.

'Yeah, I guess.' Andrea makes her way into the kitchen to make some tea.

The phone rings. It's the headmaster's secretary.

'Hello, Mrs Mitchell. We are phoning all the parents to reassure you that we are getting to the bottom of this.'

'What do you mean?' Andrea seems puzzled. The headmaster's secretary is not the police.

'Well. The only thing I can tell you is that she must have been killed *outside* the school. We all saw her leave. We had a meeting, she was present, and we all saw her leave and walk to her car at five p.m. I think she was attacked somewhere else.'

'Well. Either way there is a killer around, in the vicinity of the school, who brought the body back into the school,' Andrea argues.

'Oh, I don't think—' She tried to get a word in.

'Mrs…?' Andrea asks.

'Padmore.'

'Mrs Padmore. I understand you're trying to reassure parents, but the police will investigate.'

'It's late. We'll be in touch.' She ends the conversation abruptly.

'Okay. Goodnight,' Andrea says, knowing she's not there.

It was official. Andrea was having a bad day.

'MUM!' Sophie shouts from the kitchen.

'What, Sophie?'

'The blocks... P for Pool!'

'What?' Andrea answers irritably.

'Well, is someone trying to tell us something?' suggests Sophie.

Andrea then decides to go to bed.

'Night, all.' Andrea has given up for the evening.

'Night, Mum.'

'Night, darling,' says Greg casually, not the least bit perturbed.

Andrea tries to find a pair of pyjamas to wear to bed and then hopes for a better day tomorrow.

CHAPTER 2

The Playdate

It's eight a.m. and the girls are already up, causing havoc. They don't have to go to school today as it's closed, so they've decided to pitch a tent in the living room and watch the news channel non-stop. They have equipped their 'girl cave' with food stocks consisting of chocolate biscuits and grilled cheese on toast. Andrea comes down the stairs, looks at them, rolls her eyes and walks into the kitchen.

'Morning, darling,' Andrea says as she sees Greg.

'Morning,' he replies.

'I don't like leaving them on their own while I go to work,' she explains.

'Do you know what the other mothers are doing?' he asks.

'I don't really know them yet, but there is a group chat thing. Some of them leave their kids alone because they are thirteen and...'

'Are normal?' Greg adds sarcastically.

'Correct,' Andrea agrees.

'I just don't know what they'll get up to and they might...'

'Burn the house down?' Greg suggests.

'Exactly,' Andrea says.

'Well, call in and tell your boss. See what she says,' Greg advises.

'Okay. What are your plans?'

Greg works as a personal banker. He can hardly bring clients to his house. 'I'll check too, with Graham. Maybe we can call this annual leave.'

Andrea is nervous. She's just moved to Spring Town and doesn't know who to trust. Can she use a nanny agency? Are nannies murderers? She doesn't know the other mothers well enough to call in a favour. She has just introduced herself to them in the group chat and asked about uniforms and sports kit. Andrea decides to tell Caroline about the whole situation and gets the okay to work from home.

Greg leaves for work and the news on the TV is booming, '*A riot in New York claimed the lives of...*' Andrea's thinking that maybe they should have moved to Australia and lived in the mountains with her brother. The only things that kill you there are the spiders and snakes... and the bushfires... and the locals.

The phone rings. It's one of the mothers from the school. 'Hi, is this Andrea Mitchell?'

'Yes.'

'Hi. I'm Georgia Holland, one of the mothers from Oakville School.'

'Oh hello,' Andrea says, wondering if she should know her.

'Your phone number was circulated by the school as you are a new mum, and we'd just like to know if you'd feel like attending a coffee morning.'

'Oh!' Andrea wasn't aware of any coffee mornings.

'Sorry, it's short notice,' Georgia says in a slightly patronising manner.

'Um...' Andrea is nervous.

'It's today. This morning... at my house. You can bring your kids. Most people have no childcare arranged.'

No answer from Andrea.

'You'll get to meet everyone, and your daughters can meet the other kids,' Georgia reassures.

'Sounds great actually.' Andrea tries to sound grateful but really just wants to suss people out a bit.

Andrea breaks the news to the girls that their day of being in the girl cave will have to wait while they visit Georgia's house and try to make friends with normal people. The girls are not convinced that Andrea makes good judgments when it comes to making friends or suggesting friends for them. The girls always find something wrong with their new friends, like they have mafia parents, or they have personality disorders. Andrea finally convinces the girls that they should get dressed for a visit and meet her in the car in ten minutes.

As Andrea gets ready, her mind boggles. Will it be formal? Will it be weird? Will they be friendly? What will they talk about, besides the murder? They all jump into the family 4WD and head off. Andrea drives around the sweeping bends of the posher end of Spring Town. There are perfectly cut hedges and manicured lawns. English gardens are much less structured and wild. A lot of professional gardeners have parked up and down the road. There are vans with flowers being delivered, laundry being delivered and vans for organic vegetable and organic meat being delivered. There is a van with the sign 'Mobile Pet Baths' and another with 'Mobile Car Valet'. Andrea wonders if these people ever leave the house or is everything brought to them! The girls laugh at the writing on the vans such as *Bushes trimmed... bushes treated... bushes manicured.*

'Jeez, they sure look after their bushes here,' Sophie jests.

Eventually she finds 42 Moorcroft Avenue. It is a mansion amongst other mansions with large mature trees and neat flower beds. A lot of cars have already arrived, about eight, and Andrea feels nervous, like she's about to be interviewed.

'Oh... my... God,' the girls say in unison. They are impressed with the size of the house and are suddenly keen to get out of the car to start their playdate. Andrea drives in and is worried about where to park even though there are spaces for twenty cars.

A woman comes out. 'Hi. You must be Andrea?'

Andrea winds her window down. 'Hi. Where do you want me to park?' Andrea asks.

'Oh anywhere. Don't worry. Are these the girls?' She pokes her head in the back.

'Yes.'

'How lovely. Just park anywhere and we'll see you inside in a bit. I'm just making coffee.'

'Oh. She makes her own coffee. That's something she does herself,' Andrea murmurs.

They get out of the car and the girls run towards the front door, straight past another mother coming in with her son. They find the back door and run outside to assess the garden and pool area.

Andrea creeps into the house, clutching a bag of croissants that she brought from her larder and tries to find the room where all the noise and chatter is coming from. She looks to her right and sees that the front lounge room is full of more than ten women. It is a large room, about forty feet by twenty feet with beautiful sofas and curtains. *It was probably professionally done*, Andrea assumes. As she walks slowly in, hoping no one will notice her, everyone stops talking and turns around to look at her. She stands there and has to announce herself, as Georgia is still making the coffee.

'Hi. I'm Andrea Mitchell, we have just moved here from the UK,' she says, almost apologetically, for disturbing their perfect lives.

Andrea is then bombarded with a hundred '*Hi*'s and '*Hello*'s from various people and hands waving for her to come over and sit.

Phew, she thinks.

'Hi, I'm Antoinette.'

'I'm Maryanne.'

'Hi, I'm Geraldine.'

'I'm Nicole.'

Other mothers smile politely and say 'hi'. Georgia arrives at a room with a massive tray of coffee and Andrea looks at her wondering why 'the help' didn't carry it in.

Georgia disrupts the introductions, 'Ahh. You've met Andrea.' As she settles the tray down. 'Right. That's most people. I don't think we'll wait for any more. Let's get on with the agenda.' Georgia takes the bag of croissants from Andrea and places them next to the tray.

An agenda, Andrea thinks to herself.

'Right, Maryanne, what's first?'

Surely the murder is the first item on the agenda, Andrea thinks.

'Okay, the first item,' Antoinette announces. 'Are we still happy with the new sports uniform? The headmaster said he would phase it in, but they often say that and then—*boom*—they suddenly don't like to see the old one at all and if your kid is wearing it, then there's pressure to go and spend more money.'

'I think the new one is better, especially the cricket uniform. You couldn't tell the schools apart before,' says Antoinette.

'Yes, I guess that's important. Do we need to tell them apart though?' Georgia says as she writes that down.

They carry on and Andrea starts to have an out-of-body experience. She is suddenly involved in school matters of a school that she hasn't even been to yet because… wait for it… there's been a murder, and no one is talking about it. *When will they talk about it?* she thinks. Andrea tries to look interested, but she can see the kids playing outside and drifts off into a bit of a daydream. Is this what she's missing work for? How many of these *meetings* are going to be compulsory? Will she be ostracised if she doesn't attend them regularly?

Andrea hears splashing in the pool and some screams. She goes to the window, and so does Georgia.

'Oh, I didn't know your girls were going to swim. I haven't had the pool cleaned for a while.' Georgia looks slightly annoyed.

'Sorry. They have just assumed they would be allowed. This is swimming weather for them.

'Mmmm,' says Georgia. 'What are their names again?'

Andrea assumes Georgia is about to tell them off.

'Sophie and Alice.'

Georgia sticks her head out the window and yells, 'Sophie, Alice, there are towels in the pool house and hair dryers. Don't come in here wet, please,' Georgia says it in a nice enough tone. Andrea is relieved and embarrassed.

'They're a lively pair, aren't they?' Georgia says with minimal sarcasm.

'Sorry. They are… independent,' explains Andrea.

'Well, they'll liven the place up a bit.' Georgia seems determined not to let the pool invasion ruin their potential friendship. They re-join the other mothers who seem to have started talking about the murder.

'It's probably a heart attack,' says Geraldine.

'Or a stroke,' suggests Nicole.

'She was young though,' adds Maryanne.

'We'll have to wait for the coroner, I guess,' Andrea adds.

The other mothers on the sofas further down the room all turn around to look at her as if their heads are rotating on a screw in their necks. They don't say anything but seem puzzled that she has an opinion on the matter.

'What do you mean... Coroner?' says Antoinette.

'Umm, the policemen said "coroner"... so... and the news said...'

'Andrea,' interrupts Georgia. 'Let's heat up the croissants.' Georgia tries to get Andrea away from the group and they go into the kitchen together.

'These ladies have rose-tinted glasses,' Georgia explains.

'Oh!' Andrea is surprised by Georgia's bluntness.

'They don't want to talk about anything negative. They don't watch the news because it depresses them. They go to the gym, take their pills, work on their bodies and marry wealthy men.'

'Oh,' Andrea says to hope for more information. Even though she found Georgia to be slightly inappropriate.

'Sounds as boring as hell to me,' says Georgia.

'Mmmm,' Andrea agrees.

'There are other mothers at the school though, ones who have jobs and I'll have to introduce you to them. They are not here today because they have nannies, and they are very aware that there has been a *murder* at the school.'

'Oh, I see.' Andrea is relieved.

'I'm just trying to keep this lot from going hysterical. I've put a little something in their coffee,' Georgia says casually as if it was normal.

'Sorry... What!' Andrea is shocked that Georgia has admitted to drugging her guests.

'It's usual,' Georgia explains.

'Is it? How will they drive home?' Andrea asks.

'They don't. They sleep here on the sofas until pick-up time,' Georgia explains.

Andrea doesn't know what to say.

'They know I do it. They expect it. It's a joke that everyone knows. If there was no alcohol in the coffee, they wouldn't turn up,' Georgia reinforces.

'Gosh.'

'Yours is not spiked though because I don't know you very well and wouldn't do that to a stranger.'

'Oh. Thank you.' Andrea sighs.

'These ladies have been known to go berserk.'

'What do you mean?'

'Well. Last year, they took a dislike to the previous deputy headmaster and ganged up on him... and I mean... he was really scared.'

'Oh?' Andrea needs to know more.

'They walked into his office and threatened him about the compulsory after-school clubs. Also, at the soccer matches... well... they can get a bit physical on the side-line. And then there's the time the police were called to the school because one of the dads brought his new girlfriend to the cricket match when his wife was there, and a cat fight broke out with several of the mums involved.'

'Jeez.' Andrea is now wondering if she chose the right school for the girls.

'Yes. It was violent. I hate to say it, but they are *New Money*.'

'Oh.'

'You know. No class. No manners.'

'Gosh.'

'Yes, I'm just going to try to keep them calm so they don't bother the police or take their children out of the school. Without their funding, the school could close,' Georgia explains as if she is on the board of governors or something. Andrea really doesn't want to know whether she is or not. It has been a busy couple of days and she was now wishing that she had some alcohol in her coffee too.

They walk back into the sitting room where all the mums have nodded off. Georgia gives her a detailed run-down of their personalities and background.

'Now that's Antoinette, with the dark hair. She plays tennis and doesn't stop talking about how good she is at it. She is on her second husband and she is a bitch.'

'Oooookkkkaaay,' says Andrea, grateful for the heads-up.

'Yes, a real narcissist. She talks about herself incessantly, always must take centre stage.'

'Gosh.'

'That's Susan next to her. Her husband died and left her millions. She has nothing to do all day but insists on doing all her own housework and is as tight as a duck's ass.'

'Interesting.'

'Geraldine next to Susan. She is nice really but a little cold and aloof. She decided not to have a career and regrets that.'

'Nicole is married to a famous plastic surgeon and is constantly having work done on her face and body. She'll turn into a Barbie doll soon.

'Victoria is a rude bitch. She thinks she's better than everyone but has no real talent or achievements to back up that claim.'

'Marie is a psychopath. She's constantly going to see a therapist and has real vendettas against the other mothers. I think she tried to poison one of them once, but I can't prove it.

'Anne with the freckles is a real motor mouth. Don't get stuck talking to her or you'll never get away. She has mild Tourette's syndrome.'

'Wow,' Andrea says whist thinking that she has definitely

chosen the wrong school.

'Shall I go on?' There were more mothers dozing on various antique sofas that needed to have their stories told but Georgia could see the blood draining from Andrea's face.

'Basically, just watch your back is what I'm saying,' Georgia warns Andrea.

'Yes, I will, thank you.'

'You look exhausted, but I swear I haven't dosed your coffee. Do you want to lie down?' Georgia offers.

Andrea is wondering how to get out of there and go home. She might have to use an excuse like sickness or mental illness or something. She wanders outside to check on the girls for a moment of relief and can see through the summer house windows that the girls are sitting quietly with ten other kids. The group are playing snooker and watching TV. It all appears normal. Andrea bursts in and says they have to leave as a tutor has been arranged for the afternoon, which is clearly a lie. The girls are annoyed as they have started to make friends. After several curse words from the girls, Andrea bundles them off, past the drunk mothers, into the kitchen where she finds Georgia talking to some 'help' and makes her apologies.

Once safely outside in the car and driving down the road, Andrea takes a big breath and offloads to the girls.

'What the actual fuck!' Andrea says out loud.

'Mother... language... Please,' the girls say, winding her up.

'They are the weirdest bunch of mothers I have ever met.'

'Surely they can't top the ones in the UK?' says Alice.

'Oh, they do!'

'Are you sure it's not... you?' says Sophie cheekily.

Andrea is not even worried about the insult from Sophie but explains that there is no tutor booked for this afternoon and that it was just a ruse to get out of there. The girls are excited and planning their afternoon with various acronyms so Andrea can't understand them. The twins had devised their own military terminology to confuse Andrea and Greg. It's not as if they come from military parents. For example, TIT means Tent in front of TV. Please COCK is to place the Crisps On Couch Kindly. PENIS is Pizza Evening with Nachos In Sauce... etc.

The drive home seems to take forever even though it's not far. The girls wind Andrea up further with their opinions and theories. They are very curious and notice things that others don't. They like to hypothesise and show-off their cleverness. On the way home, they try to draw Andrea into a discussion of a comparison between humans and chimpanzees.

'Mother...'

Andrea doesn't know which one said that but doesn't reply.

'It seems that even though we have evolved from chimps millions of years ago... we still behave like them,' explains Sophie.

Andrea says nothing.

'Yes. No matter how much money a family has... they still have the usual monkey toys in the garden... such as a tree house and swings,' Alice adds.

'And all kids want to be swung around by their parents, like monkeys, and bounce on a trampoline,' Sophie explains.

'Yes. Try swinging a dog or cat,' Alice says to Sophie as she knows her mother is not interested.

'And adults like to swing in hammocks,' Sophie points out.

'Grandparents like rocking backwards and forward on a rocking chair... why do we need this movement?' asks Alice.

'Yes, and think of the equipment at schools too; the monkey bars, the parallel bars for gymnastics...' Sophie points out, as Andrea is still not responding.

'What about the roller coasters at theme parks? Why do we enjoy that?'

'Swing rides, merry-go-rounds?'

'Why is bungee jumping a sport?'

'Humans like to be thrown about. It's a fact,' states Sophie.

'It's a mystery,' Andrea butts in. It seems she *was* listening.

'We haven't evolved *that* much. Think of the food we eat too. Some of our favourite things are peanut butter and bananas,' explains Alice.

'We're not that similar to monkeys,' Andrea says and is annoyed now. 'If you keep spouting off about evolution in the US, you will annoy the religious people.'

'We beg to differ,' says Alice as she speaks for both of them. 'I think if adults swung around more, they wouldn't need anti-depressants,' Alice whispers to Sophie, but loud enough for Andrea to hear.

'I bet that's true. It gives you a rush and grown-ups probably miss it,' says Sophie.

'We should tie Mum to the swing when we get home,' Alice suggests.

'Good plan,. That might cheer her up,' agrees Sophie.

CHAPTER 3

The Stalker

It's Wednesday and Andrea walks down to the kitchen to find the girls have erected TIT again, Tent in front of TV. They pop their heads out to ask if they might be going to school. They watch as Andrea looks at her phone. The headmaster has sent another text around to all the parents, reading, '*Police are still working at the school. Do not try to drop your children off this morning. Please await further instructions. The police will be interviewing some parents so please do not leave town without informing the police.*'

The girls see Andrea put one hand on her forehead and have surmised that there is no school today and fist-punch the air. Andrea informs the girls, eats, showers and says goodbye to Greg. He's going to work from home to make sure the girls don't terrorise the neighbourhood and hold people captive in their TIT.

Walking to the car, Andrea calls Caroline to let her know that she will come into the office today as she has no house viewings. As she approaches her car, she sees a jigsaw piece on her windscreen held down by a wiper. It has a picture of a girl's face on it. She thinks it's weird but jumps in the car anyway and puts the piece in the glove compartment. Driving along to work Andrea thinks about how everything is new to her here; the roads, the food, the washing detergents. She smells her clothes knowing they have a foreign smell but wishing they didn't. *What else will be new?* She thinks to herself. But in some strange way, she is still glad that they moved from England. It's a chance to start over and she can start over with Greg. He had been distant for the past few years, as he grew more and more tired of England. He hadn't really made any friends in London. He had acquaintances to go to the pub with, but whenever he asked someone over for dinner, they seemed to find an excuse not to make a definite date. Andrea always knew that people just tolerate Greg.

Andrea arrives at work, having day-dreamed her way there, remembering to drive on the 'wrong' side of the road. Getting out of the car at work, she notices a man in the carpark with a hoodie pulled up over his head. He turns his back on her when she looks at him, which makes her feel uncomfortable and she quickly goes inside. Once she gets into her office, she looks out the window. He is still there, looking up but not directly at her, as if he doesn't know where her office is. She hides behind the window blinds anyway.

Caroline comes bursting into Andrea's office. 'Great you're here. You can meet the team.'

Andrea quickly forgets about the man and looks forward to the first meeting. She wants to be part of a team and just assumes that Americans would be welcoming.

'There's a meeting room down there.' Caroline points to the end of the corridor 'Room twenty-four and we'll have our weekly meeting at eleven a.m. Don't worry, they don't bite,' says Caroline cheekily.

'Okay.' Suddenly, Andrea's not so keen.

Andrea had brought more things to settles into her new office. She has brought a plant and some photos of the girls for her desk, her own stationery, pens etc. She manages to fill the time before the meeting by checking emails, her online diary is now working, and finds where the coffee machine is.

It's eleven a.m. and Andrea is anxious. *Will they be drinking coffee with alcohol?* She wonders. Andrea has met people individually at work, in passing, but hasn't met the whole team yet. She starts to remember her theory of office politics. There is always 'one of every type' in the office setting. There's always one narcissist, one arsehole, one nice person, one backstabber, one liar and one pathetic individual who has a nervous breakdown and ends up in an asylum. No wonder she's anxious when she knows what she's in for. Regardless, Andrea enters the room, exuding fake confidence.

'Hi, I'm Andrea. I'm new,' she says as she attempts to sit down.

'Oh no, not there. That's where Clive sits,' says a brunette, in her twenties.

'Okay. Is here okay?'

'Umm yes,' says the brunette.

'Where are you from, Andrea?' asks a man opposite her

'The UK. London.'

'Oh, that's nice.,' he replies.

'Nice and violent.' Andrea tries to make a joke because she's nervous.

'Really?' says another staff member.

'Well…' Andrea attempts to qualify her joke when Caroline enters the room.

'Hi, everyone. This is Andrea Mitchell, and she is here on a permanent part-time basis, seeing as we need to ramp things up a bit.'

Andrea receives a lot of '*Hi*'s and '*Hello*'s from around the table and people yelling out their names to her.

'Let's kick off because we have a lot to go through. Firstly, we should have a drink night for Andrea to welcome her, so can someone organise that?' Caroline orders.

'Yep,' says someone.

'Okay. Now... sales are semi-good for the houses that we know would sell. For the houses that we knew wouldn't sell... we need to come up with a strategy otherwise they will sit on our books.'

'Mmmm,' says everyone from around the table.

'Let's start by talking about the elephant in the room,' Caroline says pensively.

Andrea is wondering whether she's going to talk about the murder at the school... but no!

'There have been stories about houses being haunted. About things moving around the rooms. This is a very superstitious community, and we need to give them a message that these houses are safe to live in if they want to upsize,' says Caroline.

'Things moving around?' Andrea asks.

'Yes. Some people have said that things have moved in front of them. There could be someone playing tricks on us. So can people have a good look around their properties and check that we're not being sabotaged. It may be our competition down the road,' Caroline suggests.

'Yes,' says a man at the meeting.

'Or just kids,' a woman suggests.

'Check that no one is living there. It may mean going up into the loft,' Caroline asks.

'Are we covered by the insurance for that?' Andrea asks.

'Yes, darling,' Caroline reassures.

'A lot of kids have left home from here, from Spring Town.' Caroline turns to Andrea to bring her up to speed on the gossip in Spring Town and how it affects the real estate industry.

'Really!' says Andrea. *How much weirder will this get*? She thinks to herself.

'Yes, it's like they just go. They leave a note for their parents,' says another woman at the table.

'It's weird,' says someone else. She had forgotten their names.

'Then their parents leave the area, and no one wants to live in those houses. It's like the house has a curse or something,' explains Caroline.

'It doesn't help that a girl was found drowned with her leg caught in the bicycle wheel. The parents moved away. No one wants their house either,' Clive divulges. Then wishes he hadn't. 'There seems to be a dark cloud over the town,' he explains.

'Gosh.' Andrea is shocked.

'Yes, and what was weird was that her backpack had cocaine in it,' says a man at the table.

'Mark... don't,' Caroline says, as she didn't want him to scare Andrea.

'Really. I guess teenagers can get into drugs,' says Andrea, trying to stay calm.

'She was twelve,' Mark says.

'Twelve!' yells Andrea.

'Mark, you'll scare her away,' shouts Caroline. 'The police are still investigating. I guess they don't want the drug dealers to know that they are on to them. So, you won't hear much in the news about it.' Caroline reassures Andrea that things are being looked into.

Great. So, there are drug dealers in Spring Town, Andrea thinks.

Andrea drifts off into another daydream and before she realises, the meeting is over and she doesn't know what she's missed. She doesn't really care though. Instead, Andrea goes back to her office and starts searching for other schools that her girls could attend.

The afternoon drags on. She makes phone calls and books

house viewings. Andrea leaves the office at four p.m. and plans to do the rest from home. She takes the stairs to the underground car park. Having forgotten about the man in the hoodie she is shocked to see him again, or another man... she's not sure... in a hoodie, smoking in the carpark. She freezes for a second then keeps walking to her car. He doesn't see her, and she manages to get into her car and lock the doors in one smooth choreographed swoop. She starts her car, and he turns his head to look at her.

'Fuck,' she says quietly. She tries to act normally and drives out of the carpark, trying to look at him out of the corner of her eye on the way past. He looks like that man who was watching her when she got the blocks out of the mailbox the other day.

Why does he stare? she thinks.

'What the fuck?' she screams once she's turned the corner. 'What is it with this town?'

She calls Greg.

'Hi, hon—,' he says

Before he can finish his words, she yells at him.

'Some weird guy is following me.'

'Are you sure?' He has recently been unimpressed with her level of paranoia.

'YES,' she yells.

'Well. Come home and see if he follows you,' Greg says, in a vague attempt to give her some advice.

'Nooooooo. I don't want to do that,' she yells back in a critical fashion.

'Well... go somewhere... shopping... and see if he follows.'

Andrea's not impressed with Greg's advice and decides to go straight to the police station because she would feel safe there. She looks in the rear-view mirror and can't see a car or a bike following her. Andrea finds the police station by using her sat nav. Pulling up outside the station, she looks behind her and waits for a few seconds before unlocking the door and running into the station. There is only one person at the desk who is just finishing with the duty sergeant.

'Excuse me,' she interrupts the duty sergeant as he fills in some forms.

'Yes, ma'am,' he says without looking up.

'I think there is someone following me,' she explains calmly.

'Are you sure?' he asks, again without looking up.

'Yes. He was waiting outside my office all morning and he looked at me strangely. It's hard to explain but I think he's been watching me before, at my house. I get this funny feeling that someone is watching me quite a lot.'

'I see.' The duty sergeant finally lifts his head and looks at her. He looks her up and down in his effort to assess her mental state.

'Yes. There's a man with a black hoodie who I've seen two or three times and—'

'Let me just stop you there, ma'am. Two or three times does not constitute stalking,' the sergeant patronises.

'So, I should wait until he follows me a few more times?' she questions.

'Ma'am. I'm busy. With *real* stalker cases and trust me if you were being stalked, you would *know* it… you wouldn't just *think* it… or *sense* it… Now, I'm very busy here so if you would like to let me know when you are *sure*—' he tries to finish his sentence.

'Yes, I can imagine you're very busy in this town.' Andrea demands his attention.

'What is that supposed to mean?' He is annoyed now.

'Well with all the drug dealing, murders and drownings, I bet Spring Town's finest are run off their feet.'

'Keep your voice down, ma'am.'

'Why? Is it a secret?' she says sarcastically.

'Listen,' he whispers.

'No. You listen. I worked in intelligence in the UK so get me a bloody detective because I have a series of questions about this weird town,' she whispers all of this with her face very close to his screen.

'Okay. Okay.' He relents and picks up the phone while looking her up and down again in a confused manner. He calls someone and says there's a lady from an intelligence agency in the UK her name is... He looks up at her. Andrea tells him her name. He waits for a few seconds then puts the phone down.

'Take a seat, ma'am.'

She sits down and the duty sergeant keeps looking at her over his glasses. She starts to question herself again. Is she paranoid? *Greg could have been a bit more helpful,* she thinks..

There are people sitting around her. They look normal but they don't make eye contact. Andrea remembers being followed in London sometimes. She was sure she was being followed along the Thames near MI5 but could never prove it. Her boss was very good to her and arranged for a car to pick her up and drop her home each day until she finally freaked out and left.

After about ten minutes, a good-looking, man walks towards her in the police station waiting area. He is maybe Italian. Well shaven. Tall. 'Hi, I'm Detective Cameron,' he says holding his right hand to her.

'Hi. I'm Andrea Mitchell.'

'Come this way.' They start walking down the hallway to his office.

'You're living here now or just visiting?' he asks.

'I'm trying to settle here, but there's been so much going on...' They walk into his office.

'Coffee?' he offers.

'No thanks.' She's frightened of offers of coffee now.

'Take a seat.'

'Firstly, I think someone's stalking me.'

'Okay, how—?'

She cuts him off by saying. 'I think that there could be a kid trying to send me messages. Is there a child missing at all?'

'Umm, no. But... kind of...' he tries to explain.

'Kind of?' Andrea asks.

'I can share this with you as I've just been in touch with your London office.' He had checked that she worked for MI5 whilst she was in the waiting area.

'Oh, I don't work there any more really.'

He looks at her strangely and sits down and starts to explain things to her about Spring Town. Andrea is on the edge of her seat and quickly forgets about the stalker.

'Some kids have run away. They write to their parents, but the parents don't really know where they are. It's very worrying. They are mostly older teenagers, sixteen, seventeen, and could support themselves, but they are still technically missing... and we don't know where they are.'

'Okay. The day that the teacher was found in the pool, someone put children's alphabet blocks in my letterbox. The blocks read letters P for Pool, amongst other letters,' Andrea explains.

'I see.' Detective Cameron seems genuinely interested.

'It could be a coincidence.' She says, not wanting to come across as paranoid.

'Yeah, but thanks for sharing. Anything else?' he asks.

'I work in real estate and my boss thinks that people could be living in the lofts of the empty houses. We were going to search them. I don't know if you're interested in helping us.'

'Yes. If you want,' he says. 'Does she think kids are living in these houses?' he asks.

'Well, there are noises, things moving. So, it's plausible,' she explains.

'I see.' He seems concerned.

'I must sound crazy to you.' She smiles and hopes that she hasn't said too much too soon.

'No. It's the little things that help in detective work.'

'I'm really worried about the murder though.' Andrea fishes for information.

'Yes, I can't disclose anything about that.'

'Are you close to finding the killer though?' she asks.

'I can't say, Mrs Mitchell. Have you had any other messages or puzzles given to you?'

'Well, ummm, there was a picture of an octopus on my front door mat the other day. I didn't think anything of it at the time but the tentacles sort of look like a map of some sort.'

'Right,' he says as if Andrea has just confirmed a thought in his mind. He reaches for his phone.

'Um and someone put a jigsaw puzzle piece on the bonnet of my car this morning. It was a piece of a girl's face.'

'Okay.'

'You probably think I'm mad.' Andrea is still embarrassed about what she is saying. It could just be kids messing with her.

'No, not at all. My girlfriend works with missing persons and has a theory about puzzles. I want you to meet her and show you what you have so far.'

'Who is she?

'Hang on.' He calls his girlfriend. 'Natalie... I have someone here I want you to meet. Yeah, I think you'll find her interesting... Okay, okay... mm. Okay.' He hangs up. 'Can you meet her tomorrow, like for a coffee at the diner down the road?'

Detective Cameron explains how to recognise Natalie and they say goodbye.

Andrea walks down the corridor then turns around and has to say one more thing to Detective Cameron. She is glad he is still there in the doorway.

'Detective Cameron,' she says, and he looks up from some papers he has in his hand. 'I heard about the drowned girl too. Is it true that her backpack full of cocaine and was only twelve years old?' she asks.

He looks sad and nods his head. They share a concerned look and then she turns to leave.

Andrea leaves the police station and forgets that there could be a stalker following her. She drives home. Her head is full of questions. At the traffic lights, she texts Greg saying, '*Been to the police. Can we upgrade the home security?*' Her phone makes a sound as if he has responded, but she doesn't care to look at it. Andrea has a low threshold for going to the police. In the UK, she would notice things and call the police whilst driving along. If there was a lorry at the side of the road, with lots of bottles of water and leftover food near it on the ground, she would presume that it was full of asylum seekers who had been left there by their driver to freeze in the cold. Sometimes, they were abandoned beside the road because the driver had been paid already. She would also notice when someone was acting suspiciously. A man walking along the road in a suit with a briefcase, but looking up at every open house window, is a potential burglar in her mind, particularly if they are wearing trainers with the suit. There is no real training for being observant. Andrea had studied criminology at uni but didn't know if it would lead to a job. She was good with puzzles and cryptic crosswords. That's how she got the job at MI5, scoring highly in an intuition test when she applied. There were loads of uni graduates there from many different specialities, all hoping to be offered a job.

Andrea arrives home and can't be bothered to look in the mailbox again. Another letter or clue will just keep her up all night. The girls have ordered pizza so there is no need to cook. Andrea flops down in front of the TV with Greg and the girls and they all watch *Seinfeld*. Just another normal day!

CHAPTER 4

The Bugging

Andrea awakes after a night full of bad dreams. She keeps forgetting how cheese on pizza gives her nightmares. One of her dreams involved her girls with backpacks full of cocaine and they were riding their bikes around and around the front garden in a figure of eight, near the rose bushes. In the dream, Greg is chasing them saying 'Don't do it.' And Georgia, the coffee spiker, is chasing them also and yelling out formulas for making crystal meth. *How weird*, she thinks. Another nightmare involves the stalker, who eventually catches up to her and she stabs him in the eye with a pen. He pulls it out of his eye and just walks away. There was another nightmare, but she can't quite remember it.

The girls start acting up first thing in the morning.

'Mum. I think I'm pregnant,' says Sophie.

'WHAT?' Andrea says.

'Look, it's a food baby,' Alice says, pointing at Sophie's tummy which is poking out.

'You get it from messing around with chocolate cake,' says Sophie.

'Strawberry tarts can give you a food baby,' laughs Alice.

'And cream doughnuts,' Sohpie adds

'None of them can be trusted.'

'I think it was the gingerbread man...,' says Sophie.

'No, it was the ice cream man in the van who got you

pregnant,' says Alice.

Andrea ignores them and pours her coffee into the sink, grabs her keys and bag and waves goodbye to the girls sarcastically as if she is glad to be going to work. She opens the door to Louise, a newly acquired tutor. who was about to knock and says, good morning' to Andrea.

Andrea comes close to saying, '*No, the fuck it isn't*,' but her English manners override her and she manages to say 'Morning,' in a high pitched tone, then shuffles past to escape for the day.

Louise enters the kitchen where she finds the girls in hysterics, holding their abdomens, because they're laughing so much. She asks them what is so funny, and they start on her with their food baby jokes.

Andrea's frustration at her cheeky children is quickly forgotten when she remembers that she has a meeting with the mysterious Natalie today. Halfway down the drive, she stops the car and jumps out to check the mailbox again for clues before pulling out of the drive. There's a jigsaw piece of a train tunnel. Again, Andrea is not sure if someone is messing with her. She jumps back in the car and puts the new clue into her bag with her others that Detective Cameron told her to bring to show Natalie.

Andrea heads for the diner. She feels a bit weird that she's going to a diner instead of a detective's office. Either way, at least someone wants to listen to her. *But who is Natalie? Is she a real cop or maybe FBI?* Andrea's imagination goes wild with images of Natalie having maybe a foreign accent and dark sunglasses, a dark suit with guns bulging out the sides, and a slim waist.

The diner is a 1950s style; long caravan, silver metal sheeting on the outside, something that's rare in the UK. These diners are everywhere in the US. Andrea parks and enters up the steps. She spots a typical waitress dressed in a 50s style uniform with a name badge '*Sally*'. The walls are plastered with various pictures of American desserts and old movie stars. Andrea is not sure how she will recognise Natalie. She sits down in the last seat at the very end, away from people so they can talk privately when Natalie eventually gets there.

After five or ten minutes, a woman enters the diner and looks straight at Andrea. She walks towards her past all the other customers as if she already knows who Andrea is. She is slim, wearing a dark pants suit and has long flowing brown hair past her shoulders.

'Hi, I'm Natalie Bellino,' she says in a foreign accent.

'Hi. I'm Andrea Mitchell.' She holds out her hand and they shake hands.

Natalie sits down.

'How did you know it was me?' Andrea asks.

'You're the only one here who looks out-of-place,' Natalie explains.

'Oh.'

'Yes. I hear someone has been sending you puzzles.' Natalie's accent sounds Italian.

'Yes. But first I went to see Detective Cameron because someone was stalking me.'

'Oh.'

'Yes. But I'm not sure if it's all connected.'

'What is?' asks Natalie.

'The puzzles. The stalking. The murder in the pool.'

'Murder?' Natalie says calmly as if she already knew about it.

'Yes. The murder at my kids' school, in the pool, of a teacher reflects one of the puzzles sent to me. I think the puzzles are sent by children. Children have gone missing from Spring Town.

Children may be living in the houses that I show as a real estate agent. I am new here and I think someone wants my help or wants something else... I don't know... Then I heard at work yesterday that a twelve-year-old girl drowned with a backpack full of cocaine,' Andrea stops to take a breath.

'Yes. That's a lot of things you have on your mind,' Natalie says in a supportive manner.

'Yes. Detective Cameron said you are working on missing people and puzzles...' Andrea asks.

'Yes. He said you worked at MI5.'

'I worked there, though as an analyst.'

'Look, I think I can trust you considering your background. I work in a special branch of the police force. It's mostly missing persons unit, but it touches on murder and drugs. Puzzles have been sent to other families too. They appear to be childlike, you know... toys and games. They are not sent to the police though.'

'Really?'

'Have you brought me some to look at?' asks Natalie.

'I have brought these things for you.' Andrea empties her bag on the table. 'The octopus is weird. I don't know what it means. But it looks like a map,' Andrea explains, and Natalie agrees. 'They bend at right angles here and here,' Andrea explains.

'Yes, it could be. I need to check the archives at the station, the roads, the subways etc. Okay, thanks. What else do you have?' Natalie is fascinated.

'"I" for ice cream was just put in my post box... mailbox, on the first day we got here and I just remembered it this morning. Does it mean anything to you?'

'It's possible. Ice cream vans could be used for drug trafficking. Children get involved in selling ice cream at the local fairs and school events too.'

'Really? And these were put in my post box a few days ago P for Pool, S for Sweets, B for Bike, M for Maze...'

'I've seen other puzzles that could also be a message.'

49

'Blocks?' Andrea asks.

'Well, yes, usually a picture or a letter. Not just a toy.'

'Do you want to take these? I have jigsaw pieces of a girl's face and a railway tunnel this morning.'

'It's fascinating that you picked up on this. Most people would have ignored it. I really need you to be my liaison, to get close to the mothers... to work for me... spy for me... just watch them. Their routines.'

'Ummm.' Andrea is overwhelmed. She didn't know she would be getting involved.

'It's important and I don't have enough staff to watch them,' Natalie insists.

'Ummm. But can't you tap their phones or triangulate... or something?' Andrea is not sure how much help she will be or even if she wants to.

'Yes. Their phones are tapped. But they say very little over the phone. Can you get a bug into their cars and houses? I've tried to but they're always at home.'

'I guess so.' Andrea isn't sure why the other mothers would be involved.

'Maybe even the place where they do yoga. Then listen to it in the evenings after work. Tell me what they talk about. Don't give up the real estate job though. It's a good cover.'

'Ummm.' Andrea would rather run a mile from this town.

'And get a burner phone. Call me on that when you want to meet.'

'Ummmm.'

'Are you frightened?' Natalie asks.

'No. Yes. But strangely excited.'

'I'm so glad you came to live here.'

'I'm not,' says Andrea seriously.

Natalie laughs and orders some coffee and pie.

'We think that children are hiding here somewhere and sending us messages. We've looked in the vacant houses and found nothing. It's as if they are frightened of the police too,' Natalie explains. 'The problem is that we don't know what they are hiding from. It's as if everyone is guilty here,' Natalie divulges.

'In what way?'

'Well, the people are weird.'

'That's for sure,' Andrea agrees.

'I don't know if you've noticed but the children rarely look like their parents. I don't know if there's a lot of sperm donor children here. It's just a theory,' Natalie says.

'Gosh?' Andrea is strangely interested and hangs on Natalie's every word.

'There could be dodgy adoptions. I have so many theories and haven't ruled anything out. Anything is possible in Spring Town. It's so weird.'

'That's for sure.'

'There is some gossip that unmarried mothers are told that their children have died after birth, but they are really handed to another couple on the adoption waiting list.'

'Jesus.' Andrea is shocked.

'I think the children are mixed up in some drug smuggling racket.'

'Without the parents knowing?' Andrea asks.

'I'm not sure but I think the school could be part of it.'

'What?'

'Yes, the teacher that got killed… she was a detective working undercover for me.'

'Jesus Christ. You knew her?'

'Yes. She was a lovely person and a good detective. It can't be a coincidence that she's been found dead a few weeks after I sent her there.'

'Jesus. I need to send my kids to another school.'

'No. If I'm right, all the schools are involved in this area.'

'What do I do then?' Andrea says loudly.

'*Shhhhhh*. Sign them up for home-schooling but make up an excuse to do that... say they are behind in their education or something, otherwise people may get suspicious if you're not sending them to school.'

'I think I'll go back to the UK.'

'Well, that's an option for you. But seriously, I'd like you to work with me on this, as a consultant. I can pay you. The detective who died was young and brave. I want to find the killer.'

'I don't know.' Andrea is getting very stressed. She is fidgeting and starting to sweat.

'And you are on the inside with the mothers,' Natalie persists.

'Not if they're home schooled.'

'There will be play dates and coffee mornings.'

'Oh, I've been to one already and the woman hosting it puts a little something in everyone's coffee.'

'Drugs?'

'Some sedative or alcohol. She said she was trying to keep them calm.'

'Weird,' Natalie says with a puzzled look.

'And they didn't really discuss the murder the way normal others would.'

'Yes. Nothing is normal here.'

'So, it's not just me... everyone is weird here?'

'Look, Andrea. I could really use you here. Please stay and

help us. The police chief doesn't want to know about my little theories about toys and puzzles. He could be in on it for all I know.'

'Umm.'

'I'll pay you cash out of a fund we use to pay my informants. We'll meet in secret so even the police force won't know that you're helping me.'

'Umm.'

'Come on. If children are running drugs for a cartel, I need to stop it. Something has spooked the children here and I need to get to the bottom of it. I want to find *all* the so-called missing children and help them. They could be living on the streets for all we know.'

How could Andrea refuse? She had fantasised about getting out from behind the desk whilst working at MI5 and now she can do some fieldwork. Her kids would be safe as long as they don't attend any schools. She tells Natalie she will do it then leaves to go home.

Driving home everything goes through her head. *Children pushing drugs! This town! A murdered teacher/detective. Maybe London was safer,* she thinks.

Andrea goes straight home to buy all her new equipment online. There was a great spy shop in London near Selfridges that was full of gadgets. It had cameras disguised as cans of coke. Sunglasses with binocular lenses etc. She was going to try to have some fun with this morbid situation. She spends the afternoon ordering things and then planning how to get inside some of the mothers' houses!

First on the list was Georgia Holland, the coffee spiker. She phones her from the list of contacts sent from the school when they first registered.

'Hello.' Georgia answers the phone.

'Hi, Georgia, It's Andrea.'

'Oh. Hi, we haven't scared you off then?'

'No of course not.'

'What can I do for you?'

'Yes, well, I was wondering when I could taste some of your famous coffee? Hehe.'

'Oh. You are funny. It's just a bit of Baileys. Not Rohypnol.' Andrea was shocked at her mention of the drug.

'Well, I'm new in town so...'

'Yes sure. Or I can come to you...'

Damn it, Andrea thinks. She wants to bug the house. Well, she will just have to bug her handbag instead.

'That sounds lovely.'

'Okay. Well tomorrow or Friday?'

'Yes. Friday is fine with me. Are you inviting anyone else?'

'Um. I'm not sure if I know anyone well enough to just call them up'

'Oh. Shall I bring a select few?'

'Yes. Thank you, Georgia.'

'I'll see who's around and they can meet you.'

'Okay.'

'So, what time is afternoon tea served in the Mitchell house?'

'Is two p.m. okay?'

They arrange to meet and Georgia calls a few of her friends to make up a group of them.

The next morning Andrea's surveillance equipment arrives. She has small devices that can be placed inside handbags and even small enough to be pressed onto the side of sunglasses. She has bought these in many shades of colour so they match the handbags and can't be detected. They are the size of a pin head.

'Wow, Mum's got lots of boxes arriving,' says Alice, as she tries to shake a box.

'Yes, nothing for you though.'

Sophie picks up a box.

'Give me that!' Andrea grabs it from her.

'Heeeyyy, I know this company. Are you spying on someone?' Alice asks.

The girls were once caught spying on their teachers. There was no punishment though as long as the footage was destroyed.

'It doesn't concern you.' Andrea is annoyed again.

'Tell us. Maybe we can help you,' says Sophie.

'No.'

'We have experience with this sort of thing,' Alice says in a confident manner.

'I'm sure you do. I just need to bug a few empty houses to be sure that they haven't got squatters.'

'Oh.' The girls don't believe her and look at each other as if to say *what the hell is Mum up to?*

'Yes. Someone is scaring all the potential buyers away.'

The afternoon tea date approached just as Andrea had spent time reading the instructions of her new gadgets whilst trying to bake scones.

The doorbell rings and Andrea feels nervous and starts to sweat.

'Georgia, hi!'

'Hellooooo, Andrea, I've brought a posse.'

'Great. Hi!' Several women enter her house. It is daunting

for Andrea as she hasn't met them before.

Introductions are done in the entrance. 'This is Lynette, Kate and Michelle.'

They all say '*Hi*'.

'Welcome,' Andrea says and invites them into the lounge room to sit on the sofas that had finally arrived. These women have left their children at home with nannies. They all run their own companies so can juggle coffee morning with work. They compliment her on her lovely house.

'So, Andrea. I hear you're from the UK,' says Lynette.

'Yes.'

'What part?' Kate says.

'Well, I worked in London and lived on the outskirts.'

'Really? What did you do in London?'

'I worked in insurance.'

'Really?' Michelle says

'Yes, it was a bit boring but paid well.'

'How do you like it here?' asks Kate.

'Umm I'm getting used to it. It's a lot like the UK really.'

'Is it?'

'Yes. At least everyone speaks English, and we eat similar food.' Andrea is nervous and doesn't know how to make conversation with them. *These people could be drug traffickers* , she thinks Andrea takes orders for coffee and tea and goes into the kitchen.

During the conversations, Andrea learns about these new, more interesting mums, as Georgia put it. Michelle has her own interior design company and employs two people who work in her renovated barn beside her house. Kate is a lawyer and works from home.

'What about your husband? I hear he's American,' asks

Susan.

'Yes. He wanted to return home to the US.'

'Oh,' Kate says, fishing for more.

'It's not a good time to arrive in Spring Town, is it?' says Michelle.

Andrea is surprised that someone actually wants to talk about the murder.

'I was shocked actually. Do we know any more about the teacher?' Andrea asks.

'Oh no. I was talking about the winter coming. It can be very cold,' Michelle explains.

'I don't mind the cold,' Andrea says, trying to look indifferent about the murder.

The conversation goes on with the usual boring stuff. Andrea never really did like small talk. But in Spring Town they specialise in it. Eventually Andrea gets her first opportunity to plant a bug. Kate wants to go to the bathroom and leaves her handbag beside the sofa. The other three are jabbering away and Andrea tried to distract them so she can reach down and stick the bug on the inside of the bag. She gets them to look at the garden and as they all glance out the window she quickly leans down and plants the bug. Just then Michelle turns around but doesn't suspect anything.

'What have I missed?' says Kate, who re-enters the room.

Andrea starts to sweat. *Did she see me? That was a quick loo trip. Is she planting a bug on me in my bathroom?* Andrea says to herself. But Kate sits down as if nothing has happened.

'Are you okay, Andrea?' says Georgia.

'Yes. Just felt a bit tired.'

'There's no alcohol in the tea, is there?' Georgia jests.

'No.'

The ladies all laugh.

'So, you know about the boozy coffee mornings?' says Michelle.

'We're usually working first thing in the morning when Georgia has them. So it's lovely to have an afternoon thing so we could attend,' says Kate.

The ladies all talk about themselves as a way of informing Andrea that they are semi-important in the community. Andrea settles into the conversation and feels more relaxed. *Would these women really be allowing their kids to push drugs?* Andrea sits there thinking, whilst pretending to be listening. Regardless, Andrea is feeling pleased with herself as she has planted her first bug. They discuss the after-school club. Apparently, the headmaster drops them home afterwards. *How weird is that?* Andrea thinks to herself.

An hour and a half passes by and the mothers start to leave. Georgia stays behind for a bit and sees the women off as if she had hosted the tea party herself. This gives Andrea a chance to plant a bug in her bag also. She chats to Georgia in the kitchen whilst cleaning up the coffee cups. Then, when Georgia is not looking, she plants a light blue bug inside Georgia's bag. *Eureka*! She thinks, assuming that she's probably going to be the best one to listen to.

Georgia leaves and Andrea collapses into a chair and tries to think of her next move. If the kids are delivering drugs, then they need to be put under surveillance. Natalie has probably tried this but maybe a tracking device can be placed on them somehow. Andrea goes back to the Internet catalogue for the spy shop. There are trackers that look like keyrings. *They could be attached to the kids' school bags,* Andrea thinks to herself. *But how do I convince them to put them on their bags? Especially when Sophie and Alice are not seeing the other kids regularly.* She scrolls down.

There is a patch that is almost invisible, and it acts as a tracker. Andrea thinks of placing it on the kids' backpacks but again… how would she get close enough? Andrea knows she needs access to these kids. She needs to create a large gathering, a party, or something, but the kids need to be in school uniform, so the tracker gets stuck to their school bag, as they're delivering drugs in their school uniform, probably.

It's impossible, Andrea thinks to herself, and she plans to follow the children one by one in the after-school period to see if they leave when they're supposed to be in an after-school club.

CHAPTER 5

The Strangers

The school has reopened suddenly. Alice and Sophie can hear the school bell ringing from their kitchen. It's the first time it has rung for a week. They are anticipating the arrival of their tutor, Louise, who has been late for the first few days. There was a weird feeling about the fact that they don't have to go to school. As Louise is late, they decide to walk down to the school to watch the kids arriving. It is a kind of morbid curiosity.

'Tardiness is a sin,' says Sophie, referring to Louise.

'Why can't she be organised like us? With a schedule that she could stick to,' says Alice.

'I know,' agrees Sophie.

'Still, what's the point of it anyway?'

'I know.'

'We should be tutoring *her*!'

'Yes. Quite so.'

Several cars start to pour into the school. The girls can see some of the kids that they met at the drunken coffee morning and are almost jealous that they are allowed to go to school. Andrea wasn't very clear on the reason they had to stay home. They just assumed it's because there is a murderer on the loose. She just said Andrea was being 'paranoid and protective' for a while until things settle down. Once outside the school, Alice and Sophie can see the children getting out of various large cars, and each one looks tired and pale. In the UK, kids usually run in and can't wait to see each other, but not here. The girls comment on how unenthusiastic everyone looks. A few of them turn around and see Alice and Sophie watching them over the fence. The girls try to wave at them, but then see the headmaster and hide.

'Have you noticed anything about these children?' asks Sophie.

'Umm, they're ugly?' Alice says seriously.

'Besides that. They don't look like their parents.'

'That's true. Yes, I had noticed. I just assumed they were all mutants or something.'

They both laugh.

'If we're going to have any friends in this country, we need to find a way of making some,' says Sophie.

'Yeah, but maybe stalking them at the school drop off is not the way.'

'Possibly.'

'What if we invite them over?' Alice suggests.

'We hardly know them though, and what if they don't like being tied up and playing "interrogation" games?'

'We can play normal games.'

'BOORRRIIIINNNGGG!' Sophie complains.

'Well, we need to try something.'

'What about joining a club with kids of similar interests?'

'We're not allowed out,' says Alice.

'We'll be allowed out soon though.'

'Let's hope.'

'I've seen a paintballing place near here. That would be fun.'

'Let's ask boys just in case the girls don't come.'

'Do you think we'll be allowed to do that?' says Sophie.

'Let's hope.'

'Have you noticed that black van keeps going past?' Sophie says.

'No. Where?'

'I think it's gone now.'

The girls feel a bit deflated and decide to walk back home to see if Louise has arrived yet.

Just as they look down at their phones, the black van slows down on the road beside them. They had always been told by Andrea to run if a car or van slows down near them.

'Be cool!' Sophie tries to warn Alice.

'What?'

'Don't look.'

'Where?'

'Three o'clock. The black van,' Sophie says.

'Fuck. It's following us from the school.'

'Hope no one's getting kidnapped.'

'It's turning around now and coming this way,' says Alice, as she uses her phone as a mirror.

'Are there batteries in your screech alarm?' Sophie whispers.

'I brought my stun gun instead.' Which is typical of Alice.

'Fuck. You brought the taser?'

'I brought the stun gun, not the taser. There's a difference.'

Sophie used her phone as a mirror also and can see the man getting out of his van and walking closer their way. He's a big build wearing black T-shirt and blue jeans. He's oldish, about fifty with grey hair, or could be sixty. She doesn't really know but is trying to memorise a description.

'Should we call the police?' asks Alice.

'They won't get here in time.'

The girls walk quicker and pretend that they're not scared. They have a fake conversation to try to put him off.

'Dad arrested someone yesterday,' Sophie says, pretending their father is a policeman.

'Did he?'

'Yes, he shot him in the head then arrested him.' Sophie tries to sound calm.

'Oh.'

'Yes, that's how he likes to do things. Shoot first and ask questions later.'

The fake conversation doesn't slow down the man who is trying to catch up to them.

He continues to walk quickly and is soon only a few paces behind them.

'Ladies, can you please tell me where...' Before he can finish his sentence, Sophie and Alice have prepared answers for him.

'Sorry, we're in a hurry!' Sophie says sternly.

'Our mum is waiting for us around the corner.'

'Can you show me where...'

'I'm afraid we can't talk to strangers.'

He puts his hand on Alice's shoulder and says, 'Hang on...' stopping her from walking.

Just then as Alice steps away from him, she flicks the safety switch on the stun gun and then lunges at his abdomen, holding it there, stunning him for a few seconds. He doesn't know what is happening to him. He yells and falls down. The girls run down the street and leave him there shaking.

'Maybe he's someone's Dad?' Sophie says while running.

'I don't think so.'

They stop when they get two streets away.

'Fuck!' says Alice.

'Well, that worked well,' says Sophie in a calm voice, trying to cheer up Alice.

'Yeah, it was good to try it out,' Alice says and they both laugh.

Just then, Andrea pulls up between the girls and the curb.

'What are you doing?' she yells.

The girls are too out of breath to answer.

'The tutor rang me to say you weren't at home. I had to turn the car around. I'm supposed to be at work.' She has no idea that a creepy man has just approached her girls.

'What are you doing at this corner?'

'Oh, the tutor was late, so we wanted to see the kids,' Sophie says.

'Why?'

'Um.'

There was no way they were going to tell Andrea how close they got to a possible kidnapper, or that they may have just stunned an innocent man asking for directions. But the fact that he placed a hand on one of them was enough for them to be scared. They would only be in more trouble if they told Andrea about using a stun gun. Alice and Sophie didn't talk on the way home. The reality hadn't sunk in even though they were strangely excited by what had just happened.

'Are you two okay?' Andrea asks, knowing that something is up?

'Yes, Mother,' they say simultaneously.

Andrea pulls into their driveway and the girls get out.

They walk inside, pensive, looking around and assessing their safety.

'I think I'll set some traps,' says Sophie.

'I was just thinking that,' agrees Alice.

'For what?' Andrea hears them.

'I'm not sure if there's mice,' explains Alice, even though she was thinking of human traps.

'Oh. Okay. If you're sure. But watch your toes in the middle of the night. I don't want you being caught in a trap!' Andrea warns. Sophie and Alice appreciate the irony of what Andrea just said.

'Louise is waiting for you guys in the kitchen.'

The girls seem strangely happy to see Louise and settle down to their lesson. By about lunchtime Alice goes upstairs and hears a noise in the loft. She decides to get a micro camera from her stash of espionage gadgets under her bed. She's thinking it's probably mice but after today's drama, she doesn't want to take any chances. Armed with some mace, she places the camera just inside the hatch door. By the time it's three p.m., Louise has finished teaching them Latin, History and French and is just hanging around the house to wait for Andrea to get home. The girls rush into their bedroom to turn on the software for the micro camera. They get a shock.

'Fuck a duck,' says Sophie. 'There's a squatter in the loft.' Their hearts race and they become more scared of this person than the man they had just stunned.

'Shit. How long has someone been there, spying on us?'

'He has small feet. Look!'

'It's a kid!'

'What?'

'It must be.'

'Can you turn the camera around?' They move the camera up and down remotely to see a boy, maybe about ten years old, sleeping in their loft. They decide not to tell Andrea or Greg for fear of scaring him away. They try to think of a plan that will coax him out.

Over the next few days, Alice and Sophie monitor the situation in the loft. He seems to sleep through the day and is awake at night, coming down to steal food, and clothes such as T-shirts and socks, and tracksuit bottoms from the laundry. Sophie sees him wearing one of her tops during their review of the surveillance footage one day. And on another day, he's wearing Alice's wool scarf to bed to keep warm.

'This has gone on too long,' says Sophie.

'What do you mean?'

'Well, he should come down and meet us. It's no life for him up there.'

It seemed ironic that the girls wished for a friend and didn't know that they had a potential one living in their own house, above them.

'Let's write him a note,' suggests Alice.

'Good idea.'

'Let's invite him to a midnight feast.'

'Yes, that sounds good.'

'We'll need to be very quiet or "The Borings" will wake up.'

The girls conjure up an invitation which he can't refuse.

Dear Loft Dweller,

We are happy that you have taken up residence in our house and would like to extend to you an invitation for an evening of food and games. Could you possibly sneak out of the house tonight at three a.m. and meet us in the garden shed? We will prepare games and storytelling. Dress for the cold weather and no need to bring anything.

Kind regards
Sophie and Alice.

'I think that sounds brilliant,' says Alice.

'Yes well, I would go, wouldn't you?'

'What games and storytelling do you have in mind?'

'Well, he looks about ten years old. So maybe Harry Potter and some Monopoly? I don't really know.'

'Let's see how he is. He might be frightened of us.'

'Yes, let's see.'

The invitation is planted whilst the boy is sleeping. The girls reach into the loft hatch and put it just inside so he will see it when he attempts to exit and raid the kitchen again. They set their alarms for two thirty a.m. but not so loud as to wake "The Borings". They go to sleep with smiles on their faces.

'I hope he's funny,' says Sophie.

'Yes. He's obviously quite adventurous.'

'And how clever not to be caught for all this time.'

'Yes.'

The alarms go off and they rush to get the thing they need for the garden shed with blankets and pillows to sit on. They bring a cool box and some torches.

'Mum and Dad shouldn't wake up,' confirms Sophie.

'They've drunk enough wine to sleep through.'

'Yes, that's one thing you can count on.'

The girls kit out the shed and await their guest.

'What time is it?' Alice asks.

'I dunno. I left my phone inside.'

'Me too.'

'I have night vision glasses though.'

'Have a look. Is he coming?'

Just then, a small boy pokes his head in the door and nearly scares the shit out of them.

'Hi,' he says.

'What the fuck!' Alice says without thinking.

'Augh!' Sophie screams.

'Sorry. I got your letter. Was it meant for me?' the boy asks.

'Yes, yes. Come in. Come in.'

'Hi.'

'Hi.'

'Ummm, I'm Alice.'

'I'm Sophie.'

'What's your name?'

'Do I have to tell you?' he asks.

'No. No.'

'Can I have some food?' he asks.

'YES. Please do.'

He picks up a slice of cake and nearly eats it in one mouthful.

Alice and Sophie look at each other with wide eyes.

'Can I have a drink, please?'

'Yes.' Sophie hands him a can of ginger ale. He drinks it all in almost one go.

'How long have you been living in our house?'

'Do I have to answer that?'

'No.'

'I just thought this was a picnic,' he says.

'It is. It is not an interrogation.'

'It's been lonely up there. Thank you for the letter.'

'You're welcome.'

'What games have you brought?'

'Umm, Monopoly.'

'Can I be the ship?'

'Yes, of course.'

Alice opens the box and sets out the board on the blanket. They watch the boy as he makes every move, looking at his curly hair in the darkness and wondering if he has had a good wash recently. He is excited to be playing Monopoly and it seems to be a good ice breaker. It allows social interaction without the usual questioning. He seems gentle in the way he rolls the dice. He has manners and offers them another turn if they are not happy with the cards they pick up. They giggle a bit, and he seems comfortable with human interaction.

'It's your turn now,' he would say. As the girls are in a trance, they keep forgetting whose turn it is. To get him talking, they try telling him about themselves, hoping he will follow.

'We're from London.'

'Yes, I figured you were English. Why did you come here?'

'Well. Our parents wanted to. Dad's American,' Sophie says. He nods.

'Do you like it here?' he asks.

'Yes, so far,' they lie. They've been cooped up and they are not sure if he knows about the murder.

'There's a couple of odd things that have happened,' Sophie says, hoping to be able to ask the question about whether he has been putting blocks in the letterbox. But he freezes and looks at her like a rabbit caught in the headlights. She refrains from further small talk about unpleasant topics.

'We're home schooled. But you probably know that,' Alice says, to change the subject.

'Your turn,' he says.

'We have loads of gadgets,' Sophie says, trying to engage with him. He looks up.

'Yes, we have traps, cameras, motion sensors… which we haven't used yet… a stun gun…' says Alice.

He looks excited.

'Yes, in fact, we used it the other day!'

'Don't!' Alice warns. She thought the story it might scare him away.

'On a stranger…,' Sophie says. Alice rolls her eyes.

He looks interested. 'Can I see it?'

'Yes, we can show you another time.'

'We can show you how to set traps and how to spy on people… if you're interested.'

He grins. What ten-year-old boy wouldn't want to see their traps? He seems to feel around them, like they can somehow protect him from whatever he is hiding from.

'Will your parents throw me out?' he asks.

'No.'

'You can meet them if you like?'

'No! Please. I don't want to.'

'Okay. Okay. That's fine.'

'And don't tell anyone please,' he begs.

'We won't,' says Sophie.

'We don't really know anyone and we're new here,' says Alice.

They all start to yawn as the end of the Monopoly game draws near.

'Okay, well… walk behind us as we take you back to the loft.'

'Okay.'

The girls camouflage him with a blanket in case their parents wake up and look out the window. They help him up into the loft even though he obviously doesn't need help. They hand him a book of *Harry Potter* and say goodnight. The girls go to their room and get ready for bed.

'This place just got a whole lot more interesting,' says Sophie.

'Yeah, didn't it,' agrees Alice.

'And I didn't realise that I miss being a kid and playing Monopoly.'

'Yeah, me too.'

The girls discuss how they were going to set up some motion sensors, a trip wire and maybe more traps in case the man in the van knows where they live. They have to make sure the boy doesn't get caught in them though. They go to sleep discussing how they are going to protect him.

CHAPTER 6

The Aquarium

It's the weekend. As the girls have been cooped up inside for so long, Andrea and Greg decide to take them out.

'BOORRRIIIIIING!'

'What! I thought you liked the aquarium?' asks Greg.

'Can't we just go shopping?' Sophie asks.

'Dad hates shopping. I'd rather we just have some family time,' says Andrea.

'Fine.' Alice moans.

'Whatever.' Sophie agrees.

Secretly, the girls like the idea of going into dark spaces with crowds where sharks swim overhead but they would prefer to spend more time with the loft dweller, even though he probably sleeps all day. The girls prepare some food for him, leave a note and gave him a burner mobile phone with only their phone numbers on it.

'Bring stun guns,' Sophie whispers to Alice, as they are feeling scared at the thought of leaving the house.

Sophie then mimics the effects of being stunned, standing and shaking, so that Andrea and Greg can't see.

Alice laughs.

Sophie then gestures strangling someone around the neck.

Alice laughs again.

Sophie then pretends to throw a rope and lasso someone.

They are both in fits of laughter.

'Well, you two have brightened up,' says Andrea.

'You both have bags under your eyes,' Greg adds. He usually doesn't notice anything.

'No. Have we?' asks Alice, looking in the mirror.

'Anyway, you shouldn't criticise the way your daughters look. That could affect our mental health,' warns Sophie.

Greg doesn't know how to respond.

They jump in the car and head for the aquarium. Greg drives past the place where they assaulted their first American victim and they look at each other and laugh. To pass the time, they discuss possible names for the loft-dwelling boy. They start searching the Internet on their phones for American boys' names.

'OMG... Imagine the rollcall at an American school. The teachers would nearly shit themselves when they read out some of these boy names...,' says Sophie.

Sophie reads out names as Alice simulates answering to the roll call.

'Yeah... like... Hunter?' Sophie says.

'Present, miss,' Alice replies and they continue.

'Gunner?'

'Yes, miss. Present.'

'Blade?'

'Yeah.'

'Magnum?'

'Yes, miss.'

'Smith?'

'Yes, miss.'

'Weston?'

'Yes, ma'am.'

'Canon?'

'Here.'

'Lance?'

'Yes, ma'am.'

'Bow?'

They continue until they get bored of the subject.

They drive through the centre of Philadelphia to get to the aquarium. The girls have their windows down and are soaking up the outdoor scenery when they smell the stench of urine from the homeless people sleeping rough. They start to quiz their parents about homelessness. Alice and Sophie have a serious concern about homeless people. Even more so now that they now have made friends with a homeless boy.

The city looks old in parts but is mostly very modern. They miss London, the architecture, the familiarity. They were excited about moving to the US, but it hasn't quite worked out the way they had planned. They start to feel slightly subdued. In the UK they could go to their friends' houses who had indoor swimming pools. They had made a lot of friends with wealthy parents at their private school. Some of the parents were 'Sir' this or 'Lady' that. They would have staff to help with the playdates or even host them whilst the parents went out! They speculate as to what their friends might be doing now. They don't want to seem too desperate by contacting them all the time, but they had set up a chat group to keep in touch. The girls like to pretend everything is bigger and better in the US.

The family discuss other things on their journey. It's the perfect time to catch up with their parents as they are a captive audience for the whole drive.

'How's banking going? Any fraudulent accounts? Money laundering? Dodgy transactions?' Sophie asks her dad.

Greg doesn't know what to say.

'Leave your father alone,' Andrea says.

'I was reading something on the Internet that the banks know about money laundering but choose not to report it because they would lose so much revenue.'

'Umm. I wouldn't know anything about that,' he says. Greg just deals with small accounts.

'Change the subject,' says Andrea.

'Okay. Let's talk about what's really going on in this town,' Sophie says, in a threatening voice.

'Yeah. I think you guys are keeping secrets from us,' Alice adds.

Greg and Andrea look at each other. Andrea is keeping secrets from everyone. Greg is oblivious to the weird town and the people in it.

'What do you mean?' asks Andrea.

'Well... other kids are back at school...' complains Sophie.

'The murder is not solved yet,' Andrea says sternly.

'Some murders never get solved but people don't live indoors for the rest of their lives,' complains Alice.

'You won't be indoors forever.'

'Well, until when?'

'I don't know.'

'Well, we look anaemic.'

'No you don't.'

'Things will change soon, and we'll get back to normal,' Andrea says.

'What things?'

'Shush. I'm trying to drive!' Greg ends the argument.

Parking in the carpark at the aquarium, they notice some of the school children they met at Georgia's house arriving with their parents. Andrea doesn't know if she wants to go over to them or not. Walking around the entrance, the first tank is full of blue lobster.

'Hi, do you like Lobster Mornay?' Sophie says to the lobster tanks.

'Yeah, and salad?' Alice adds.

'Stop it,' says Andrea.

'I wonder if the "guests" know that they will be on the menu in the restaurant?' Sophie says.

'Oh, let's go to the sharks,' Alice replies.

'Okay.'

Andrea and Greg follow.

'Did you know that sharks have two penises?' Sophie says, determined to annoy her parents today.

'Umm yes,' Greg says.

'Why though?' Alice asks.

'They're called "claspers" actually,' says Andrea.

'Ummm.' Greg doesn't want to get into this. He is still getting used to the fact that they are going through puberty and seem to enjoy asking awkward questions.

'What would a group of sharks be called?' asks Sophie.

'A shiver,' says Alice.

'A group of whales?'

'A pod,' Alice answers.

'A group of stingrays?' asks Sophie.

'A fever,' says Alice.

'A group of salmon?' asks Andrea.

'A run,' says Sophie.

'Have you guys practised this?' asks Andrea.

'A group of tortoises?' asks Greg.

'A creep,' says Alice.

'A group of turtles?' asks Greg.

'A bale,' says Sophie.

'Did you look all of this up on the way here?' Andrea asks.

'What do you call a group of claspers?' asks Sophie.

'A government,' Alice says.

The girls giggle.

'Look, a hammerhead!' shrieks Sophie.

'He certainly wouldn't win a beauty contest,' says Alice.

'Some people's heads look like that,' says Sophie.

The hammerhead seems to take a dislike to the family and comes over to bump the glass.

'Wow. Bugger off!' says Sophie.

'Language,' says Greg.

'What a bloody cheek,' Alice adds.

'I might have to order hammerhead and chips later,' Sophie says nastily, looking at the hammerhead swim off.

'Don't antagonise the fish,' Greg warns.

The girls run off and try to get away from their parents.

'Wow, little penguins!'

'How cute.'

'Jesus, there's piranhas down there, let's go that way,' Sophie says as they run off.

'Stay close,' Andrea yells out.

'Yes, Mother.'

Just then, Andrea stops to talk to a mother she met at the boozy coffee morning. She has forgotten her name but acts very friendly. She has brought some bugs with her and reaches into her handbag. Then touching the other mother's handbag manages to plant one just inside, whilst complimenting her.

'Oh, I love your shoes!' Andrea says to Antionette.

'Oh, thank you!'

'How have you been?'

'Oh fine.'

'The kids are back at school we haven't seen you there.'

'Yes. Well, the girls had different education and I'm just getting them home schooled for a while.'

'Oh. That would drive me insane.'

'Yes, well I'm getting out of the house. I go to the office and show houses so that I don't go insane.'

'Great,' the mother interrupts, looking disinterested.

'Are you here with your children?' Andrea asks, feeling like that was probably an obvious question.

'Yes. River and Paris.'

'Lovely names!'

'Yes.'

'And yours are Sophie and Alice?'

'Good memory!'

'Well, they have become quite popular on social media. My kids have seen their postings. They're quite the comedians.'

'Really! I must have a look.' Andrea is confused. She doesn't know what they are posting.

'Anyway, nice to see you.'

Sophie and Alice run up to Andrea saying, 'We're going to the gift shop.'

They run to the gift shop excited about an idea they have just had.

'Look, shark's teeth jewellery. Just what I thought,' says Alice.

'A necklace,' says Sophie, trying to put it on herself without getting scratched.

'Look how sharp it is.' Alice says as she feels the tooth.

'I love it!'

'Let's get one each.'

They spot a whole wall of stuffed animal toys and decide to buy some for the Loft Dweller. There are masks and hoods which cover their heads and look like whales and dolphins. They try them on and, just then, they hear some women talking about Andrea.

'Shush! They're talking about Mum,' says Alice. They leave their dolphin hoods on as a disguise and try to listen in. They listen to the conversation of two woman.

That new English family is here.

Andrea and what's-his-name.

Really?

I don't believe the whole home-schooling excuse.

Why not?

Well, we googled her and there wasn't much on the Internet.

That's suspicious.

Do you think she works for the police?

Is she spying on us?

She's acting strange though.

How?

She just looks nervous. She doesn't look you in the eye. Like she knows something.

How much could she know? She's only been here five minutes.

Well, I have to go and find my kids.

Yes, me too.

Keep me posted.

Okay.

The girls wait until they can't hear the voices any more and take their hoods off.

'What was that?' says Alice.

'I dunno. But Mum's not a spy,' says Sophie.

'Or is she?'

'Don't you think it's weird that she has bought spy stuff?'

'What is she doing?'

'I thought she worked behind the desk at MI5?'

'She must have. She didn't do fieldwork or she wouldn't be home by seven p.m. every night.'

'Yeah, I guess.'

'Those ladies are nuts if they think Mum's a spy.'

'Yeah.' Alice laughs.

'Could you imagine it?'

'No. Not really.'

The girls purchase their shark tooth jewellery and some gifts for the Loft Dweller and continue their tour of sea life. They come across Andrea talking to the mothers that they were just eavesdropping on. They watch from a distance.

'She's fondling that handbag,' says Sophie.

'Yeah. No wonder they're suspicious of her.'

'She's really sucking up to them.' Sophie is intrigued. She watches her mother now in a new light.

'Yeah and Mum doesn't really like those sorts of handbags. She's trying too hard to make friends,' says Alice.

'Hang on. Look.'

'What?'

'I think she just put something in that handbag,' Sophie whispers.

'Like a bug?'

'Yeah.'

'Why would she bug them?'

'She's up to something.'

'Gosh.'

'I'm grilling her later… Fuck… Why don't we get told anything?'

'Yeah!'

Andrea has planted her third bug in Susan's handbag. The girls run up to Andrea and Greg and decide to go to the aquarium restaurant for lunch to try to interrogate their mother. Sitting down at a spare table in the restaurant, Sophie and Alice can't help but to stare at their mother. They had never seen her plant a bug before.

'Well, you've been busy, Mother,' says Sophie sarcastically.

'Oh?' Andrea doesn't know what they are talking about.

'Just saying… you've obviously got an agenda today.'

'What do you mean?'

'Never mind.'

Sophie is starving and decides to scour the menu instead of questioning her mother at this point.

'Mother,' Alice says. 'What exactly did you do for employment back home?'

'I've told you. I was an analyst at MI5. You haven't told anyone though, have you?'

'No. No.'

'It's a strange thing to ask me at the aquarium,' Andrea says.

'Yes, very strange,' Sophie pipes up from behind the menu. 'Bugger! No hammerhead on the menu.'

'Seriously!' Greg says. 'Don't say bugger out loud.'

'It's not a rude word,' says Sophie.

'It is!' says Andrea.

'No, it's not. A bugger is someone who plants bugs.'

Andrea's eyes open wide as she stares at the girls. She wonders if they saw her. *Was I not stealthy enough? Jesus*, she thinks.

'Well, I'll have to eat some of the other inmates then.'

'What?' says Greg.

'The squid or something.'

'Can we have a big share platter? Prawns, scallops, oysters, lobster...' Alice goes on.

'Will you eat it all?'

'Yes. Yes, Mother.'

Sophie and Alice sit in wait of their seafood platter and examine Greg and Andrea's faces in the meantime. Andrea seems to have aged since they got there. She hasn't found a decent hairdresser yet and her roots are showing. She would always go right into London to have them done near Selfridges. Greg is also going grey, and his hairline has receded more. He has more wrinkles, more than Andrea, and looks depressed. Andrea and Greg don't talk to each other and seem to drift off into a daze, each looking around the room for something to fix their eyes on even though their two daughters are sitting opposite them. The girls have often felt that their behaviour is too much for their parents and that it exhausts them. But they can't seem to stop or act normally.

After lunch, they drive home because the girls have had enough of the aquarium, and Andrea has had enough of the girls. On arrival, Andrea goes to the mailbox and the girls run inside, having made plans to bake cakes. There is nothing in the post box and Andrea feels a bit deflated. She has planted three more bugs, but she usually doesn't get anything juicy from listening to the recordings.

Muriel sees her from across the road and waves. Andrea feels caught. It would be rude to turn around and go inside so she waves back and walks over to Muriel's front garden to greet her with an ulterior motive. *Muriel must know a thing or two about this town. Bugging her house would surely prove fruitful,* Andrea thinks.

'Afternoon, Muriel.'

'Hellooo, Andrea, do you have time for tea?'

'Oh yes, please. I've just been to the aquarium.'

'Oh, that's a bit of a drive. Come on in.'

Entering Muriel's house, she sits down in the living room with excitement and anticipation. Looking around to survey her surroundings, she sees a mixture of interior decorating styles. Three-piece lounge suite is chunky, probably 1950s but reupholstered. The room is dark and gloomy with many gilt framed photos dotted here and there. The coffee table is probably 1970s and the curtains probably 1990s. So, it looks like Muriel only redecorates every few decades. She walks in holding a tray with Country Rose pattern China. It all seems over the top, but Andrea assumes that she doesn't get many visitors.

Muriel is not very inquisitive when it comes to Andrea's life, more the other way around. After the general chit-chat, Andrea tries to pin Muriel down regarding any gossip or weird happenings in the suburb. Muriel sits ladylike, sipping tea, answering questions where she can, and refraining from those that she can't. She is aware of the many children that have run away and how this has led to people leaving the town. She has no theory for this. Andrea doesn't know what to make of Muriel. She looks like a 1950s hairdresser with a teased up purple or blue rinse hair-do. But she behaves in a superior manner.

To explore the house more, Andrea asks to use the facilities. The cabinet above the bathroom sink proved interesting with a large collection of medications. She did not understand the names but took photos of them all with her mobile phone. *Now, where to plant a bug?* Andrea thinks. There is usually a landline in the hallways of most houses. On the way back to the living room, she sticks a bug under the hallway table.

'Ah there you are,' Muriel says as Andrea re-enters the living room.

'Lovely house,' Andrea compliments.

'Thank you.'

'Well, I must get going and see what mess the girls have made of the kitchen.'

'Oh?'

'Yes, they were going to bake cakes so the kitchen will have white flour everywhere, looking like a... (Andrea nearly says "Crack Den") a Victorian bakery.

'How nice.'

'I'll tell them to bring some over to you if you like?'

'Ooh that would be lovely. Thank you!'

Andrea goes home and has an instinct to go straight to the bugging software in her study to see if Muriel phones anyone. And she was right.

Andrea Mitchell has just been over for tea, Muriel says on the phone.

Andrea is surprised that she would mention her name. She can't hear the other person's replies, but only Muriel talking.

Nice lady.

Asks lots of questions.

Oblivious.

Goes to her post box a lot and takes things out.

Well, that depends on whether her children run away or not.

A cold chill goes down Andrea's back. Who is Muriel talking to and why are they talking about her children running away? Andrea decides to bug the girls' bedroom while they are baking in the kitchen.

What Andrea doesn't know, however, is that the girls have a bug detector that they've brought over from London with their other gadgets. They now 'sweep' the rooms they enter, and rather than remove any bugs, they act out fake conversations. That evening, the bug in their bedroom made the following recording for their own amusement, knowing Andrea would listen to it. That evening Andrea listened to *Tape 1 girls' bedroom*.

'*Louise looked well-put-together today, as they say,*' says Alice.

'*Do you think?*' Sophie responds. Although it's difficult for Andre to tell their voices apart.

'*Yes.*'

'*Is it possible that she is dressing up for us?*'

'*What do you mean?*'

'*Could she be bisexual?*'

'*Or a lesbian!*'

'*I guess it's possible.*'

'*Have you seen her looking at you?*'

'*Just at my breasts.*'

'*The aquarium was fun today.*'

'*Mum was behaving weirdly though.*'

'*Yes.*'

'*She's not very good at planting bugs.*'

'*No, she's not.*'

'*Anyway, night.*'

'*Night.*'

Andrea is shocked that they saw her planting bugs and doesn't want to listen any more so she turns it off.

CHAPTER 7

The After-School Club

The following morning, Andrea knows she will have to put up with the usual horsing around from the girls during breakfast. The girls are talking in the kitchen whilst eating their cereal and Andrea comes downstairs to get her breakfast.

'How is everyone this morning?' Andrea asks hopefully.

'Annoyed,' says Alice.

'Really! What are you annoyed about?' Andrea didn't really want to know?

'Dad. He pretends he can't do stuff just to get other people to do things for him,' says Sophie.

'Like what?' demands Andrea.

'Ironing, using the dishwasher,' Sophie explains.

'Well...' Andrea isn't too bothered that the girls do chores for him.

'I bet he didn't do stuff for you when we were babies either.'

Andrea was stumped. They know just how to win so many conversations.

'Did he change our nappies? Or did he say, "I'm not very good at that..."' Sophie mocks how Greg would speak.

Andrea says nothing.

'Did he say that he is not very good at feeding the babies?'

Andrea was stumped again.

'Yeah, and the whole breast-feeding thing is a complete con,' says Alice.

'What do you mean?' Andrea asks.

'Men have nipples, Mum. They just pretend they don't work,' explains Sophie.

'They definitely don't work,' Andrea says.

'How do you know? Where is the evidence that they don't work?' says Alice.

Andrea doesn't want o entertain this subject.

'Hey. We should strap a milk pump to Dad's chest when he's asleep,' suggests Sophie.

'Yeah. We could check it for milk in the morning, then put it in his coffee,' says Alice.

'Stop it. Get dressed. Louise will be here soon.' Andrea orders.

'No. She's usually late,' the girls say together.

'What do you mean?'

'She's always late so it's quite good really,' Sophie explains.

'Yes, it gives us time to check the stock market and things,' Alice says seriously.

'We're teaching her English History,' says Sophie.

'Yeah well… there's not much she can teach us,' agrees Alice.

'I'm not paying her to be a student. I'm paying *her* to be the teacher!' Andrea says angrily.

'Fat chance of that,' Alice whispers.

Andrea decides in her mind that she needs the girls to be at home with *someone* and Louise is just a glorified babysitter whilst all this turmoil is going on. Louise arrives and Andrea collects her keys and bag to leave the house. As Andrea turns to tell Louise not to answer questions about breast feeding, she can't be bothered and just says, 'Bye.'

The girls yell out, 'Bye, Mother,' as if they had just had a normal conversation.

Andrea doesn't have time to go to the letterbox but rushes to a house viewing. She conducts the viewing as if on automatic pilot, thinking all the time that she is going to be doing her first stakeout or stalking of young children this afternoon. That would sound illegal, if she was doing it alone and not with Natalie.

After the day passes quickly, it's finally three thirty p.m. and the kids are coming out of the school. Andrea is parked across the road in Caroline's car. She asked if she could borrow it using the excuse that her's was not working. Andrea has binoculars and a long-distance hearing gadget. Greg will be coming home early to mind the kids when Louise leaves. So, she is all organised and has packed plenty of water and chocolate into her bag for provisions, not knowing how long she will be on the stakeout.

After about thirty minutes, all of the parents cars have left and other children have started their the after-school clubs. Andrea can see into the classrooms with her binoculars and can see the headmaster talking to about ten children. They pick up their backpacks and leave the classroom. Andrea can no longer see them. She waits in the car though as the headmaster may recognise her. She had met him once when they looked around the school months ago. There certainly wasn't any information in the brochure about a late club called Drug Trafficking. He seemed like a normal guy back then and there was nothing to alert Andrea. A few minutes later, she sees a child, possibly a boy, leaves the school on a bike with a backpack and seems to be in a hurry. This is Andrea's chance. She starts the engine and drives behind the bike at a safe distance. The bike takes a left turn down a lane that is not designed for cars. Andrea goes to the next street on the left and tries to double back hoping to find the bike rider. Nothing. No bike rider in sight. She then parks, gets out of her car and walks down the lane that the bike took. It's lined with garages, and she thinks that the child could be in any one of them.

Andrea goes back to the car. She waits and waits. Then after about thirty minutes, when Andrea is not looking, the boy on his bike rides out of the lane and past her car. She follows it and finds that the boy has ridden back to school. This is just what she had suspected. That the after-school clubs are used to deliver drugs. But where? To one of the garages? The boy takes the bike into the back entrance of the school and is met by the headmaster at the side gate.

Andrea can't wait to meet with Natalie and fill her in. She calls her on her burner phone, and they meet at the diner.

'I knew it!' says Natalie. 'I followed a few kids at different times and then they just disappeared.'

'Well, I waited, and he emerged just where he disappeared. I'm not sure, but I think he took drugs to a garage in Baker Street.'

'We've searched those garages though,' says Natalie.

'There must be something there.'

'I've used so many resources that the chief won't throw any more money at this.'

'Let's follow another kid tomorrow. Do you have time to do that?'

'Yes sure. Okay. Meet me here at three p.m.'

'Okay.'

The following day, Natalie picks up Andrea at the diner carpark. They go to the school and park outside.

'There!' Andrea says as she points at a girl leaving the school on her bike and heads in the same direction. Natalie starts her engine and travels behind at an inconspicuous speed.

'Let's get to the lane before them.'

'Okay, good idea. I'll overtake.'

They park where they can see down the lane except for a stack of wooden boxes.

They wait and see the bike travelling up the street behind them. The girl passes without noticing them, rides down the lane, goes behind the boxes and then… they can't see anything.

'What?' says Natalie.

Natalie gets out of the car and runs down the lane.

'She's gone. And she didn't open a garage door,' says Natalie.

'Where is she?' Andrea whispers to herself.

'This is what keeps happening. I would follow them and then they would just disappear. My boss thinks I'm crazy.'

'Okay but we need to be able to see the whole lane. Let's go up onto the top of the garages and we will see where she emerges from in about thirty minutes,' Andrea suggests.

'Why thirty minutes?'

'She has to be back at school before after-school club finishes,' Andrea explains.

'Yes. That's true.'

Natalie and Andrea climb up onto the top of a garage and lay low. They can see the area clearly now and they should be able to see which garage the girl emerges from.

'Any minute now,' Andrea says.

'What?'

'It's nearly twenty-nine minutes.'

'Okay.'

'I can't hear a garage door opening, can you?'

'No, but what's that?'

The ground near the boxes is opening like a trap door and the girl shoots out on a bike as if there was a slope for her to ride in and out. Before Andrea can get a close look with her binoculars, the trap door is shut.

'What the hell?' Natalie says.

'Did you see that?'

'That's why they were disappearing. The road is underground,' Natalie yells in excitement.

'Are there any underground passages that you know of?' Andrea asks.

'Shit!'

'What?'

'Thank you... thank you... thank you. I wouldn't have got this far without a partner. I wouldn't have got on top of a garage without a lift up for a start.'

'It was nothing.'

'I'm so excited. We're going to catch these bloody drug pushers and free the poor little kids from child slavery.'

'Yes!' Andrea says, full of adrenaline.

'We need evidence, photos next time.'

'Sure, and a schedule of what, who, when.'

Andrea drops Natalie back and drives home. When she gets there, she realises Greg's car is not outside and Louise would have left hours ago. She enters her house to find it suspiciously quiet. She calls out to the girls and hear them whispering. Andrea is immediately panicked. Her mind goes wild.

'Up here, Mum!' Sophie yells.

Phew, Andrea thinks, and she starts climbing the stairs. But she hears different voices.

'Where?'

'Up here.'

Andrea enters the girls' room to see a boy sitting on Alice's bed.

'You have a playdate?' Andrea asks nervously.

The three of them say nothing. The boy looks frightened.

'Is everything okay?' she asks. Then looks at the boy.

'Are you friends with my girls?'

He looks down.

'Alice… Sophie… who is your friend?'

'He lives here, Mum.'

'What do you mean?'

'He moved in before we got here.'

'We found him a few days ago while looking in the loft,' explains Sophie.

'We convinced him to let you meet him,' says Alice.

'Oh… um… what is your name?'

He doesn't answer.

'He doesn't talk much.'

'Why?' asks Andrea.

'I think he's traumatised, and he shudders sometimes when he does talk,' says Sophie.

'Oh… umm…' Andrea is wondering what to do.

'We told him you wouldn't call the police,' Alice says.

'Oh… well… someone may be looking for him.'

'Please, Mum. Just let him stay until we work out what's going on in this town.'

'What do you mean?'

'Come on, Mum, we're not stupid. We know you're doing some investigating…,' says Sophie.

'Um… okay…'

The boy looks relieved.

'What is your name?'

He doesn't answer.

'Can we call you… um… Luke?' Sophie suggests.

He nods.

'Okay that's what we'll call you for now.'

'Let's go downstairs.' Andrea says.

'No, Mum, he may be seen through the window.'

'I'll bring him some food up here,' Alice says.

'Oh, okay.'

'Don't tell Dad.'

'Why?' Andrea asks.

'You know what he's like. He's never even got a speeding ticket. He is not going to harbour a child runaway.'

'You're right.'

'He can stay in the loft,' Andrea says.

In a weird way, Andrea is glad that she has sort of found one of the lost children, or that he has found her. She has a million questions for him but while they were keeping quiet, she knows she would have to take things slow. The girls take food up to Luke, and Andrea wonders how she is going to keep this from Greg.

Later that evening, Greg arrives home and they go downstairs to stop him from coming up. Luke goes back into the loft and they all try to act normal. Andrea cooks dinner for Greg and they have their usual conversations, asking about how their day was. Andrea goes to the study and listens to see if there are any recordings of the bugged handbags. As usual… nothing. They are either speaking in code or have noticed the bugs and are saying nothing. She goes to bed and thinks about arranging to meet Natalie the following day to tell her about Luke.

In the morning, Andrea wakes up early and manages to get out of bed without waking Greg. She reminds the girls that Louise is coming and that they need to feed Luke before Greg wakes up. While she's saying that, she realises that they have managed to feed him for several days without anyone noticing. She leaves a note for Greg, arranges to meet Natalie at the diner, and tells Caroline she will be in work late today.

Andrea walks straight to the post box as if expecting to find something. She considers questions that she wants to ask Luke to see if he is the one leaving her messages. *Did he mean to use the block P for Pool? Had he seen the murder? Is that why he's scared? Did he go to that school?* Andrea has her own witness that she can gently interrogate at some point when he feels like talking. Luke can do nothing but help her, she thinks.

She opens the post box and there is a leaflet for the ice cream restaurant. She is about to crumple it up when she notices that someone has circled the picture of the owners in red pen. It seems weird to her. Usually, a leaflet is a leaflet. But this one seems to be a message.

Natalie is waiting at the diner for Andrea and has started eating pancakes when Andrea arrives.

'Hi. How do you stay so thin?' Andrea asks.

'I don't eat much of an evening meal, so I can justify a big breakfast.'

'Oh.'

'Also, the stress of this town burns fat off.'

'I guess that's one good thing about Spring Town.'

They laugh.

Andrea fills Natalie in about the boy living in her loft. Natalie agrees that the boy should not be disturbed and should carry on living with Andrea. Natalie says that these kids could easily run away again. In the meantime, Natalie is going to run a check on missing persons with Luke's description.

Natalie shows Andrea a map of tunnels on her laptop that she has found online. The tunnels were used by the people to shift alcohol during the prohibition period. The map has a central part with eight tunnels that lead away from it in different directions.

'This map is in the shape of an octopus!' Andrea says.

'Yeah, I guess. I think the school kids could be using these old tunnels.'

Natalie gets a map of Spring Town up on her laptop and enhances the tunnel map over it. The centre of the octopus is now the Sacred Heart Hospital, but it used to be a brewery.

'That's weird.' Andrea says.

'I guess they were storing the alcohol there or making it there.'

'All the tentacles come from there,' Andea notices.

Natalie and Andrea examine the routes that children could be using to move drugs around Spring Town. The tunnels have exit points and one of them is the lane where the girl on the bike disappeared and reappeared.

'We need to go down these tunnels,' says Andrea.

'It's organised crime though,' warns Natalie.

'So?'

'I should do this without you,' Natalie says, reassuring Andrea.

'Do you think your boss will give you more resources now?'

'To be honest, I don't trust the Chief of Police here.'

'Really?'

'Yes. For all I know, he is aware of it and is taking a cut.'

'This is getting serious, Natalie. My instinct is to move away.'

'And Luke? Will you take him too?'

'No, of course not.'

'There are children out there somewhere, Andrea, hiding, too scared to come home. There is a dead cop posing as a teacher.

A dead girl with a backpack full of cocaine and God knows how many others,' Natalie explains.

'Okay.' Andrea reluctantly gives in.

'Have you had anything else in your letter box?'

'Only this ice cream restaurant leaflet.' Andrea shows it to Natalie. It's an ice cream parlour but the menu is full of ice-cream disguised as restaurant food, like steak and chicken wings. There seems to be a chain of them.

'Okay. Did you circle this face on the back?' Natalie asks.

'No.'

Natalie looks on the underground map to see if it is close to any of the tunnels.

'Look. It's near the end of this tunnel. I think we should check it out.'

'Tomorrow?' Andrea suggests.

'Yes.'

'I have to go to work now,' Andrea says.

'Yes, great. I'll pick you up here in my car around eight p.m.?'

'Okay.'

That evening Andrea wants to ask Luke some questions. She refrains from this as it may scare him off and decides to grill the girls instead. She goes up to their room whilst Greg is watching TV and finds them whispering.

'So why didn't you tell me straight away?' Andrea demands.

'Well, he was scared, Mum, and you might have frightened him away.'

'He looked terrified,' Alice says.

'I wonder what he has been through... where his parents are... whether they are still alive?' Andrea says, hoping the girls know more than they are letting on.

The girls look at each other, not knowing what to say to their mother.

'Sometimes I just want to leave this place,' Andrea moans, as she is finally telling the girls how she really feels.

'I don't,' says Sophie.

'Really?'

'Yes, well Dad is happy here and we've met some kids already and well...one......' Alice adds.

'Things will improve,' Sophie says.

'Yes,' Andrea tries to say positively.

'Once we get back to school things will seem normal again,' Alice says positively.

'After a while we can ask Luke... or whoever he is... whether he wants us to go to the police.'

'Yes.'

'I just don't want to scare him off, Mum,' Sophie begs.

The girls can seem so sweet at times. Like they really do have empathy. Andrea has wondered sometimes...

CHAPTER 8

The Carnage

It's another morning full of anxiety and Andrea comes down to the breakfast table in anticipation. Greg also tries to toast some bread without being drawn into a debate about any trivia. Alice starts on Andrea...

'Mother. What was your favourite pet as a child?'

'Um, I had a cat called Sparkle.'

Sophie and Alice giggle.

'And what was your favourite childhood cake or pastry?'

'I liked cupcakes.'

The girls fall about laughing while Andrea and Greg wonder what is so funny.

'And, Dad, what was your favourite pet?'

'I had a dog called Oscar.'

'And your favourite cake?'

'Carrot.'

The girls can't stop laughing and giggling.

'What is it?' Andrea demands.

'Well to figure out what you could call yourself if you became a porn star, some people use things like favourite dog and a food or something.'

'So, you could be "Sparkle Cupcakes," Mother. And Dad could be called "Oscar Carrot"!'

'Well, we fell for that one,' Greg says.

'We have asked loads of people, and some of the names are hysterical.'

'Fascinating,' says Andrea.

'Yes. Our teachers in London have porn star names like Mavis Muffin, Patch Pavlova...' says Alice.

'Daisy Sticky Toffee, Milly Mudcake, Jack Jelly...' Sophie adds.

'Okay... okay,' Andrea stops them.

'I bet you couldn't wait to ask the teachers at *this* school,' says Greg.

'Yes, what a shame we're home schooled,' Alice replies.

Another so-called normal day in Spring Town. Andrea goes to work, completely preoccupied with the police case she is working on. She enters the real estate office building and walks past people, saying '*Hello*' but still not really knowing their names. Some of them say '*hi*' and some don't even look up. There are various phone calls taking place and she can hear that her colleagues are struggling to sell houses. They repeat things like 'No, I don't think there are squatters', 'No there's no news on the murder' and 'I don't think there's a poltergeist.'

Andrea stares out the window in her office, she looks down to see if the stalker is there. For some reason she is not frightened of seeing him again as she works for the police now. She checks the Internet for news of the murder. Nothing. Caroline pops her head in...

'Morning!'

'Morning!'

'How are things?'

'Okay. I'm not having much luck though.'

'How's your car?'

'Sorry.'

'Your car... is it fixed?' Caroline asks. Andrea forgot she made up an excuse to use Caroline's car.

'Oh yes. I got the gear box fixed.'

'Ouch. I bet that costs a fortune.'

'Yes.'

'What garage did you use?'

Andrea's not sure she likes all the questions and is feeling paranoid.

'Umm. Greg sorted it out. I don't know.'

'Okay. Well, I'm down the hall if you need anything.'

'Thanks.'

Caroline walks off looking a bit puzzled.

Andrea's day is mundane, and she can't help but to search the Internet. She searches for any news about this town. There seems to be nothing.

She drives home in yet another daze, thinking. Trying to piece it all together. Greg comes home, has dinner, goes to watch TV and Andrea makes her excuses and leaves to meet Natalie. She is relieved that some people need to view houses at night. It's a good cover.

Natalie is waiting for Andrea at the diner, and they drive off in Natalie's car to check out the ice cream restaurant. It's about a fifteen-minute drive so they have plenty of time to talk. Andrea wants to know more about the woman she is helping so much. Who is Natalie really? She talks mostly about her fiancée, Detective Cameron, or Peter, as she calls him.

They arrive on the street near the ice cream restaurant, and it appears that all hell has broken loose. There are lights flashing from police cars, ambulance, and a fire engine. The area closer to the restaurant is cordoned off and Natalie tells Andrea to stay in the car while she goes to see what is happening.

Natalie flashes her badge at a policeman in uniform and asks him what's going on.

'Carnage,' the policeman says.

'Details please' demands Natalie.

'Some guy working in the ice cream restaurant went nuts with a machete. He cut a guy's hand off and sliced a few bellies and was yelling out like he was hallucinating.'

'Shit!'

'Yeah, we shot him,' says the policeman in a nonchalant manner.

'Oh. How many injured?'

'Three bled out. Five still living.'

'Shit,' Natalie says.

Natalie walks away. It's not really her area. She works on missing persons, not violent crimes. Getting back into the car she tells Andrea about what happened but leaves out some of the gruesome details. She's worried she might frighten Andrea away.

'It's a bit weird that I get a leaflet and then the exact same restaurant has a madman on a rampage,' Andrea says.

'Yes. I think it's all connected,' says Natalie.

'Lovely,' Andrea says sarcastically. This only complicates things. Andrea likes to work things out to find answers.

'Don't get discouraged, Andrea.'

They sit in the car and realise that the whole, *using children for drug trafficking thing,* just got more serious. They watch from a distance while ambulances and the coroner vans turn up. People are crying outside the restaurant, as if they are relatives or friends of casualties. They decide to follow an ambulance on its way to the hospital. It was Andrea's idea. Natalie is confused by this but trusts Andrea's instinct. Two ambulances leave at the same time.

They are not sure if they are carrying the dead bodies or the injured ones. Natalie keeps a safe distance, so they don't get noticed.

'There is no blue light so they must be either well enough or dead,' Natalie says.

'Or just a few cuts and... WATCH OUT!' Andrea yells.

One of the ambulances takes a sharp left and nearly causes an accident.

'Where are they going? That's not the quickest way to the hospital,' Natalie says.

'The hospital is that way,' says Andrea, pointing in the opposite direction.

'Where are they going?' says Natalie.

'I don't know.'

The ambulance takes another sharp turn and Natalie has to stop for a red light so they can't follow.

'Quick!' says Andrea, knowing that they may lose it.

Natalie turns around the corner and there is no sight of the ambulance.

They double back, slowly driving past dark alleys and lanes.

'Shit. We've lost them,' Natalie says.

'Where are they taking that body? Or person?'

'I don't know but they want to hide someone.'

'Could the ambulance guys be involved?'

'I don't know... Oh Andrea. I'm tired of losing people,' says Natalie.

'They could have gone down a tunnel, let's check this street on the map. Do you have it?'

'No,' says Natalie. 'I don't want to blow your cover. I'm driving you back to your car and we'll talk tomorrow.'

'Okay.'

'Check the online maps when you get home and listen to the bugs again.'

Andrea goes home, checks on the girls and whispers to them, 'How is Luke?'

'He's okay, Mum.'

'Goodnight.'

'Goodnight.'

Andrea resigned herself that she is up to her eyeballs in whatever the scandal is. She is also hiding a boy in her loft, and she knows about the headmaster, the drugs pushed via bicycles, the ice cream restaurant owners are somehow connected, and the ambulance service may also be involved. Her mind works overtime while she tries to piece it all together. She can't discuss it with Greg. He may do something to blow her cover, like tell the police.

Andrea goes to the fridge and gets some post-it notes. She remembers the blocks she was given and the clues as well as the other objects and gets them out of the kitchen drawer. She writes the name of each clue on a post-it and puts them into groups. There is a group for clues that she has already worked out, and another group for clues that she hasn't. Then there is the jigsaw piece of the girl on her windscreen. Could this mean that there is a missing girl, like a missing piece of a puzzle? Then there's the ice cream restaurant leaflet, where an employee started hallucinating and cutting people.

The drugs must be in the restaurant or part of the whole trafficking process, Andrea thinks to herself. *But they shot him. How can questions be answered now? Maybe that's why they shot him!* she wonders.

Andrea decides to pour a glass of wine, as it helps her think, and start an incident board, similar to ones she saw when walking past an office at MI5. She gets a notice board off the wall and turns it around to stick everything on the back. She starts by pencilling out the octopus picture and then placing Post-Its of people and things on it. She remembers the stalker, which had slipped her mind, so he needs to go on it too. She draws a picture of him in a hood, also a stick man picture of the headmaster, the dead teacher, the dead child and backpack, the ice cream restaurant, Luke, the coffee mornings, and the missing children.

She links each piece of information to each other with bits of string. *The drugs could be made in an ice cream kitchen. The headmaster could be getting the children to travel there to either collect and/or deliver them. The children get sick of this and leave or hide, such as Luke. The stalker is following her because she is new in town and could blow the school's cover. The toy blocks could be left by someone who knows that a teacher was found in a pool, a bike is involved, the maze is the tunnels. The octopus is also either the tunnels or a road map linking the school to the ice cream restaurant, or both. The other mothers may be in on it, and are taking a cut?* Andrea is not sure. *Surely, they should be suspicious by now.*

The morning news says nothing about the carnage from the night before. *Typical Spring Town propaganda,* Andrea thinks. *Would the news reporters be in on things too?* Andrea calls in sick as she can't keep making up reasons why she hasn't shown enough houses in the past week. She has a full computer file of bugged handbags to listen to and so she wants to concentrate on that.

The girls come downstairs and don't seem to say much for a change. They look a bit sullen, not their usual selves. Their long blonde hair seems lifeless and their usual energy level seems low.

'Everything okay?' Andrea asks them.

'Well, Mum (they only call her mum when they're miserable or it's something serious), we have no life here.'

'Yeah. It's just one boring day after another,' Sophie says.

'Louise is boring,' Alice adds.

'And poor Luke. Living in the loft. He's too frightened to play outside with us in the day time.'

'You were both in good spirits yesterday.'

'Yes, but it gets boring! We want to go to school.'

Andrea is worried. The thought of them going near that school fills her with fear.

'It's not possible,' she snaps at them.

'Why?'

'Well. I'm not sure it's all that safe here.'

'What does Dad think?' Sophie asks.

'Well. I haven't exactly told him.'

'Why?'

'Well. I'm waiting to find out more before I tell him. And, if it's not safe here, we'll move.'

'How long will it take for you to decide?' Alice asks.

'I don't know. But you have a new friend, and it would help if you gently interrogated him. Find out where he's from, which house I mean, and make sure he's happy staying here with us.'

'Okay.' The girls agree.

They eat their breakfast in silence. Andrea takes her coffee upstairs and starts on the computer file which is labelled 'Kate's bag'. Hours go by and Kate is just meeting people and chatting. She must have left her bag in the hallway to her house because nothing much can be picked up on the bug except doorbells ringing and people exchanging deliveries at the front door. Kate takes that handbag to work a few times and, as she is a lawyer, Andrea isn't sure if she should be listening in on conversations with clients. However, one of them got interesting. Andrea listens to a consultation between Kate and a woman possibly in her office at work, from a few days ago.

'Hi, Kate. I've been thinking about the legal side of things.'

'Of what?'

'Well, the adoption.'

'Yes.'

'Well. We haven't signed anything yet.'

'We keep the adoption agency out of it and just inform the courts.'

'Which courts?'

'The family courts.'

'Oh.'

'Yes, the adoption agency is being investigated so we won't be using them.'

'Oh, I see.'

'I've submitted the paperwork to the Family Court, and you will be the legal guardians of Gabrielle in a few weeks. I'll let you know.'

'Okay thank you, Kate.'

'My pleasure.'

Andrea is puzzled but goes on to listen to one of Georgia's handbag bug files. She fast forwards until she gets to something that sounds interesting. She can hear Georgia's voice mention the ice cream restaurant. She thinks she may be talking to her husband in her kitchen.

'It's all kicked off at the ice cream restaurant,' says Georgia.

'Oh?' a man's voice says.

'Yes, someone went berserk and killed people.'

'Oh well, that's the fast-food industry for you. Really low-class people.'

'Do you think it's drugs?'

'Probably.'

'There were cops everywhere, apparently,' Georgia says.

Andrea wonders how Georgia knew that. It wasn't on the news yet.

Andrea's not sure if this means anything but she's too tired in the evenings to go through all the recordings. She's still a bit shaken from the ice cream restaurant massacre. And to think she used to love ice cream. This has definitely put her off!

She keeps trying to make sense of this weird suburb. *If adoptions that might not be legal! It may be connected with the missing people. If people are not going through the adoption agency, where would all the records be?*

Andrea decides to go to bed and sleep on it. When her mind is completely clear and drifting off to sleep, that's the time when she thinks of solutions. She looks up to the ceiling and remembers that Luke is on the other side, sleeping, and hopefully finding refuge from whatever he has come from.

CHAPTER 9

The Complete Family

The following afternoon, Andrea reaches into the post box again and there is nothing unusual this time. However, she sees a letter from the London Adoption Agency which has been redirected. She becomes breathless. Several months ago, she wrote to the adoption agency about a baby boy she had given up for adoption in the UK in her youth. She had become pregnant to her university professor, and he wanted her to have an abortion. She couldn't face doing that, so instead, she started wearing bigger clothes and deferred her second year at uni. The baby boy was born in the UK and was adopted by an English couple.

Trembling in front of the house, Andrea opens the letter.

Dear Andrea Stevens (her maiden name),

We have passed on your request to your son who has stated that he would very much like to meet with you. He grew up with UK parents who have since moved to Canada, and they have recently provided an address, where he now resides in the US. The address is listed below with his mobile number. Regards...

Andrea screams and drops the letter. Not only does he want to meet her, but he is less than a three-hour drive away instead of having to fly to another country. She squeals again.

'Andrea. What is it?' Greg yells out the kitchen window.

'It's okay. I have news.' She goes running into the house to tell the family. They knew about the baby she had given up and had been trying to convince her to get in touch with him.

'Mum, you must go,' says Sophie, as they all stand in the kitchen watching Andrea to experience her every expression.

'Yes. Now,' says Alice.

'Shall we come too?' says Greg.

'No. I want to meet him first. Shall I call him first?'

'No, surprise him,' says Sophie.

'Oh. I can't believe it!' Andrea stares into the room at nothing. The girls know they are now taking second place to an older brother but are suddenly excited.

'Wow. A brother,' says Sophie.

'Are you okay with this?' Andrea turns to Greg.

'Of course!'

'A brother!' says Alice, as if it hasn't sunk in.

'Well, let's see what he's like,' says Andrea in an attempt to make the girls feel more important.

'Yeah, he could be an axe murderer,' laughs Sophie.

'Sophie!'

Andrea grabs her bag and the letter which has his address and rushes out the door.

'I'll ring you and tell you how it goes,' she says as she runs out.

The girls and Greg look excited for her.

'Is he going to live here?' they ask Greg.

'I don't know. I guess he could. Let's see what your mum thinks and make sure she likes him first.'

'Of course, she'll like him. It's like saying that she may not like us some day,' says Sophie.

'That's not entirely impossible,' says Greg.

'Very funny.'

'Oh, Dad. Double negatives are sooooo—'

'Okay. Okay. I was kidding.'

'Can we stay up and see how it goes? She has to drive three hours to get there, then they talk, then she drives back.'

'Help me with dinner and you can stay up.'

'Yeah, it's not like we have a school to go to.'

'Mmm.'

'Mum,' Sophie yells at her as she's leaving. 'What is his name?'

She turns slowly as she smiles and says, 'They called him "Harry".'

Andrea drives for hours with so much adrenaline in her veins that she has to keep watching the speedometer and slowing down. She had dreamed about their first meeting for the past twenty years. *Will he look like me? Will we have things in common? Will he call me 'Mother?' Will he want to live with me? Did he get an education? Does he have a job? Is he on benefits?* All these questions go through her mind as she starts to worry. She wonders if he's not the sort of person that she could have in her life. *What if he's committed crimes?* Andrea thought, as she really knew nothing at all about him. At least if she still worked at MI5, she could have done an unauthorised check first. But there's no time to waste now. It seems that she has already wasted twenty years that she could have spent with him.

Andrea plays out the other scenario in her head, seeing as she has so much time on her hands during the journey. She considered the possibility of leaving uni at the age of nineteen and looking after her baby. She could have lived at home with her parents,gone back to finish her studies part-time and completed her degree at the age of twenty-five or twenty-six. Then gone straight to work at MI5, met Greg at the coffee shop close by,got married, had the girls...

No, she thinks to herself. Any change in the past could mean that she may have never met Greg and the girls would not exist. This way seemed better somehow. At least she has three children and is about to get to know the third one all over again.

Memories of the birth come flooding back to her. She did a lot of yelling at the nurses. *No one tells you about the pain*, she thinks. *Or the heartache about the adoption process.*

A tear rolls down Andrea's face. She was young. She was in two minds about the adoption. On the one hand, she was relieved that she could continue the enjoyment of her youth without the constraints of a baby. But on the other hand, she missed him desperately from the moment they took him. She could hear him crying all the way down the corridor and whispered, 'One day, I will find you. I will find you. And you will be mine again.'

Her mobile rings. 'Mum. Are you there yet?' Sophie says through the handsfree.

'Nearly. Are you guys okay?'

'Yep.'

'Did Dad cook dinner or was it sandwiches?'

'Sandwiches.'

'Oh well. I'll see you later, with Harry hopefully, unless he turns out to be a psycho,' She laughs nervously.

'Well, he has the genes for it,' says Sophie.

'Thanks.'

'No problem.'

'Okay, see you at midnight. That's probably when I'll get back.'

'Bye.'

'Bye.'

Andrea finally comes to the front of the house that Harry is staying in. She has driven for over three hours due to the traffic and her heart is racing. She tries to get out of the car without undoing her seatbelt. Her eyes stay focused on the house as she removes the belt and walks up the long path to the front door.

She looks for a bell but there is none. The house looks shabby. Paint falling off. She feels as if she has come to rescue him. *He is definitely coming home to our place tonight,* she thinks to herself. She knocks at the door. Several minutes pass with no reaction from the occupants. She thinks that maybe he has changed his mind. *Is he hiding in there? Does he hate me for giving him up? Has he had a terrible time and is now damaged?* She thinks.

The door opens abruptly and a young man with blond hair says, 'Yep. You lost, lady?'

She knows the blond boy is not Harry because he should have brown hair and hazel eyes. She leans forward to look at his eyes to be sure that the blond hair is not peroxide.

'Blue eyes,' she says.

'Okay, lady, what do you want? I don't date older ladies and if you've been sent here by a dating website, well, it wasn't me who clicked on your picture so—'

She interrupts him, 'Does Harry live here?'

'Yeah.' He looks her up and down before calling Harry. 'HARRY. SOME CHICK HERE TO SEE YOU.'

'What?' a voice yells out and her heart stops.

He lets her in. Harry sees her and ducks behind the armchair. Andrea immediately recognises him as the stalker who had been following her.

'YOU'RE THAT GUY!' Andrea yells and points at him. 'You're that stalker. What are you doing? Are you pretending to be my son now? As well as stalking me.'

'I am your son.'

'I don't believe you.'

'Can't you tell we look the same? You're Andrea Hanson. Pregnant at nineteen. My birthday is eighteenth June.'

Andrea's not convinced. He could have hacked a computer to get that information.

'You had me in London at the Royal London Hospital. I was given up for adoption to a couple who moved to Canada. You wrote to *me*, lady, and I was checking whether I wanted to meet *you* before... to see what you are like... so I stalked you a bit. It's not a crime.'

'Heavy!' one of his house mates pipes up.

'You frightened me. And it *is* a crime.'

Harry's housemates laugh.

'I had to check you out and make sure you weren't a weirdo.'

'It wasn't an invitation to follow me around and scare the crap out of me.' She walks closer to the armchair and puts her face into his, checking his features.

Harry cowers and puts his hands over his head to protect himself from Andrea.

'Why didn't you just ring me? I've been frightened for two months.'

'Two months?'

'Yes.'

'No, I've just been stalking you for two weeks.'

'Rubbish,' She says.

'It's true. I just got here from Canada two weeks ago.'

'He's telling the truth,' one housemate says. 'He just flew here a few weeks ago.'

'I did see some other bloke following you though, last week.'

'What!' She's not sure if she believes him.

'Yeah, I just thought it was another one of your illegitimate children.'

Another housemate laughs.

'Why didn't you call the police if you knew I was in danger.'

'And say what? "Oh, I'm just stalking a woman and could you please come and arrest the other stalker?"'

'Is it really you?' She looks at him closely. 'Are you Harry Chandler, my son?' He is overweight, a nice face though, pleasant looking, attractive... possibly. Long brown hair down to his shoulders and hazel eyes.

The housemates look at each other in surprise.

'Yes. Sorry to disappoint you.'

'Look, we can't talk here, Harry,' she says softly.

The state of the house left much to be desired. It was a typical man cave with a rabbit running around leaving small poos and beer cans stacked so high that they have made an Eiffel Tower that almost touched the ceiling.

'Nice artwork,' Andrea says in a more pleasant tone.

'Thanks.'

'Look, come back to my house and meet my family... we can talk, get to know each other. Pack some things. I'll wait in the car.'

Harry is not sure.

'You decide. Sorry it wasn't a more memorable reunion. I've been stressed.' She leaves the house, feeling slightly deflated that she has just interrogated her son and sat in the car, hoping he would follow her.

The group of young men look confused. Harry stands still for three seconds as if unsure about whether he wants to get to know Andrea further. Then suddenly, his mind is made up and he frantically picks up clothes from the floor and shoves them into a bag and collects the bunny on the way out, saying, 'Later, dudes', before the door slams on his way out and they yell out, 'Don't forget the rent.' Harry runs down the brick path, nearly tripping.

Suddenly, he wants to know her. She forgave him so quickly for the stalking so that must be a bonus. He opens the back door of the 4WD and throws the bags on the back seat and straps the bunny in with a harness from his bag. He had been taking it for walks, like a dog, with a chihuahua dog brace and lead. Harry sits in the front seat with her and there is an awkward silence as they drive for a few minutes before anyone says anything.

'I'm sorry I scared you,' Harry apologises.

'It's okay. I'm worried about the other stalker now.'

'Could he be another son?'

'NO. Look, there's a lot going on in my life at the moment. I don't want to scare you but the less you know the better. Also, there was a dead body at my kids' school.'

'COOL,' Harry says while he looks at Andrea. She looks back at him in a confused manner.

'The houses I'm trying to sell are haunted.'

'EXCELLENT!'

'And, well...'

'Your life sounds pretty exciting.'

'Oh?'

'Yeah, I was worried that you would be some boring old housewife.'

'Ummm... well...'

'But every cloud has a silver lining,' he says

'Oh really?'

'Yeah. We found each other and I think you're nice.'

'Well, that's good because we're driving towards my house and you're going to meet my kids.'

'Kids! How many?'

'Two girls.'

'Girls! Thank God. I'm your only son. Whooeeeeeee. No competition. No male ego shit.'

'You're pleased.'

'Hell yeah!'

'Your parents… what were they like?' Andrea is concerned about whether he had a good upbringing.

'Oh, they were really cool.'

'Oh, good.'

'Yeah, they were always so stoned that they didn't know if I was at school or not.'

'Great,' she says sarcastically.

'Yeah, and they'd go outside and shoot wild birds with their shotguns and then fall asleep in the garden, drunk.'

'Lovely. Don't tell me any more. Did you go to uni after school? Do you have a job? What do you like doing?'

'Hell. Is this a job interview? I like computers.'

'Oh, that's good.'

'Yeah, I've kinda educated myself.'

'Oh?' She seems disappointed.

'Yeah, I can track people, find out what their habits are… you know, clone their phones and stuff.'

Andrea starts to smile. He *is* her son. It's confirmed. He is just like her and the girls.

'Okay, I get it. The girls like that too.'

'Excellent. I can't wait to meet them.'

'Oh, trust me… they're interesting. They are always giving people advice… you know like as if they have lived longer than them… They are wise beyond their years. They are identical twins so… they have this whole twin thing going on and it can be hard for other people to break into their little unit. Sophie is the more dominant of the two though. Alice waits for Sophie to do something mischievous then she joins in. It can be hard to tell them apart so, if you're not sure, the one acting up is likely to be Sophie.

'Okay. Sounds like fun!'

'Well, that's one word for it.'

Andrea wants to find out more about Harry though. 'So, you've *had* jobs?'

'Oh yeah. Don't worry, I can easily get a job. I did study computer science at uni in Canada. When I say I educated myself, that's because I found the work quite remedial... you know, basic? I did some extra classes online which really helped to give me more advanced knowledge.'

'Sounds interesting... What do you like to eat?'

'Wow. It *is* an interview. Umm... I guess I like steak, fish and chips, regular food. My parents weren't really into anything spicy.'

'And do you have a girlfriend?'

'Not at the moment. I'm in-between relationships... which is a nice place to be actually. I tend to pick up the psychos.'

'Oh. Interesting.' Andrea sounds worried that there is going to be a psycho ex-girlfriend turning up at her house. 'Who were those people you're living with?'

'I only know one of them well. I went to uni with him, the others are his friends really.'

After about an hour of catching up, Andrea pulls up at a gas station and gives Harry money.

'Go in and pay for forty dollars of gas and buy yourself some snacks.'

'Yes, Mum.'

Andrea smiles at him and is surprised at how quickly he's using the 'Mum' word.

He joyfully goes into the gas station shop, almost skipping. The shelves of chocolates and sweets make up a small smorgasbord that he can hardly choose from. He lovingly looks out of the window and gazes at the mother he never had and is slightly concerned to see a man talking to Andrea. It is worrying that the man is standing so close to her. Harry throws forty dollars at the cashier and walks out quickly to the car.

'Hey, buddy!' he says to the man.

'Hey, son.'

'How did you know I was her son?'

'Take a walk so your mother and I can get acquainted.'

'I don't think she's your type,' Harry says calmly.

'What?' says the man.

'Yeah, she only likes men with teeth.' Harry doesn't like the look of the man. He looks like he has been in prison.

'Just piss off, son.'

'Once again, she likes men with teeth.'

Andrea looks scared.

She shakes her head as if to say *'don't escalate this'*.

'If you run inside and tell that office manager, we'll be gone by the time you come back. And look, my plates are so dirty that no one will get the number. So just piss off if you know what's good for you. I have a gun in my pocket.'

'If you had a gun in your pocket, we wouldn't still be talking,' Harry says, and Andrea is visibly shaking as the man tries to take her arm. Just then, there's a loud noise.

BANG! Harry shoots the man's foot without removing the gun from his hoodie pocket.

'What I didn't contribute to that conversation is that *I* have a gun,' Harry says calmly.

The man yells and falls to cradle his foot. Harry steps on the man to get past him and into the car. Andrea screams and gets in the car and they drive off. Harry is high from the excitement. They drive down the road. Andrea is at the wheel, breathless and still shaking, trying to drive straight.

'What the hell did you do?' yells Andrea.

'What? I saved your arse, literally.'

'You can't go around shooting people.'

'Yes, you can... In the USA, we have the right to defend ourselves. This is not England, Mother.'

'You're crazy.'

'That's not very nice. If it wasn't for this gun, we'd be buggered. Or... you'd be buggered. I don't think he was hot for me.'

'Why didn't you tell me you had a gun?'

'Because we just met, and I didn't know if you were a psycho.'

'I'm planning to introduce you to my daughters and you're insane.'

'Haaaayyy. You shouldn't criticise your children. You should always praise them first and *then* give constructive criticism. All the parenting books say that.'

'Shush. I'm trying to drive.'

'Look, I'll take the bullets out and give them to you once I'm sure that Eileen is not chasing us.'

'Eileen?'

'Yes, *I lean*... Get it. He can't stand up straight now, so he has to lean. Or I could call him Footloose... Maybe we should call him Hop-a-long... or—'

'STOP. This is not funny.'

'I think it is. He said "I have a gun"... then BANG! He didn't know *I* had a gun. That's funny, Mother.'

She shakes her head. 'It's GBH. Do you know what that stands for?'

'Good Boy Harry?'

'Grievous Bodily Harm and there are probably cameras filming at the station.'

'Look, Mum… just chill.'

Again, she can't believe he's calling her 'mum' already.

'He's a shit. No one will care. If he goes into a police station and reports me, the police will take one look at him and not give a shit.'

'Really?' She starts to calm down.

'Yeah. They will count the number of missing teeth with the number of tattoos and divide it by his predicted IQ and tell him to fuck off.'

'What?'

'He's not going to go to the police and report it because he'd have to hide his gun first.'

'How can you be so calm?'

'Because I'm young and all young people think they are invincible.'

He's like the girls. He has an answer for everything, Andrea thinks.

'Jesus,' she says.

'It's probably all the hash I've smoked passively since birth.'

'I'm trying to drive.'

'Okay.'

'And don't tell my family.'

'Do you want me to drive?' he offers.

'NO!'

They continue for a few more miles in silence with Harry trying to think of something to say to change the subject.

'So, tell me about you and why did you come to the US if there are guns here?'

'I'm not that scared of guns. I worked in Intelligence.'

'What?'

'Well, I was an analyst for M15 and—'

'Fuck off!'

She looks at him with a strange look and says, 'Language.'

'You're a spy?'

'No, just an analyst. So, I would look at the behaviour of people, make predictions based on data and look for trends.'

'Oh okay. Still cool though.'

'But I guess I got to know how horrible the world is.'

'Yeah. Like what?'

'Well, the last thing I worked on was a blackmailing racket and it led to lots of arrests.'

'Wow.'

'I don't think they caught everyone.'

'Wow.'

'Yes. I feel as if I made a difference though. But really, I just want a normal life now. You know… normal,' Andrea stresses.

'Yeah.'

'I don't want to be looking over my shoulder all the time. People see me leave the MI5 building in the evenings. They look at me strangely and a couple of times I thought I was being followed home.'

'Oh.'

'I just had enough of London.'

'So, you came to the US where all the mad gun owners are?'

'Well, it must sound stupid.'

'I'm not judging.'

'And my husband is from Philadelphia. He really wanted to get back to the sunshine.'

'Yeah, me too, Canada sucks. It's so cold that your balls freeze. Seriously. I don't know if I can have children.'

'I'm sure you can. Don't mention that you shot a man in the foot to my husband.'

'No problem.'

'Or to the girls. It might give them ideas.'

'Really?'

'Oh yeah, they're into weird games like "Hostage" and they set traps in the house and garden.'

'Should I be frightened?'

'Yes.'

'Great,' he says worryingly.

'And one more thing, there's a ten-year-old boy living in our loft. My husband doesn't know yet. The girls are bringing him food. We don't know his name. We call him Luke. Please avoid him. You might scare him off.'

'Okay,' Harry says with a puzzled look.

'What's that noise?' she asks.

'My bunny.'

'You brought the bunny? Oh, the girls will love that...'

'Oh, I know what I want to ask you.'

'Oh no. I think I know what it is.'

'Well... Who was my father? Do you even know? I mean if you're not sure who knocked you up, then that's okay.'

'Harry!' she interrupts him. 'He was my professor at uni and... I'm sorry to say... he didn't want me to have a baby because he was married and had kids of his own. He thought his wife would leave him and his kids would hate him so...'

'Soo... does he know that you stayed pregnant? Does he know I exist?'

'No. Sorry.'

'Oh.' Harry goes quiet for a few seconds.

Andrea looks at him to gauge his reaction. 'Are you upset?'

'Well. Some dude didn't want me to be born. I don't know how I feel to be honest. I think I want to meet him and beat the crap out of him.'

'Be my guest. He lives in London though.'

'Arsehole.'

'Yeah,' Andrea agrees.

Andrea and Harry finally arrive at her house. Andrea had telephoned Greg, so they know to expect Harry. As he gets out of the car Harry feels like he is in heaven. The white house with the perfect fence. He can smell home cooked food coming from the neighbour's house.

The front door swings open, and the sees two identical girls run down the stairs to greet him.

'Hi, bruv!' says Sophie.

'Hi, bruv!' says Alice almost at the same time.

They throw their small arms around his waist and their heads are almost buried into his abdomen.

'Wow. Soft,' says Alice referring to his soft tummy.

'Yeah soft. You could be our new pillow,' Says Sophie.

'Girls! That's rude.'

'Sorry, Har... arrghh! A bunny?' Sophie exclaims.

'Can we keep it?' asks Alice.

'She's called Thelma,' says Harry.

'You bought us a bunny?'

'Well, um, yes, do you like it?'

'Love it,' they say in unison.

'Welcome, Harry.' Greg extends his hand.

'Thank you, sir.'

'Call me Greg.'

'Okay.'

They all walk inside the house with Thelma in a harness and dog lead held by Sophie.

Harry looks around from the hallway, almost doing a three-hundred-and-sixty-degree turn. It's homely. No smell of weed.

Normal pictures on the walls and no painted hippie murals. Finally, he felt he had come home and could experience 'normal' for a change.

'Girls, take him up to the spare room. Show him where the towels are and let him have a shower... on his own... without a video camera.'

'Killjoy.'

'SOPHIE!'

'Okay, Mummy.'

Harry wonders why they need to be *told* not to film him in the shower.

'Alice, can you keep an eye on her?' Andrea knew it was a futile request, as they were just as cheeky as each other.

Andrea walks back into the kitchen to tell Greg all about it. He pours Andrea a glass of wine.

'Well. How did it go?' Greg is keen to find out all the details.

'Well, we had a long drive back and talked a lot. He's definitely my son. He's so much like the girls.'

'Really?'

'Yes. You know I feel as if we finally have a compete family. I feel complete. Does that make sense?'

'Yes. It does. How long do you want him to stay here?' Greg asks.

She gives him an angry look.

'I'm just curious. Is he going to be calling me Dad?'

'Let's just see what he wants first and whether it's feasible.'

'The girls love him already,' Greg says, trying to make up for his previous question.

'Yes, but can he cope with them? They have a victim now to practice their karate on.' Andrea laughs.

'Yeah, they may give *me* a break. I think I like him already,' says Greg.

She laughs as she heats up a pizza.

'He has a similar personality as the girls. It's weird. At times when we were driving, I felt like I was talking to them. You know, Greg… we had a bit of trouble at the petrol station and Harry protected me.'

'Really? He flexed some muscles, did he?'

'Something like that.'

'Is he aggressive?' Greg asks.

'No,' Andrea lies. 'He told some guy to stop talking to me.'

'Well, he can stay as long as he likes,' Greg says, as if it was his decision.

'Thank you.' She kisses Greg on the cheek. But did not need his approval. 'My baby boy is finally home.'

Greg laughs. 'A rather large baby.'

'Don't be mean.'

'I'm just saying… I could get him running with me in the morning,' Greg suggests.

'Just leave him be… He'll lose weight running away from the girls.'

'Yeah.' They laugh and drink wine, waiting near the oven for their pizza.

Later, Andrea decides to check on Harry. She walks into the spare room and finds him sitting up on the bed with a T-shirt and joggers on.

'Are you comfortable here?'

'Yeaaahhh,' Harry says enthusiastically.

'I'm heating up a frozen pizza so come down and get it later.'

'Oh, I've already had three pizzas today. This is a king size bed.'

'Yes.'

'When people stay over, do they sleep three in a bed?'

'No.'

'Then why so large?'

'Everything is big in America,' she explains.

'Yeah, that's for sure.'

'Did the girls annoy you?' she asks.

'No. They just hid my towel and I had to walk out of the bathroom naked.'

'Oh sorry.'

'I think they took a video. Will they post it on the Internet? I'm not bothered if they do.'

'I'll sort it out… GIRLS,' she shouts.

'DELETE THAT VIDEO!' she shouts down the hall.

'IT'S ONLY OF HIS FACE. WE'RE NOT PERVERTS!' Sophie shouts.

'THAT'S NOT THE POINT!'

'WHERE'S THE POINT?' Alice says cheekily.

'WITHIN A FEW MINUTES OF A MAN ENTERING THIS HOUSE, YOU HAVE MANAGED TO SEE HIM NAKED.'

'No,' says Sophie. The girls came down the hallway to Harry's room.

'NO?'

'He covered his vital parts as he walked around looking for his towel. We saw nothing,' Alice explains.

'Go to bed.'

'She's in a bad mood again,' Alice says to Sophie as they scamper off.

'Menopause probably,' says Sophie.

'I can hear you!' Andrea yells.

'Do other thirteen-year-old girls do that?' Harry asks.

'No. I blame the Internet. I try to block things, but they find ways of getting around it. I checked their search engine one day and nearly had a heart attack. Anyway, I'm going to go and give them another bollocking and take their phones off them or they won't sleep.'

Harry laughs. 'Bollocking? What's that?'

'It's an English term for a telling off. I would have thought your parents knew that word. Don't answer that. Now try to sleep. You've had a big day. You've saved my life and you've survived an introduction to my daughters.' She walks to the door to leave and turns and looks at him with motherly eyes. 'Will Thelma be okay in your backpack?' Andrea can see her nose peeping out.

'Yeah. She's used to it.'

'Night, Harry,' she says. 'Oh, and pretend you don't know about...,' she points to the loft where Luke will be sleeping.

'Sure. Night, Andrea... Mum.'

She turns the light off and leaves the door ajar, like she would for a young kid.

Harry is content. He likes the weirdness. He can hear Andrea bollocking the girls and smiles to himself and he goes off to sleep.

CHAPTER 10

The Liberty Bell

Andrea awakes to remember that her son is now living with her. She jumps out of bed and goes to his room. He's not there so she goes downstairs and finds him with his head in the fridge and his bottom sticking out over the top of his tracksuit pants. The girls are sitting around the breakfast table giggling and looking at his exposed buttocks.

'Morning,' Andrea says.

'Oh, morning.' Harry lifts his head out of the fridge. 'I just thought you might have pancakes in here like other perfect American families.'

'Ummm,' Andrea says.

'We're not perfect,' Sophie says.

'You know like on TV those perfect families... they always have pancakes for breakfast,' he says.

'You've been watching too much TV, Harry,' Alice jokes.

'I can make pancakes,' says Andrea. She'd make him a four-course meal if he wanted it.

'Really? That would be so cool.'

'So, Harry,' says Sophie.

'Yes, Soph... umm, Al...' He can't tell them apart.

'I'm Sophie.'

'And I'm Alice.'

Andrea looks at them because they have just lied. *But does it really matter?* she thinks.

'Do you have a job?' Sophie asks.

'Umm. I'm currently freelancing…'

'Oh, I see.'

'Did you go to Uni?' asks Alice.

'Ummm, yes and no. I did computer science but basically taught myself and didn't go in that much.'

'Where is Thelma?' asks Alice.

'Oh, under the bed. She gets nervous. Ummm, what do you guys do on Saturdays?'

'Terroise the neighbourhood!' says Sophie.

Harry looks shocked. He didn't believe her but just thought it was a weird thing to say.

'But since that became illegal, we had to curtail our weekend hunting expeditions,' says Alice.

Harry looks bothered.

'Chill,' Sophie says. 'She's joking.'

'We are more like boys when it comes to hobbies.'

'Oh.'

'Yeah, we like to build forts in the garden and practise air-rifle shooting.'

'Yes, we got these really cool targets off the internet last week.'

'Do you wanna see?'

'YES.' Harry is excited about the hobbies of his sisters

'Go and show him the guns, girls, and I'll cook the pancakes.'

'Okay.'

That reminded Andrea. Where was Harry's *real* gun? *Is it in the car?* She wondered.

Andrea goes out to the car but remembers that there could be post on a Saturday, and more importantly, there could be another clue in the post box. She opens the post box to find nothing there. Looking around to see if anyone is watching her, She sees Muriel from across the road. She is at her curtain and quickly moves away from the window when Andrea sees her. There are some people jogging in the street. Andrea doesn't really know the other neighbours yet, nor is she too keen to meet them.

It's the first Saturday with her long-lost son. She is now torn. She wants to meet with Natalie but also wants to spend a nice normal day with the son that she hasn't known for so many years. Peering out the back window, she sees the three of her offspring setting up targets to shoot. She smiles. *The complete family*, she thinks to herself. Somehow, she feels that the girls are safe with Harry.

Greg wakes up and is like a bear with a sore head.

'I think Harry was sleep walking,' he says.

'Oh. Why?'

'I heard someone moving around last night.'

'Oh. Sorry.' Andrea knows it could have been Luke but doesn't want to tell Greg.

'What do you want to get up to today?'

'Well, I guess we could show Harry around Spring Town. Maybe go out for some lunch?'

'Okay.'

They are setting up to do some shooting in the back yard first.'

'Oh. I'll have a bath then.' Greg goes off for a long soak. He puts headphones on, as usual, whenever the girls are practicing their shooting. Andrea finishes the pancakes and brings them out to the garden. She sneaks one into the loft for Luke seeing as Greg is in the bath. He is asleep but she leaves it just inside the loft hatch.

After a morning of garden target shooting, they come in and the girls tell Andrea how impressed they are with his skills.

'He's a dead shot!' says Sophie.

'Really?'

'Yeeahhh!' says Alice.

Andrea knew he could shoot at close range, from the Gas Station. But long range is a different skill altogether.

'How do you fancy a look around town?' asks Andrea.

'Yeah, we can show you the secret tunnels,' Sophie says.

'TUNNELS!' Andrea yells as she can't believe her ears. To think that the girls know about the tunnels that may have been use for drug trafficking recently.

'Yes, Mum. The tunnels that were used during prohibition. It's on the website and we were going to take a school trip there, but we've been at home instead,' Alice explains.

'So, there was a school trip organised?'

'Yes. Why are you freaking out? It was supposed to be next week,' Sophie says.

'Jesus!' Andrea says loudly.

'What?' Harry asks.

'I have to ring…'

'Who?' Sophie asks.

'No one.'

'Are you okay, Mum?' Harry asks.

The girls look at each other, as he has called her "Mum."

'Yes, but no one is to go near those tunnels,' she demands.

'Why?'

'Just trust me on this.'

Andrea rings Natalie who has left for the weekend with Peter for a romantic getaway. She leaves a message saying that a group of school children are going to be taken to those tunnels and that maybe the children will not be safe. Natalie rings her back and agrees that they should have some surveillance on the school trip and that they will discuss it on Monday. She tells Andrea that she went down the tunnels with a video camera and walked around as many of them as she could. She's going to try to explore more when she gets back from her trip with Peter.

Andrea feels calmer and decides to take her family to see the Liberty Bell in the centre of Philadelphia. It is more to help herself forget about the goings on in Spring Town and to try to have a nice day out. They all get dressed for the trip. Harry feeds Thelma and the girls leave more food for Luke.

The journey starts with the usual questioning from the girls, although this time they are firing questions at Harry.

'Sooooo, Harry… She abandoned you?'

'Girls!' Andrea says.

'Ummm, yes, I guess.'

'And you're okay with that?'

'Ummm, I had great parents. It's not like I suffered or anything.'

'Mmmmmmm,' Sophie says, suspiciously.

'Have you had a girlfriend?' asks Alice.

Harry was shocked by the random question.

'How many friends do you have on social media?'

'Forty close ones only.'

'Have you been to Europe?'

'Not really.'

'What things are you good at?'

'Well, mostly nerd things.'

'I'm listening,' says Sophie, and they both look at him more intensely.

'I like hacking into computers, stealing people's passwords

and messing with them,' he says.

'You steal money?'

'No.''

Andrea looks at Greg as if she's not sure if that part was true.

'You're kidding?' says Alice.

'No.'

Andrea smiles from the front seat, as he tried to impress them.

'That's soooo cooool,' the girls say.

'Can you show us how to do it?'

'Well, I'm not sure Andrea would be too keen. If you got caught, you might get some time in juvenile detention or something.'

'What else can you do?' asks Alice.

'I'm good at electrics. I can rewire things and get things to work.'

Andrea is thinking of how useful he can be, and he could maybe help her with her consultancy work for Natalie.

'What kind of electrics?' Andrea asks.

'Radios, walkie talkies, Garage doors...'

'Mmmmmmm,' Andrea says, thinking of more possibilities.

'We're kinda similar,' says Alice.

'How so?'

'Well, I don't know if we can trust you yet. Soo...'

'Okay, I get it.'

'Let's just say we have a lot of equipment.'

Harry's intrigued.

'Do you like it here in the US?' Sophie asks.

'Yeah. It's too cold in Canada.'

There's a pause while they look Harry up and down.

'So, what kinda women are you attracted to?' asks Sophie.

'Oh um… well…'

'Let me guess… tall… long hair… glamourous… takes care of herself…'

'Well, yes, but they are hard to hold on to… if I manage to get one of them in the first place.'

'Don't bother, Harry,' Alice pipes up.

'Yes, she's right, Harry. Women like that are not real. They spend a lot of time making sure that they look amazing all the time. How boring is that?' Sophie explains.

'Yes, they are fake. They skip meals to look good. They are constantly obsessing over their looks,' says Alice.

'They're always looking in a mirror,' Sophie adds.

'So basically, what we're saying, Harry, is that you can't have a relationship with a woman who is just having a relationship with herself.'

Andrea is listening and wondering where they get their info from.

'Now are there any female nerd friends that you can think of?'

'Well yes… but…'

'Now think of them with makeup on and a bikini.'

Andrea pulls a face and wonders when the topic is going to be over.

Harry concentrates and stares into the distance, trying to imagine his friend from Uni in a bikini with red lipstick on. Greg is trying not to laugh at his thirteen-year-olds giving dating advice when they have never been on a date.

'If you ask a nerd girl out for a date, she *will* put makeup on for you *and* a nice dress *and* get her hair done. But she just doesn't do that for every guy to see who walks past her in the street,' Sophie explains.

'Yes. Do you really want a girl who needs attention from every man in the vicinity, every day?' Alice asks.

'No... um... that makes sense. You guys are pretty smart! You should have your own blog.'

'We're thinking of setting up an online thing where people can ask us for advice!'

'Oh really?'

Andrea is trying not to laugh.

'Hey. I've just realised... as your name is Harry, the first letter of our first names makes up the word shaag!' Sophie announces.

'Oh! Back to being immature,' says Andrea.

'Well... Sophie, Harry, Andrea, Alice and Greg... our first initials spell shaag!'

'That's brilliant!' Alice says. 'They used to spell saag!'

'What's a shag? We don't have that word in Canada.'

'Sex. Harry,' says Alice.

'Oh,' he says, slightly embarrassed.

'We knew a *posh* family in the UK... Petula, Oliver, Sebastian and Harriett.'

Harry laughs. and adds his own. 'What about a *trashy* family?'

Alice helps with this one. 'Yes. They could be calledTrevor, Ricky, Ann, Sharon, and Yvonne.'

'You could have Peter, Octavia, and Oliver... the *poo* family.'

'What about *smell*?' Harry says, to encourage them.

'Sarah, Melanie, Elaine, Louise, and Lorretta.'

'*Snog*?' Harry says.

'Sorry, you're my brother,' says Sophie in a fit of laughter.

'Noooooo, can you make up names for it?'

'Stephanie, Natalie, Olive, George,' says Alice, quickly to dilute Harry's red-face.

'So, you have snogs in Canada but not shags? Interesting,' says Alice.

'What about the *devil* family?' Harry asks.

'Donald, Evelyn, Victoria, Iris and Leslie.'

'You guys are great at this,' Harry says, genuinely enjoying himself.

'I knew a family that had nearly all the names of the royal family... Sarah, Harry, Charles, Elizabeth...'

'How weird,' the girls say together.

Andrea looks over at the three of them and smiles.

They arrive in Philadelphia downtown and want to go straight to the Indoor Market. Greg drops them off while he parks the car. They enter and immediately see chocolate being sold in all the shapes of human parts.

'Cooool,' says Alice. 'Look at the chocolate kidneys.'

'Oh my God,' says Sophie. 'I'd like to try the testicles.'

The market is busy, so Sophie and Alice take each of Harry's hands and drag him around the crowded aisles of stalls. Andrea follows behind in a state of euphoria, looking at how lovely her son is and how easily he fits into the family. They wander around, wide-eyed. The variety of food is something Harry has never seen before. They don't have quite the same sort of indoor markets in Canada. There is an open-planned eating area and Harry considers eating again even though they had pancakes for brunch.

After about twenty minutes, Greg finally returns, having parked the car and wants to go directly to the Liberty Bell. The girls complain. But eventually they wander off in the direction that Greg is leading them to and fall in line.

'Wooooooo!' says Sophie.

'Look at that big crack.' Pointing to the Liberty Bell.

'I guess it was rung a lot over the years.'

'No that happened the first time they rung it when it was delivered from London.'

'Reeaaallly?' the girls say together.

'Why do they call it the Liberty Bell?' asks Alice.

'It was called that when it became a symbol of liberty for the Abolitionists. The people who wanted to abolish slavery,' explains Greg.

'I think slavery was disgusting,' says Alice.

'Yeah. I can't believe people were treated like that. It's horrible,' says Sophie.

'Yes, it was,' says Andrea. 'And how can people today ever forget that their ancestors were treated so badly?'

'They were bought and sold!' Sophie says angrily.

'Yes. Horrible,' says Harry.

'We are so lucky now that it is over,' says Alice.

'No, well, there are still people being enslaved but not on the same grand scale.'

'What do you mean?' asks Alice.

'Forced labour,' Andrea says as she was thinking of children trafficking drugs. 'Forced marriages…'

'Why did they *take* people from other countries and bring them here?' asks Alice.

'They justified it in those days by needing a lot of people to work,' explains Greg.

'But if they needed workers, they could have done what we do now… you attract people to your business with benefits, salary, sometimes a house to live in, and rights!' says Sophie.

Workers have rights to work in a safe environment now and

to be treated with respect and dignity. You don't just *take* people against their will!' says Alice.

'Sometimes I'm ashamed to be white,' says Sophie.

'Me too,' says Alice.

'A lot of the presidents owned slaves,' says Harry.

'God!' says Sophie.

'The big North versus South Civil War was partly fought because the South wanted to keep people enslaved.'

'How greedy,' says Sophie.

'Yes. They knew they would have to pay proper wages if they didn't have slaves,' explains Greg.

'Eventually the male slaves were given citizenship in the late nineteenth century, but they still suffered because people couldn't accept them as equal,' Andrea explains.

'What happened?' asks Sophie.

'They segregated them, and they shut them out of voting houses so they couldn't vote anyway,' Greg adds.

'God. There should be compensation,' says Sophie.

'Yeah, for the descendants,' says Alice.

'There is a movement trying to do that,' Says Andrea.

'Really?' the girls ask.

'There were slaves in the UK too, but it wasn't taught that much when I was at school,' Andrea says.

'We learned about it,' says Sophie.

'Yeah?'

'They go on about it being "abolished", but actually the black people revolted, which helped things along,' explains Alice.

'Yeah. Sometimes, a revolution is what is needed to make things change,' Sophie adds.

Greg and Harry wander around the visitors' centre trying to get to know each other. They meet up with Andrea and the girls and Harry looks like he had been sweating.

'Everything okay?' Andrea asks.

'Yes, we've been having a chat,' Greg says.

Andrea looks worried and thinks Greg might have frightened Harry off. She wants him to live with the family, but Greg might not be so keen on the idea. Like all men, they say they're okay with something then start to complain later and change their minds. They all wander back to the Indoor Market and find a table in the middle for lunch. Harry lines up to get everyone cheese steak sandwiches. The girls are wondering if Harry will eat two of them and start giggling. Greg goes off to have a look around the centre and they remember that Luke will be on his own at lunchtime.

'We left him some food,' says Sophie.

'He will be okay. He will probably come down out of the loft while we're here,' Andrea reassures them. 'I wonder where he lived?' she asks.

'Maybe there. In that house.'

'Has he told you very much?' Andrea asks.

'No. Not really. We don't know anything about him,' says Sophie.

'Well, probably best not to probe him for information. It might scare him off,' Andrea says cautiously.

'Just wondering though, Mother… why haven't you told the police?'

'Well… ummmm… I'm still not sure who he is frightened of. You never know… he could be hiding from the police.'

'Really?' says Harry.

'So, let's wait until he opens up a bit.'

'Should we tell Dad now?' Alice asks.

'Nooooo,' Andrea says. 'He will want to tell the police straight away.'

'Yeah. True,' Says Sophie.

The drive home was sombre. The girls looked out of the car windows as they left Philadelphia and looked at the people sleeping rough. They were mostly black people. They had built little houses made of blankets and tents, in front of churches and on patches of grass in the street. They had realised how lucky they are, not to have been slaved. But mostly, they realised how horrible white people had behaved.

Harry slept on the way home. His two cheese steak sandwiches were causing him to burp in his sleep. Andrea didn't notice as she had too much on her mind. She needed to meet with Natalie again to go through things and was eagerly awaiting her return from the loved-up weekend.

In the time left to travel home, Andrea manages to have a quick nap in the car and has a dream. Her dream is set in her university years. She is at a party with loads of uni students. She is dressed scantily as nineteen-year-olds wore skirts that just covered their bottoms. And they wore tops which showed their abs.

In her dream, she is talking to a very hot Italian student who is studying art. She leans in to kiss him and then he is suddenly wearing a hoodie, like the stalker, so she stops herself and runs away. She runs out to the garden and sees a body of a woman lying face down in the pool. The headmaster is in the dream and is walking around the pool, saying, *'Well, I told you not to look in there.'* The dead person lifts her head and says, *'Look in the tunnels.'* Just then, there is a police car pulling up outside the party house. The police get out and come into the garden to drag the woman out of the pool. She is no longer dead and starts talking. She is not the dead teacher now but turns a mother who has lost her children. She is yelling, '*Where are they? Where are they... the children. Where are they?*' There is a crowd gathering around the pool and then a man approaches, like the one from the petrol station, where Harry used his gun. He looks at Andrea who is watching the whole performance. He reaches into his pocket and pulls out a gun just like Harry's. He says, '*I found your gun*' and points it right at Andrea's forehead. There's a BANG and Andrea wakes up.

'Sorry, I just caught the letter box as I pulled in.'

'Jesus, Greg!'

The girls are laughing loudly.

'Sorry. I can fix it,' Greg says.

Harry wakes up too and says he also had a dream. Andrea doesn't want to ask. They all walk into the house and whisper to each other that they must check on Luke and Thelma, in that order.

Andrea has had enough for one day and collapses in front of the TV. They order takeout, which keeps everyone happy.

CHAPTER 11

The Hiding

It's seven a.m. and Andrea is woken up by Detective Cameron's phone call.

'Andrea... it's Peter.'

'Peter?' She can't remember who he is as she's half asleep.

'Detective Cameron.'

'Oh. Hi... how's—'

'I think Natalie has been poisoned. I'm taking her to the hospital.'

'Oh God!'

'I think you guys could be in danger.'

'WHAT?' she yells down the phone.

'I'll explain later. Get your family across the road to Muriel's house.'

'Muriel?' she asks. *Why does he want us to go there?* she thinks.

'Yes, she's FBI,' Peter says.

'WHAT?' Andrea yells.

'Yes. Semi-retired. Please just do it, I'll explain later. Oh, and Andrea... don't take any phones or you can be traced,' he says then hangs up on her.

'Wake up, wake up!' Andrea says as she shakes Greg and runs into the girls' room. Luckily, they were awake.

'Get Luke and Harry, we need to GET OUT OF HERE NOW. Put your dressing gowns on and DON'T bring your phones.'

'What's going on, Mother?' they ask together.

Sophie and Alice look at each other but know it must be serious if they can't take their phones and jump out of bed. They put their dressing gowns on and get bags from under their bed, which are already packed, as they're survivalists. Sophie wakes up Harry and Alice goes into the loft. She convinces Luke to come down, which doesn't take long. In the meantime, Andrea tried again to get Greg out of bed.

'Are you sleepwalking?' he asks.

'We need to go NOW!'

'Where?'

'Across the road to Muriel's. She's FBI.'

'Wake up, Andrea, you're sleepwalking,' says Greg, finding the whole thing too ridiculous.

'Just get up, Dad. Mum's not kidding,' says Sophie, as she runs into their bedroom.

'Yeah, put a dressing gown on,' Andrea says.

Harry grabs Thelma and shoves her into a bag. The whole family moves quickly and rush down the stairs. Greg sees Luke coming down the loft ladder.

'What the…? Who—?' Greg asks.

'I'll explain later,' says Andrea.

'Is it safe to go outside?' asks Harry.

'Well, I don't think we're safe here,' Andrea replies anxiously. 'Did everyone leave their phones behind?'

'Yes, but can I have my gun back?' Harry asks.

'GUN?' yells Greg.

'No, let's go,' demands Andrea.

The six of them gingerly leave their house in dressing gowns and pyjamas, hoping they won't draw attention to themselves.

There are very few neighbours around. As they cross the road, Luke is hiding behind Andrea and Alice. Sophie is holding Harry's hand and Greg is rubbing his eyes and looking at Luke, puzzled, thinking he might be a friend of the girls. Muriel's front door is opened, and Andrea can see her waiting for them. A hundred questions are going through Andrea's head but she just walks into her hallway and asks the most important ones.

'Muriel. Do you know what's going on?' Andrea asks.

'Natalie's been recognised when she looked around the tunnels.'

'By who?'

'The cartel. Does anyone have a phone on them?' Muriel asks.

'No, I've asked them not to bring them.'

'The police think they may have poisoned Natalie as a warning for snooping around the tunnels. They may have seen you near the tunnels too so they might try to scare you off.'

'So, it's true. They use the tunnels and the school kids to push drugs,' says Andrea.

'Yes.'

'CAN SOMEBODY TELL ME WHAT'S GOING ON?' yells Greg.

'Ummmm, it's complicated.' Andrea doesn't want to deal with him now. They enter Muriel's front room.

'They knew you would be useful here,' Muriel says to Andrea, whilst ignoring Greg.

'Who?'

'MI5.'

'Oh, I've left there... I have left and I was only an analyst.'

'They sent you... *here*,' Muriel says in a patronising manner.

'No. No. I *chose* to come here.'

143

'Did you *choose* this suburb, or did someone *suggest* it? *And* the school?'

'Umm, well, yes, my boss... OH FUCK.' Andrea realises this could be a secret plan by her boss, so that he doesn't lose her entirely.

'Yes, check your bank account in the UK. I bet you're still being paid,' Muriel says, again sarcastically.

'FUCK! FUCK! FUCK!'

'Andrea, stop swearing,' says Greg. 'Are you telling me my wife's employers put her and my family in danger here?' Greg asks.

'Well, they nudged her in this direction and knew she would pick up on things and follow them up which is what she's been doing since she got here.'

'No. She's been working in real estate.'

Andrea walks away and shrinks down in Muriel's comfortable sofa.

'Andrea, what's been going on and who is this kid?'

'Look. We don't have time. My intel says there could be a warning sent to Andrea this morning,' Muriel explains.

'A WARNING?' Greg yells. 'What does that entail?'

'Anything from a bullet through the window to a dead animal on your doorstop,' says Muriel.

'REALLY!' he yells at Andrea and Muriel. They are not perturbed by his outbursts as they have more important things to think about.

'Yes, calm down, you're scaring the children,' says Andrea.

'*I'm* scaring the children!' he says sarcastically.

'Have you got my gun?' asks Harry.

'No, it's in the house. Sorry,' explains Andrea. 'Or in my car. I can't remember.'

'Why does he have a gun?' Greg demands.

'He… ummmm… saved me with it so I let him keep it.'

'What do you mean he saved you?'

'He shot someone in the foot who was harassing me and—'

'WHAT?' Greg yells as he puts his hands on his head.

'Cool!' the girls say.

'You won't need weapons,' Muriel says as she reaches into her TV cabinet and pulls out two handguns.

'Jesus,' Sophie says.

'Coool!' says Alice.

Luke looks surprisingly unshaken by the sight of guns. He feels safe at Muriel's house. She seems like a grandmother figure. Alice has got some snacks out of her 'survival bag' and the girls sit on the sofas and start watching the conversation like it's a movie. They share their food with Luke and make sure he is not too distressed.

'Now. I want us to all sit on the floor, turn the sofas around as barriers, they have metal in them,' instructs Muriel.

'Metal!' Sophie shouts, with a grin on her face.

Andrea mouths the word "*Sorry*" at Harry as he's sitting across from her behind the protective sofas. She was the one that insisted he leave that dishevelled house, but he could have been safer there. Harry feels a bit uneasy without his gun but is glad to know that Muriel is armed.

Muriel stands at the window keeping a lookout, with one gun in her pocket and the other poised, ready.

Greg is looking more and more annoyed with Andrea. He keeps mouthing the words *Who's that kid?* It becomes clear to him that Andrea has been getting involved in something behind his back and letting a kid stay in their house. He tries to start an argument with Andrea, but Muriel quietens him.

'Shush. I think there's a car driving up and down the road.' Muriel looks out the window.

'The car has stopped and they're getting out,' she says. 'I need to find my silencer.'

'What are they doing?' Andrea asks.

'They've got out of their car. Now they're walking around to the side gate... into the garden,' says Harry, who has popped out from behind the sofa to watch the events unfold. .

The girls look at each other, strangely excited, eating crisps. They're secretly hoping that they see Muriel use her guns.

'Stay there, I'll be back,' Muriel says. She grabs a silencer from her hallway drawer and attaches it to one of her pistols before leaving through the front door.

'What is she doing?' Greg whispers.

Harry stands back from the curtain just enough to see what's going on. 'She's walking over there... She's going around the side...'

'She'll get killed over there,' Andrea says.

'They won't suspect her. She looks like a grandmother,' says Sophie.

Harry watches her walk over to their house as if she's going to feed a cat. In silence, they almost count the seconds until she comes back.

'It's the perfect cover, a granny. Go Muriel!' says Alice, as the girls both chant and root for her.

'I can't believe she's FBI!' says Andrea.

'How exciting,' says Sophie.

Only Sophie and Alice would find this exciting. Most thirteen-year-old girls would be crying by now.

'And you're still MI5, Mum. How cool is that? You're on a mission here and you didn't even know it,' says Harry.

'Yeah. COOL,' Greg says with sarcasm.

'She's coming back now,' Harry says, watching Muriel walk across the road as if she's just delivered a package. She stops and talks to a neighbour with her coat still bulging.

'Is she covered in blood?' Alice asks.

'Ummmm, no,' says Harry.

Muriel calmly walks into the hallway and makes a call to the FBI on a burner phone and says, 'I need a collection at the Mitchell house.' The others all stare at each other wondering… *Why does the FBI know where the Mitchell house is? And what is a collection?*

'What happened? What happened?' everyone asks.

'They were… extinguished,' explains Muriel.

'Extinguished?' asks Greg as he sits on the floor with his hands on his head.

'Try to stay calm, Greg. You now need to keep your family safe. The cartel will think Andrea has killed them. So, you are not safe now.'

'Oh! Thank you,' says Greg as if Muriel has just made everything worse.

'After the removal of… (Muriel doesn't want to say 'bodies' in front of the kids) you'll need to go.'

'GO?' asks Greg.

'Where do we go?' asks Andrea.

'A safe house. Your family needs to stay in a safe house, and you need to stay here with me, Andrea. No one would suspect that. Send Greg and the girls, Harry, Luke and the rabbit away to stay safe.'

'Coooollll!' says Sophie and Alice with excitement.

'I've always wanted to go to a safe house,' says Alice.

Luke stands up and walks over to Andrea and sits beside her.

She puts her arm around him and says, 'We'll be all right.'

Alice and Sophie look at him as if he's the sweetest kid in the whole world.

'We know who these people are, we just needed more evidence, and you gave us that, Andrea, by finding the method of distribution. Arrests need to be made.'

'How did you know Luke's name?' Sophie asks Muriel.

'I've been bugging your house,' Muriel confesses.

'Oh,' says Andrea.

'A car will arrive here within the hour. There are clothes in the back bedroom upstairs. I suggest you make a move and get ready.'

'I'm not leaving Andrea with YOU. You're a hired hitman,' Greg yells.

'That's not exactly accurate. I've just terminated people who were about to terrorise your family. You can trust me.'

'She's right, Greg. We are too obvious as a family and will be spotted,' says Andrea.

'Get a grip, Dad,' says Sophie.

He looks at her with such surprise as if he doesn't know how calm she can be and how she is not even disturbed by this.

'It's just until the arrests, which should be all done by the end of the week,' explains Muriel.

'Are you sure?' asks Andrea.

'Yes, as sure as I can be. But some of them might go on the run and separate, so we need to get you all safe,' assures Muriel.

They prepare to go into hiding by sorting through clothes in Muriel's spare room. The girls have their own clothes in their survival bags but Greg searches for some clothes that fit him. He finds some jeans and takes the labels off them. Harry helps him by handing him trainers, socks and a hoodie. There are clothes that fit Luke and Harry and soon they are waiting inside Muriel's garage for their transport.

With the arrival of an eight-seater van, Andrea kisses them all, except Greg, and they climb into the vehicle. She goes to touch Greg and he turns away from her. Just then, Harry jumps out of the car but leaves Thelma with the girls.

'I'm staying with you,' he says.

'Harry…'Andrea says as if she's not happy with his decision.

'It's okay, I can be useful.'

'Okay, fine,' she says worryingly.

Muriel hands Greg a wallet full of money and a map showing him where the safe house is.

'Can you just write the zip code on a piece of paper for me?'

'We don't do that… and there's no navigation system.'

'There is not one in this car?' Greg yells.

'No. It could be tracked… This is the FBI, not some TV cop show. Now don't draw attention to yourself,' she warns.

'*You* can talk,' he says.

'Well, you didn't suspect *me,* did you?'

Greg says nothing.

'There are groceries in the back so don't stop for food. You'll be there in three hours. Be safe.'

He glares at her as if he wants to kill her then drives off with the girls yelling 'Bye, Mum.'

Andrea can see the girls waving at her from the back of the people carrier thing and they put Thelma's face up to the window. She looks across to her house where there seems to be a clean-up in action or "collection" arranged by Muriel. They are disguised as gardeners carrying large bags of rubble away from her house and putting them in their gardener's van. The van has signage saying, *"No Job Too Small."* Andrea wonders if they got any blood stains out of the back patio paving.

Andrea heads straight up to Muriel's bathroom cupboard to see what sedatives she may have. She looks at herself in the mirror. 'Get a grip,' she says to her reflection. 'Everyone is safe. It will all be over soon. Grow a pair of balls, Andrea.'

CHAPTER 12

The Sting

Sitting in Muriel's kitchen, Andrea realises that she is part of something big. The driver of the delivered car is invited into the kitchen for a coffee.

'This is Arnold,' Muriel says.

'Hi, Arnold, thank you for getting the car here so quickly,' Andrea says.

'Oh, I don't have much else to do these days. I'm retired too, like Muriel.'

'Oh, right.' Andrea understands from what he said that he's probably more than a driver and possibly a semi-retired agent like Muriel.

'Cool,' Harry says. Then he walks over to the sofa and falls on it like a building falling over and gets himself comfortable for a sleep.

'We've been asked to help you, Andrea, seeing as Natalie is out of action for a while.'

'Oh?'

'So, how's the investigation going?' he asks.

'You must know more than me. I thought you were arresting people next week,' says Andrea, slightly confused.

'No. Sorry, Andrea. I just said that to get rid of your husband. He would blow our cover, and he's too cranky to have around my house,' explains Muriel.

Andrea puts her head on the kitchen table with her arms covering her head.

'I need a drink,' Andrea says.

'What a good idea. It's *nearly* midday,' says Arnold.

'Have some Baileys in your coffee,' suggests Muriel.

'NO. It's okay.' Andrea wants to stay sober now.

'I'll make brunch,' Arnold says, in a happy mood.

Andrea doesn't know how they can be acting so normal after the killings in her back garden.

'Andrea, if we're going to find all the hidden secrets in this town we need to work together. We don't have Natalie's help now.'

'Did she know about you?' she says looking at Muriel.

'Well, yes.'

'God.'

'And Caroline has been gaining access to the houses and trying to bug them,' Muriel explains.

'My boss Caroline? Is she FBI?'

'Well, yes. We needed you to move into that house so you would be close to me and so you could look after the boy in the loft. We needed you to get close to the mothers. But then the teacher... cop... died and you stopped taking your kids to school.'

'Jesus. I feel like such an idiot,' Andrea moans.

'You're not, Andrea. We need you,' says Arnold. You are very highly regarded by your boss back home.'

Andrea looks at Arnold puzzled.

'Getting back to the boy in my loft, Luke, you knew he was there?' she asks Muriel.

'Yes. I used to bring him food. Until you moved in.'

Andrea sits there in a daze.

'Cheer up,' Arnold says. 'We have work to do.'

Muriel clears the kitchen table whilst Arnold cooks French toast. She starts bringing out maps of streets in Spring Town and old maps of the tunnels.

'Now, Andrea, the ice cream people are connected, don't you think?' Muriel asks.

'Yes,' Andrea says, trying to stay sharp, but it has been a stressful morning.

She is feeling a bit deflated after finding out that everyone was pretending to be someone else. She watches them draw copies of maps on tracing paper, which is really Muriel's baking paper. They then lay them over each other to see what lines up.

'Andrea, you have a map, or something don't you?'

'Yes. It's in my house though.'

Muriel won't let Andrea go back to the house but asks her to draw it on a fresh piece of baking paper from memory.

'It's a picture of an octopus that was left for me. I don't know who gave it to me. But the tentacles are bent at right angles in some places and are abnormal. I thought the head of the octopus could be the hospital. One tentacle ends at the school, see here, if I place it over here. And the other ends at The Ice Cream Restaurant where a hand was cut-off one night.'

'Ghastly... but interesting,' Arnold says.

Andrea only just now realises that he has an English accent. She's too tired to ask him about it though.

She draws what she can from memory. Muriel and Arnold watch on with anticipation. It's difficult for her to know how long the tentacles would be, in other words where they end exactly, so she can pinpoint a significant place. Muriel looks over and pulls the paper up to see what's underneath, and whether any buildings could be at the end of the tentacles.

'Well, it could be the laundrette at the end of this tentacle.

Then there's an industrial area at the end of this one and there's a hotel at the end of this one,' Muriel explains.

'We're assuming the hospital is the centre of the octopus. What if it's another place? Make this ice cream restaurant the centre or the school,' Andrea suggests.

'Never assume you know the answer, Andrea. That's the first rule of espionage. Then you can't miss anything,' says Arnold.

'Have you been trained, Arnold? In England?' Andrea didn't know why she was asking. She really didn't care.

'Well, yes. They recruited me straight out of Cambridge.'

'Oh really?' She still didn't really care.

'In those days, we didn't have mobile phones though, not until the very end. And they were a risk really because we could be tracked through them, and they could also be hacked.'

'Wow.' She feigns her interest.

'In the really early days, there were no personal computers. Our tactics would be considered very old-fashioned nowadays, but we got results.'

'I can't imagine not having that technology,' Andrea adds.

'Well, you have it now, Andrea, and where has it got you so far?' says Muriel, as if she's irritated.

'Pardon?' Andrea wanted an explanation for that comment seeing as she thought it was a bit rude.

'Well. Sorry to be blunt but can you tell us what you know?'

'Ummm.' Andrea felt put on the spot. 'I arrived here and there was a dead teacher drowned in the school pool. Someone started putting messages in my post box and under my car wipers. Do you think Luke put them there?' Andrea asks.

'No. The boy wouldn't risk going outside and being seen,' says Muriel.

'Right. Ummm, then, I went to the police because I thought someone was stalking me but also wanted to discuss the

154

messages and I was disturbed that a twelve-year-old girl was found drowned with a backpack full of *cocaine*.'

'Go on…' Muriel sits still watching and listening to every word.

'The police arranged for me to meet up with Natalie and we found that the tunnels were beng used by kids to deliver drugs. She wouldn't let me go down the tunnels and wanted to go into them on her own. She wanted me to bug the mothers' handbags for her, but it has not really given me any information.'

'Now let me stop you there,' says Arnold.

'Sorry. What?'

'Sometimes it is what is *not said* that is important.'

'What do you mean?'

'Did their conversation seem normal or forced?'

'Ummm.'

'If they are leaving out the usual things, they are being careful, because they know you are listening.'

'Oh, was it a waste of time then?' Andrea asks.

'Not entirely. If the recordings are on your computer, we can still access them remotely and get them checked in the bureau by experts.'

'Oh, okay.'

'Cool,' Harry pipes up, having just woken up from, the smell of French toast cooking.

'Morning,' Muriel says.

'Brunch is served,' Arnold yells out to Harry.

'I'm not really hungry,' says Andrea.

'Nonsense. We have a big day ahead of us so you'd better eat up.'

'Really? What are we doing?' Andrea asks, not really wanting to know.

'Well. Considering we're not sure how this map works, we

need to visit all possible buildings that could be related to drug trafficking.'

'Shouldn't we lie low?' asks Andrea.

'Well, Andrea, you *could*... but your family can't come out of hiding until evidence is collected and arrests are made,' says Arnold.

'And we're not calling for backup before you ask,' says Muriel. 'We don't know who to trust. There may be another mole in the FBI.'

'Shit,' Harry says. 'Oh sorry.' He doesn't like swearing in front of old people.

'The teacher cop got killed so quickly. She was there less than a couple of weeks. So, the school must be involved,' says Andrea.

'So, someone blew her cover,' Arnold adds.

'What really bothers me though is that children are being groomed to deliver drugs and I think their parents know about it,' says Andrea.

'What makes you say that?' asks Muriel.

'The headmaster organises the drug deliveries.'

'You're sure about that?' asks Muriel.

'Yes, he drives the kids home! How weird is that? Headmasters are not allowed in cars with kids alone these days. He has some sort of hold over the parents.'

'Why?' asks Arnold.

'He wouldn't be able to get away with it unless he was controlling the parents somehow. In any normal school, a child would just say, "Mummy, I wasn't at after-school club. I left school on my bike and delivered things for the headmaster," and then the shit would hit the fan and he would be sacked.'

They tuck into their brunch whilst Andrea gives them more

ideas of what's been going around in her head since she got to Spring Town.

'The headmaster could be running the whole thing,' says Andrea.

'Whatever is happening here is causing children to run away or hide in loft spaces,' adds Muriel.

'That's right,' says Andrea.

'So, maybe they have *seen* too much or have been threatened or just don't want to do it any more and the parents have not protected them.'

'Yes, that's all possible,' Arnold says.

'I think there could be something more sinister going on here,' Andrea suggests.

'Like what?' Harry says, with a mouth full of pancake.

'Natalie said the children write letters to tell their parents that they're okay.'

'Yes.'

'But what if someone else writes the letters to pretend they are fine?' Andrea suggests.

'What do you mean?' Muriel asks.

'Well, the headmaster would *know* their handwriting. He would have samples of it. I think he knows where they are.'

'Mmmmm. These children might not be "missing". They might be working, making drugs, being held like slaves,' says Muriel.

'Yes, that's entirely possible,' says Arnold.

'How many children have gone missing?' asks Andrea.

'About fourteen over three years. One found drowned, one is Luke, or Adam, I think is his real name, there's one more living in an empty house, being visited by Caroline. So, eleven still missing.'

'Oh my God!' says Harry.

'Let's not assume that we know the answer, but we have to be open-minded about the very macabre because our human instinct doesn't want to consider it,' explains Arnold.

'It's a cognitive bias,' says Muriel.

'Yes, I studied criminology at uni.'

'Yes… we know, and an online course in espionage,' Muriel says in a slightly sarcastic manner.

'You've done a good background check on me!'

'There weren't any courses in our day. You were just trained on the job,' says Arnold.

'I think we need to find a place where the drugs could be made… by children, undetected, underground,' Andrea says, keeping the focus on the job.

'The tunnels are so vast,' says Muriel.

'We need thermal imaging,' Andrea says.

Muriel looks irritated that Andrea has come up with a good idea.

'I know a guy. I could get the equipment,' suggests Arnold.

'Yes, fine, but let's narrow this down. Come on, Andrea… think… where would these children be working underground?' demands Muriel.

'Blimey,' says Andrea, not coping with the pressure… but then suddenly has an idea. 'Well, they wouldn't be under the school.'

'They could be making it in the science labs at night?' says Harry.

'Well, we could go and have a look but it's more likely to be one of the places at the end of this maze of tunnels,' says Andrea.

'Well, they could escape if they are allowed in the science labs, or create a fire as a diversion, or yell and scream. I think the headmaster is more a distributor than anything else. The tunnel on Baker Street only goes in one direction, so they head east, on their bikes, for about fifteen minutes travelling at two to three miles per hour. She would have arrived here... handed over the product... then travelled back.'

'Unless she has a longer handover period, having not travelled so far,' says Muriel.

'Yes, that's quite possible. She could hand it over to someone else who also travelled into the tunnels,' suggests Arnold.

'Where are they going, these school children?' asks Arnold.

'They could just be distributing it. The headmaster has his stash that he is selling or he gets paid,' says Harry, trying to get involved.

'He collects it from somewhere or it is delivered *to* him. So, these tunnels may only tell you where the drugs are delivered, not where these drugs are made,' Andrea deduces.

'Where are the children though, Andrea...? *Think*... if this isn't wrapped up tonight, they could move the children and we'd never find them,' demands Muriel.

'The ice cream people... they could be making it in their kitchens. They often have basements for storage so the kids could be working down there at night. They could also be living there. Many restaurants have accommodation for staff, and basements,' Andrea says, convinced she has had a brainwave.

'So, we need a big restaurant if they're housing eleven children.'

'Or more than one restaurant,' says Harry.

'Look at the octopus map. Move it around until it covers a lot of ice cream restaurants, or one big one.'

'What if the octopus head was a group of restaurants together in the centre of Philadelphia?' suggests Arnold.

'What if it's closer to home though... in Spring Town?' says Muriel.

'I don't think this is an octopus. The head looks like a pin head drop in an Internet map. I just assumed it was an octopus because I had received so many toys in the letterbox.'

Harry grabs the map traced on baking paper and moves it over Spring Town.

'HERE...' he yells. 'It's exactly like this area.'

'That's an ice cream restaurant.'

'Let's start there. We'll go there tonight,' Muriel orders.

'We'll need jackets just in case.'

'Oh, I don't feel the cold,' says Harry.

'*Bullet proof* jackets,' Muriel explains.

'Can't we alert the authorities and get backup and a warrant?' asks Harry.

'Are you suggesting I wake up a judge and show him our baking paper?'

'Umm,' he replies.

'We need to keep this between us. Sometimes you can't trust anyone. Arnold will come back with the thermal imaging equipment. There are more guns upstairs and we'll take bolt cutters,' Muriel says, as if she is taking the lead on the operation.

'Fuck,' Andrea says under her breath as if she doesn't know what she has got herself into. But she is now running on adrenaline.

They spend the rest of the day planning an evening sting and napping on the sofas. In the early hours at three a.m., Arnold turns up with the thermal imaging equipment. They get in his car, suited up with bullet proof jackets, and drive to the big ice cream restaurant called 'The Ice Way'. Harry is excited but nervous.

Andrea looks at him as if she can't believe the amount of danger she has put him in, just by getting in touch with him. Nobody really talks in the car during the twenty-minute drive. Finally, they get to the restaurant and Arnold shows Harry how to use the thermal imagining machine. He leans out of the window and points it towards the restaurant. It highlights furniture and stairs that go down to a basement. It shows the length of the building, but nothing to indicate live humans.

'There's no one there,' he tells them.

'Point it to the upstairs levels,' says Arnold.

Harry gets out of the car and walks around the building, pointing it to the two levels above.

'Nothing.'

'That's weird. I'm sure the staff would live up there,' says Andrea.

'What is up there, Harry?'

'Beds mostly. Just loads of beds.'

'They've left,' says Muriel.

'How would they know we are on to them?' says Harry.

'Let's go inside,' Muriel suggests.

'And break and enter?' Andrea says sarcastically.

'Yes,' confirms Muriel. 'Time is running out for these children.'

Arnold gets out of the car and finds the bolt cutters in the boot. He also has a Door Ram to push the door in is needed. Arnold tells Muriel to get in the driver's seat in case they need to make a quick getaway. Andrea, Arnold and Harry walk around to the back of the building slowly and try to enter. There is an entrance which is all chained up. Arnold attacks it with the bolt cutters and they ram open the doors. They find a steep set of stairs leading down to a basement area. Arnold gets his gun out just in case and is the first to volunteer to go down there. Then Andrea and Harry follow behind.

'Wow,' says Harry. 'Check this out!'

'What?' Andrea says, not really sure of what they've found.

'It's a drug kitchen.'

'Are you sure?' Andrea asks.

'Yes. He's right,' says Arnold. 'It looks like they have just run off and left everything here.'

Harry explains to Andrea what each workstation is for and how they make the drugs. But the most harrowing part of their exploration is the small table and chair where a child would have been working to make drugs. It looks like a primary-school table and chairs.

They all look at each other and know they have found the right place. After finding another door they go upstairs to investigate the ground floor of the restaurant. Again, Arnold goes first, and Andrea and Harry hide behind him. Andrea is more interested in the accommodation above. There is another flight of stairs at the back of the restaurant. Harry then follows Andrea up the stairs. She slowly walks down a corridor which has lots of doors open so she doesn't have to twist any doorknobs and can see into each one without entering. Arnold comes up the stairs and whispers to them that it may not be safe.

'But there was no one here on the imaging,' explains Harry.

'It's best to be careful though,' Arnold warns.

They go into each room and then suddenly Andrea puts her hand over her mouth in shock. There is a stuffed animal toy on one of the beds. She picks it up as it is similar to one that the girls both had when they were younger, sent to them by their American grandparents. It's ringing home now in Andrea's mind.

'These are children,' she says in disgust. After looking through all the rooms and cupboards for any children that may be hiding, they decide that the property is empty. They go back downstairs to the car where Muriel is waiting.

Back at Muriel's house they discuss their findings. They make plans to sleep for a while and then meet in the kitchen at daylight.

Andrea assumed she could go home across the street to sleep, seeing as the enemy has been exterminated, but Muriel won't let her or Harry and insists that they remain in her house. Harry and Andrea go to sleep in a twin bedroom upstairs. Andrea apologises again for not having a *normal* reunion between mother and son. But Harry insists that he is enjoying their time together.

Andrea goes off to sleep wondering where the safe house is and whether they had got there in one piece. She must be able to find out somehow. She plans to ask Muriel in the morning. Without her mobile phone Andrea feels slightly powerless. The events of the weird day start to catch up with her and she isn't sure if she can sleep. She goes over everything in her mind, which was something she would do in her previous job, and sometimes come up with the answer in the middle of the night.

CHAPTER 13

The Barn

The sun is up, and Andrea is sitting at Muriel's kitchen table writing on new baking paper.

Harry is making toast and Muriel comes into the room looking worse for wear with curlers in her hair.

'If they have taken the children, we may be able to find them. At least they are alive, for now,' says Andrea. 'Is there some way we can look at the traffic cameras.'

'That will be a mine field. We don't know what car they drive,' says Muriel.

'Let's work backwards. Let's see if they did a final trip to the school, to get rid of a stash of cocaine before fleeing the town?' Andrea suggests.

'Okay.'

'So, Muriel, how do we get our hands on a computer?'

'Why didn't you say so,' says Muriel. She goes to the corner of the kitchen and pulls out a large metal suitcase.

'Jesus,' says Harry.

Muriel pulls up the lid of the suitcase and exposes a large screen.

'You had that here all along?' Andrea says angrily.

'You never asked before. I'll just put in the password and you're away.' She hands the keyboard to Harry. Andrea looks at Muriel in annoyance.

Arnold arrives at the "Control Room" and has some new ideas. 'Oh, you've got the machine out.'

'Yes, well, this new generation needed it,' says Muriel, sarcastically.

'It might come in useful, Muriel,' he says.

'Mmmmm,' Muriel moans.

'We should check traffic cameras around here,' Andrea says to Harry.

'They probably went underground, literally,' says Harry.

'I don't think so. They knew the tunnels were compromised,' explains Arnold.

'Harry, let's check the cameras around this area and down these streets,' Andrea says.

'Yeah, sure.'

'Don't assume they lead them out the front door, Andrea,' Arnold suggests.

Muriel pipes up and says, 'They would have gone out the back door and possibly dressed them as adults, probably in the evening but it depends on how desperately they wanted to leave.'

'Would they be dressed as ice cream cones?' asks Harry, in a serious manner.

'Anything's possible,' says Arnold.

'I'm in,' says Harry. 'This is the area, it's kinda close to the ice cream restaurant that they would have to drive past.'

'What type of vehicle would they use?' Arnold says as if he knew the answer.

'They could be hiding in *any* of these vehicles,' Muriel says as she looks over his shoulder.

'Why don't we do this the other way around?' Andrea wonders.

'What do you mean?'

'Let's see which vehicles left the school yesterday. Because they would have done one last drop off. Then cross reference with vehicles around the restaurant,' Andrea suggests.

'Brilliant,' Arnold says.

They see a van near the school traffic lights. He seems to go down the street near the school.

'Now go back to the traffic camera near that ice cream restaurant and see, go back ten minutes,' says Arnold.

They see the same van.

'Got it,' says Harry.

'Okay now back to the school area. Check all cameras to see which way it went. First let's assume they did a quick drop off then they go towards a motorway… highway… to leave town,' Andrea suggests.

They all look over Harry's shoulder, as he searches the four cameras.

The fourth camera finally reveals footage of the van driving down Highway 95 yesterday afternoon.

'Great, now go to the next camera on that highway.' The van appears to travel for twenty minutes and then turns off.

'Check the traffic camera in both directions,' says Andrea as they can't tell which way it went. The van is caught on another camera heading north, and then disappears.

'Get the satellite map out,' she says to Harry, wondering why they didn't have satellite maps up yesterday!

'There are several farms close by. They could stop there.'

'Or they could keep going.'

'Muriel… does this have its own Internet?'

She doesn't answer because she doesn't know.

'It's like an iPad,' Arnold says. 'So yes'.

'Should we take it with us and continue the search in the car? We're wasting time sitting here,' Andrea says.

'Yes, let's get going,' says Muriel.

'Wait!' says Muriel. 'Jackets and guns.'

They suit up and Harry grabs some bottles of water from Muriel's fridge and some bananas from the countertop.

They all jump in Arnold's car and drive off quickly but not too fast as to draw attention to themselves. Harry has the computer and keeps looking at the camera footage on the highway.

'Keep checking *that* road,' Andrea shouts.

'Yes.' Harry seems to know what he's doing now.

They drive for fifteen minutes to where the cameras show the van had turned off the highway.

'I can't find any more footage of the van.'

'So, they are along here somewhere. Turn around and go up some of these long roads.'

'It's full of farms.'

'Perfect hiding place,' Andrea says.

'Not for people with lots of kids though. They will stand out a mile,' says Harry, knowing no one is taking any notice of his idea.

'Let's drive up each driveway till we see a grey van.'

They drive up a driveway with a sign saying, "Pickers Wanted". Andrea gets out of the car and goes into a barn to ask people if they have seen any people with children. The staff in the barn seem baffled but answer Andrea's questions thinking that she is a cop as she is wearing a bullet proof jacket. She doesn't suspect anything there and wants to try the next farm.

Driving up the next long driveway they spot the grey van parked just outside a very large red barn. Andrea gets out of the car and wants to walk up to the main house and knock on the door.

'I'm not sure you should do that,' says Muriel.

'Well, these children may be in danger,' Andrea replies.

'I'll cover you. But take this gun. Tuck it in the back of your trousers,' says Arnold.

'Be careful!' says Harry, who decides to stay in the car.

Andrea walks up to the wooden house and knocks on the door.

A lady comes to the door and Andrea suddenly feels a chill run down her spine but tries to act normal. The lady sees Andrea's bullet proof jacket and begins to look nervous.

The lady talks in an accent, but Andrea can't understand her.

'I'm from the police, ma'am. Could I come in for a moment?' Andrea says, not really knowing how to handle the situation.

Just then a man starts yelling from about ten metres behind Andrea and a gun goes off. She turns around to find Arnold standing a long way back and a man lying face down on the front lawn. Arnold had shot him. The lady turns and runs down the hallway towards the back of the house. Andrea picks up a vase from the hallway and throws it at the lady. The vase hits the lady's back and it throws her off balance. She falls to the ground. Andrea quickly catches up to her and holds her arms down so she can't get up. By then, Arnold is in the house assisting Andrea with the detainment of the lady.

'Here, use this.' He hands Andrea plastic zip ties from his pocket to use as handcuffs.

'Did you have to shoot him?' Andrea asks.

'Yes. He had a semi-automatic.'

'Jesus!'

'Where are the children?' Andrea says to the lady.

'The barn. The barn. Quick...' she says, panicking and pointing in that direction. Andrea instinctively knew that the children may be in danger, from the way the lady was speaking.

Arnold stays with the lady while Andrea runs down to the barn.

'Mum, are you all right?' asks Harry, getting out of the car.

'Yes. They are in the barn,' she explains.

The barn is bolted with just a piece of wood. Andrea removes it and rushes in.

'It could be booby trapped,' Harry says, who is following behind her.

'I just thought of that too,' she says.

Muriel follows them.

They enter the barn to find eleven children lying on bales of hay, looking weak and lifeless. She runs to the closest one.

'Call an ambulance,' she says to Muriel, who turns her burner phone on and makes the call.

'911 do you have an emergency?'

'Yes, I have eleven children who may have been poisoned,' Muriel says. Not wanting to tell the emergency services about the hostage in the house and the other one recently shot by Arnold.

She gives them the address.

Andrea goes to each child slowly, trying to hold back the tears. Each one can barely lift their head up from the hay to see who she is. Their breathing is very slow and shallow.

'It's okay. It's okay. It's okay,' she just keeps saying the same thing. Harry walks behind her nearly in tears.

Harry goes to the house to find milk for them to drink, thinking it will dilute anything in their stomachs. If they were injected though, it could be too late. He sees Arnold questioning the woman who is now allowed to sit up on the sofa. Harry sees plastic rip-ties on her feet too. It appears Arnold isn't taking any chances.

'She says her husband poisoned them, but she doesn't know what with,' Arnold says.

Harry takes this information back to Andrea along with some bottles of milk and mugs from the kitchen. Andrea is sitting near the smallest child, knowing that she had seen earlier where she would have worked in one of the ice cream restaurants. Andrea talks to them although they can hardly reply.

'We are here to help you. You are safe now. You are safe now.' She continues to go around to each one. Muriel stays put near the door, as a kind of bodyguard, ready for anything.

'There could be more drug dealers around,' Muriel explains.

Within about fifteen minutes, four ambulances speed up the driveway and Muriel waves them down. They don't see the dead man as he is lying in long grass.

'In here. In here.' Muriel waves at them.

They rush out of their vehicles carrying their equipment.

'We think they have been poisoned,' Muriel says. There are eight paramedics as there were only four ambulances attending, but eleven children. They do a brief glance around the room and run to the ones who appear sleepy.

'Let's give them all Narcan,' the paramedics say as they inject Narcan in the thighs of the children one by one, and then start putting cannulas in for fluids. The paramedic asks for more information as to when they would have been administered the drug, but Andrea doesn't know. They notice all the bullet proof jackets but are not bothered and carry on. Harry is helping the paramedics by handing them things and then moving the children onto their left side, in case they throw up.

'Are you guys police?' asks a paramedic.

'Sort of,' answers Muriel.

'Oh. Well, I'm Agent Mitchell from MI5, and I work with the police here,' she calls herself this to prevent them calling the police, as she wasn't sure if she could trust the police.

'Oh.' He seems interested in the story.

'I've been sent here from the UK. My colleague is FBI (she

points to Muriel) and she is helping with this investigation. And that is my son Harry.' She points to Harry who is now sitting with a child. 'I have another FBI helper called "Arnold" who is still questioning a lady up at the house.'

'Ummm, we'd rather you kept this quiet. These children may be targeted by a cartel' says Muriel.

'How, ma'am?'

'We need a hospital now and that needs to be kept quiet,' says Andrea.

'It will have to be several hospitals to deal with this number of sick children,' the paramedic says. 'We will have to split them up.'

Andrea doesn't like the sound of that. She needs to be sure no one will "bump them off", as they are witnesses to a major drug trafficking operation. She goes to Muriel and asks to use her mobile phone.

'Can I call the UK with your phone please, Muriel?'

'Yes, it should stretch that far,' Muriel says, being polite for a change.

Andrea dials her old boss's mobile number in the UK.

'Hello?' he answers.

'What the actual fuck were you playing at?' Andrea shouts.

'Andrea. How nice to hear from you. How are things over there?'

'You arsehole! You sent me on a mission. My kids are in a safe house. It's gone pear-shaped here and this was supposed to be my new life. You arsehole.'

'Okay. Okay.'

'I need somewhere to keep witnesses and one hostage,' Andrea demanded.

'Excellent, it's going well then,' he says in a jovial mood

171

which winds Andrea up.

'Listen, I need a hospital to protect and rejuvenate eleven witnesses and one hostage.'

'Well. You have exceeded my expectations.'

'It needs to be a hospital setting with a lot of security, something like an army base.'

'Done. Which one would you like?'

'One near Philadelphia.'

'Okay, I'll make a call and text you the address and the name of the head of the base.'

'Fine.'

'Oh, and Andrea.'

'Yes.'

'Good work.'

'Fuck off,' she says angrily.

She hangs up on him and goes back to tell the others what her plans are. Andrea goes to Muriel first and tells her that they have to get the children somewhere where they are safe and explains her idea to her. Muriel seems happy about this.

The paramedics make their way around all of the children who seem to slowly come around and manage to talk. The reversal drug and intravenous fluids had been given just in time. If Andrea had left it another day, they would have all died from the overdose.

'What hospital are we taking them to?' she hears one of them say.

'We're taking them to an army base. They need to be under guard. Let's get going as soon as they can be moved.'

After a text from her old boss, Andrea convinces the paramedics to follow her to the army base. She does not give them the address for fear that they will alert the police. Slowly, each child is carried to an ambulance and as they are small, the paramedics sometimes put two children on a stretcher, to fit them all in. They leave the man lying in the long grass, as they haven't told the paramedics about him.

'I feel bad leaving him there,' says Harry.

'He was aiming a semi at your mother when I shot him!'

'Okay. I don't feel bad any more.'

Andrea, Harry and Muriel get in the car. The lady hostage is sitting in between Arnold and Harry with her hands still in plastic cuffs. Arnold must have removed the ones holding her legs together. All ambulances turn around, and like a funeral procession, drive slowly down the driveway behind Arnold's car and turn left to make their way to the army base.

'Why an army base, Mum?' Harry asks.

'You can always trust the army, Harry, when all else fails, the army is rarely compromised.'

After twenty-five minutes they see the sign for the barracks and drive into the check point. The soldier looks at the four ambulances behind them.

'Are they with you, ma'am?'

'Yes, I'm agent Mitchell and they are with me.'

'We have been expecting you, Agent Mitchell. Do you have any ID?' Her wallet was one of the things she had taken from the house, although she didn't have MI5 ID.

'You have eleven witnesses and one hostage I hear.'

'Yes.'

'And these other people?'

'These are semi-retired FBI, Muriel and Arnold. Sorry I don't know their last names, and my son, Harry.'

'IDs please.'

Luckily the others have their wallets and IDs.

'All guns will have to be handed over.'

Arnold hands over his handgun and tells the soldier he has a semi in the boot, which he takes. Muriel hands hers over too.

'Is that all?'

'Oh yes, I have one, sorry. I forgot,' says Andrea. The pistol Arnold has given her is tiny and she reaches around and pulls it out from under her body jacket.

'All people out of the cars please,' says the guard. They have to be searched with their hands out. Muriel complains under her breath as if she is too important to be searched. All the ambulances are also searched, which seems like forever. Eventually they are allowed in. It is another long driveway to the main building and Andrea can see someone waiting for her at the front of the building. She is feeling all emotional as she pulls up in front of the large building knowing she has achieved an impossible feat that day and has finally brought the children to a safe place. She gets out of the car and walks towards the man who is saluting her even though she is a civilian.

'Agent Mitchell, I presume?' he says.

'Yes. Are you Major General Findlay?'

'Yes. But call me Max. I hear you have casualties and a hostage.'

'Yes.'

'Let's deal with the casualties first,' he says as a team of medics start to go to each ambulance.

'They will be safe here, no one can enter this base.'

'Thank you.'

'You've had a busy morning then?' he says with a smile.

'Yes. And these are retired FBI agents and my son, Harry, has been helping me.'

'And that looks like your hostage,' Max says, as the lady walks towards them with Arnold.

'Yes, we don't know her name, but we think she was involved in making and distributing illegal drugs. They have not seen their parents for years, so she is really a kidnapper too.'

'Well. Well.'

'And we think the children were drugged.'

'Oh. Right.'

'Luckily the ambulances got there quickly today.'

'Luckily... you knew what you were doing,' Max says, giving her all the credit.

'Oh, it was a team effort.'

Andrea is starting to act nervously. Max is a very attractive fiftyish man with weather-worn skin. She finds herself lost for words suddenly and starts blushing.

The children are taken to the base hospital wards on stretchers, where they can rest and have several army nurses looking after them. The ambulances turn around and drive out. The hostage is taken to a holding cell and given some food. Andrea, Harry, Arnold, and Muriel are shown to their quarters which is a house on the base, usually used for the army surgeon, who has left, and they are awaiting a replacement. The group are told that they will have to meet for a briefing at two p.m. in Max's office.

CHAPTER 14

The Army

The army accommodation, or quarters, are non-army like. They are given a house with everything they need, primarily, alcohol in the fridge, towels and spare army training clothes. Andrea has a quick shower and puts on some beige uniform-type training clothes that have been left on her bed. Muriel has a doze in the chair and doesn't bother to change, she's hoping to go home at some point. Arnold is hoping to be "off-duty" by the evening too. Harry flops on one of the beds and drinks a can of beer to put him to sleep. They really hadn't slept due to the thermal imaging exercise and then grey van chasing. There is a knock at the door and an army officer introduces himself and says he is to escort them through the base to Max's office. Andrea is not sure whether to tell them about the dead body back at the farm. She walks behind the officer in anticipation, wondering if she really can trust the army.

Entering the Max's office, they can see that it was just an informal chat and Max wanted to welcome them properly, feed them and make them feel welcome.

'Ahhh. Agent Mitchell and company. Welcome.'

They all say hello and sit down on his office chairs and sofa. There is a selection of snacks which looks like a cross between an afternoon tea and a mini smorgasbord. Harry starts getting stuck into some chicken sandwiches and sausages that he has spotted, and Muriel starts pouring the tea. Max gives them an update on the children's health.

'They are all doing well, Agent Mitchell, you'll be pleased to know.'

'Oh, call me Andrea. Are they talking much yet?'

'Yes. Apparently, most of them feel comfortable talking to the nurses and they'll probably have stories to tell you, which I'm sure will help you in your investigation.'

'Great. Thank you.'

'We've left the hostage alone, after offering her water and a light meal. I didn't want to interfere with your investigation by questioning her.'

'Thank you.'

'But she did say something like… my husband made me do it.'

'Oh. Well, I guess she would say that.'

'Where *is* her husband?' he asks.

'Dead, I'm afraid. We left him there,' Andrea says sheepishly.

'Oh!' He looks a bit shocked.

'I thought we should leave the scene quickly as there may be drug cartels after us.'

'I see.'

'It's a pretty big operation from what I have discovered so far.' She doesn't want to tell him everything about the school and the headmaster and the adoptions yet.

'Well, anything we can do to help… we have excellent computers here and I could give you a room to work in.'

'I just need to get Muriel's FBI computer from the car really and carry on with tracking some suspects.'

'Are there more?'

'Well, I don't know, but this thing seems to be growing bigger and bigger.'

'Well, we're here at your disposal. The officers can show you where the children are if you want to visit, and where your hostage is. We have a dance organised for this evening if you care to come to that. We can loan you some suitable clothes. It's 1940s theme.'

Muriel looks up from her piece of cake with her eyes lit up. *A dance*, she thinks to herself. Arnold doesn't seem bothered, and Harry is just enjoying the food.

'This is my extension if you need me. For any house keeping things, more towels etc., call this other extension here. Well, I hope to see you all later this evening. I think it starts at eight p.m. if you're not all too tired from your successful mission. My PA, Julia, might be able to loan you a dress or two,' he says in an embarrassed manner.

Andrea looks down at the beige clothes she is wearing.

He leaves and they all enjoy the cups of tea and huge variety of food.

'We need to find out who these children are,' says Andrea as she quickly changes the subject.

'Later,' says Muriel. 'Let them rest. It will be traumatic bringing up their horrific stories.'

'Yes, they are probably just happy to be safe,' says Andrea.

'But they may have enjoyed living in the ice cream restaurants. It's every kid's dream to live in an ice cream restaurant. I mean, as long as no one interfered with them... you know...' Harry suggests.

'I need to rest and find something to wear for the dance,' Muriel demands.

'Surely we have other things on our mind?' Andrea says to Muriel.

'Come on, Andrea,' says Arnold. 'Let's have a bit of fun. We were nearly all killed a few hours ago.'

'Okay fine, fine.'

Andrea goes to see the children with Harry. An officer escorts them to the hospital on the base and waits to escort them back. Some of the children recognise her from the barn and smile. Andrea can't help herself and starts questioning them even though she doesn't have any recording equipment. She thinks of her own daughters and what it would be like for them.

'Can you tell me your name?' she asks one of them.

'I'm Susan.'

'How old are you?'

'Fifteen.'

'And how long were you with the ice cream people?'

'Since I was thirteen.'

'Were you happy there… with them?'

'Well, we got loads of ice cream food to eat and sweets and I would write to Mum and Dad all the time and they would write back telling me what great work I was doing.'

A tear rolls down Andrea's face. The children wonder why she is crying.

Were they institutionalised? Have they forgotten about the outside world? Andrea thinks.

A guard comes in to tell Andrea that there is a woman at the main desk who wants to speak to her.He says her name is Caroline Hardy.

'Caroline! Yes. Tell her I will be out in a minute.'

Andrea is excited as she and Caroline can reveal their true identities to each other, that they now have more in common, and possibly Caroline could help her with the case.

Walking swiftly up to the main entrance desk, the guard follows Andrea, and her pace slows down as she starts to grow suspicious. Caroline is FBI undercover but how did she know where Andrea was? Muriel and Arnold had their phones so they were probably tracked. But why didn't she ring and say she was coming? Muriel would have said something if she had called Caroline.

Andrea walks up to Caroline, in the main entrance, and feels uneasy about their "reunion".

'Andrea!' Caroline says, as she throws her arms out.

'Hi, Caroline. You're a dark horse.'

'As are you. I must see the children. Where are they?'

As she says that, Caroline pulls her tote bag behind her as if she doesn't want Andrea to look inside it. 'Are they resting?' she asks.

Andrea starts to feel instinctively protective. *Who were the people writing back to the children and pretending to be their parents?* she thinks.

'They are sleeping.'

'Oh? Where are they being kept?'

'They have been through such an ordeal. The ice cream people tried to give them a drug overdose.'

'Ghastly,' says Caroline with little empathy.

'And they were treated by the paramedics.'

'Good,' she says in an almost patronising manner.

As Caroline looks towards the corridor that Andrea has just come from, Andrea thinks she is a little too eager to want to see the children when she could firstly want to know more about the operation, about how she found them. More motherly instinct comes over Andrea and her heart starts to quicken. She can feel her blood pressure rising and her fist starting to clench.

What does she have in her bag? Why does she want to see the children so quickly rather than get a debrief from me? Andrea wonders. As Caroline turns back to face her, Andrea punches her in the face with such force that Caroline falls back, and the contents of her tote bag are spread across the floor.

'What the hell…' Caroline yells.

'You were in on it…' Andrea yells.

'What! You've gone mad. Help me up!'

Andrea wonders for a minute if she was reaching a bit too far to think that Caroline is in on the whole cocaine trafficking via children thing and whether she will now be charged with assault.

'I've come here to help you.'

'Detain her,' Andrea orders the guard as if she is his superior. He draws his pistol and holds it towards Caroline whilst she stays on the floor.

'I'll tell my boss about you, you stupid amateur,' Caroline yells.

'You didn't want me to find those children. You had every opportunity to tell me who you really were. I borrowed your car and you found out about Natalie, who is now sick… poisoned.'

'Don't be ridiculous. Call off the dogs, Andrea,' she says whilst staying on the floor.

Andrea picks up her tote bag from the floor and goes through it. She finds a makeup compact for face powder. Something that hasn't been used since the 1950s. Andrea opens it and tastes the contents.

'It's cocaine. Not fucking powder,' she says to Caroline and looks at the guard.

'Fuck off, you're mad.'

'I'm going to get the major general. Keep an eye on her.' Just then, Andrea notices that Caroline has a deviated septum under her nose. She had noticed before but just thought it was from an injury. But she now thinks that Caroline is probably addicted to cocaine.

'Yes, ma'am,' he says.

'Yes, ma'am,' Caroline imitates him sarcastically.

Andrea runs down towards Max's office and tells him she has another prisoner. He smiles back at her which is puzzling.

'You're collecting them, Andrea,' he says.

'Sorry. Do you have the space? This is her handbag which she was very cagey about. The powder case is full of cocaine. And these sweets look weird, homemade.'

'Oh yes. Like I said, Agent Mitchell, we're here to help.'

'Thank you.'

He calls the main desk and arranges for the guard to have Caroline taken to a holding room.

'Why don't you get some rest? We have the dance tonight.'

Andrea can't believe he's still bringing up the dance when they just detained a suspect.

'Aren't you shocked by what has just happened, Max?'

'Well, I suspected she was not kosher, and I was watching through the security camera. The guard was ready for action.'

'Oh.'

'Yes, nice right hook, Agent Mitchell.'

'Oh, thank you.' Andrea wonders how many other people were watching her every move.

'Now, my PA Julia has been through her wardrobe, and she has dresses and shoes for Muriel and yourself. She's good at guessing people's sizes. The men have been given some clothes. They have been taken to your quarters. So… there's no way you can back out now,' he says in a jovial manner.

Andrea thinks he is a little too keen to see her in a dress. She wants to maybe sit with the children tonight, not party with strangers.

'Ummm, well, that is very kind.'

'Rest up. I'll see you at eight p.m. in the ballroom, which is just down there.'

'Will the children be watched all night?'

'Definitely,' he assures.

Andrea returns to tell Harry about what has happened, and they then go back to inform Muriel and Arnold.

'Jesus, Mum,' says Harry. 'Did you really hit her?'

'Good. That bloody bitch,' says Muriel. 'I thought she was on our side.'

'Well. Good call,' says Arnold. 'If she had got to the children, she would have killed them. I don't know if they would have been able to cope with another overdose so soon after the last one.'

'Yes, exactly. I need to lie down. My knuckles are sore.'

'Of course, dear,' says Muriel, who seems to have more respect for Andrea suddenly as she has just protected the children with her own bare fists.

After a nap they get ready and head to the ballroom. Andrea can't help herself and just wants to check in on the children again. She opens the door to the hospital ward, a nurse looks up, smiles at her, she smiles back then carries on down the hall to the party. When Andrea gets to the dance it is buzzing. All the officers are dressed up in 1940s uniforms and the female army officers have lovely dresses on. Max walks up to Andrea.

'Ah, you have decided to attend. I was worried when you didn't walk in with the others.'

'I think I need this actually,' she says, noticing how

handsome he looks in his old-fashioned uniform.

'Would you care to dance?'

'Ummmm.'

He doesn't wait for an answer and takes her hand. They walk to the dance floor where people are dancing to 'Jailhouse Rock'. But just as they get to the dance floor, Andrea feels a bit silly and doesn't really move much. The music changes to a slow song, "In the Still of the Night" by The Five Satins. Max holds his hands out as if to invite her to dance close. She walks into his space and assumes the traditional dance hold. They start slow dancing and Andrea is so weary that she puts her head on his shoulder. Finally, she thinks, some closeness, even if it is from a stranger. Greg wasn't affectionate. She has hardly got a hug from her husband for the past two years. They dance for several songs. Muriel and Arnold seem to be getting on well too. Harry has a few dances with some of the women there and gets a bit drunk. He stumbles along to the buffet section and finds the punch bowl.

Andrea feels guilty about being at the dance while the children are recovering from an overdose and a type of slavery. She goes outside for a breath of fresh air. Max follows her.

'Are you tired, Agent Mitchell, from saving Philadelphia from drug trafficking?'

'It's my first real mission. I don't really know what I'm doing.'

'You're doing fine.'

'Thank you.'

'You look lovely in that dress.'

'Thank you.'

There's an awkward silence and she can tell that he is thinking of kissing her. He gathers up his manners though and decides to be a gentleman.

'Andrea, if you'd rather walk back to your quarters, I'll have a guard escort you, seeing as it's dark. I'm sure you need the rest.'

He keeps talking about her getting rest and then insists that she has none. It's confusing for Andrea.

He turns to walk away. She suddenly doesn't want him to leave and says, 'Hang on.'

'Yes?' he says, wondering what she wants.

She steps closer to him and slowly kisses him on the lips with one peck.

He is then like putty in her hands, kissing her back and holding her face gently as if it were a precious bird. The moment passes quickly enough, and they release from each other.

'Sorry,' Andrea says.

'Not at all.'

'I needed that,' She confesses.

'As did I,' he says gallantly.

'The last few days have been unusual to say the least and I'm not used to being a detective.'

'Well, Agent Mitchell.'

'Please. Call me Andrea.'

'Andrea, follow your gut. That's what we do in the army. And put yourself in the shoes of the enemy and decide what their next move will be. Prepare. Watch. Attack.'

'Blimey, that is really good advice.'

'I'm good at other things besides dancing,' he quips.

'Just as well,' she jests, as if his dancing wasn't up to much.

He smiles and Andrea feels like kissing him again. But he turns and goes to join the others.

Just before he leaves her, he turns to give her another glance.

'Oh... and Andrea...'

'Yes?'

'Let me know if you feel like attacking me again.'

She laughs and feels slightly embarrassed.

Andrea is still shocked at what she has just done but can't be bothered to worry about it. She wonders how the rest of her family are doing. *Where they are? Are they safe?* She wonders.

It's too risky to try to contact the safe house though... even if she could find out how.

Andrea stands near the French doors and watches Harry. In some ways, this is the best time of her life, reuniting with him. But in others, everything seems so uncertain, and dangerous! Muriel is dancing around like a drunken FBI agent would, still celebrating her recent kills! And Arnold is chatting up female officers with his stories of being in the FBI and she hears him say 'Back in the day...'

Just a normal evening, Andrea thinks to herself, and stands there watching.

CHAPTER 15

The Stories

The following morning, Andrea knows she has a mammoth task. Interviews need to be recorded so that the children will be safe. She thinks Caroline came to the barracks to kill the children, trying to eliminate the evidence that the drug trafficking ever happened. The sooner she documents the interviews, the safer the children will be.

Then there's the hostage. Andrea needs to learn from the ice cream lady if there are any more "dens" that have children working in slave labour. How can she get the lady to talk to her in better English, as she wasn't sure what language she spoke? Although, why would she tell Andrea anything if she had friends who were doing this too? She remembers the ice cream restaurant massacre and goes through things in her mind. *Are they connected... related...? Who is running the show?* She decides to get Harry to help and she also needs equipment to tape interviews. As for Caroline, Andrea decides not to talk to her, or to do it last.

Andrea starts with the children. She goes to their bedsides with a video camera on loan from Max. Each child is interviewed as they sit up in bed and tell their stories. It seems they all attended Oakville school, and they know the headmaster, Mr Smith. They say he would give them sweets which made them feel funny but good. If they wanted more sweets, they had to do deliveries on their bikes. This was done in after-school club but during hockey practise for some older kids. Then they were allowed to leave school permanently if they agreed to live at the restaurants and work. The children loved the sweets and ask if Andrea has any. One child says he had to go deep into the tunnels on his bike and talk to a man in a black hoodie and gave him the contents of his backpack. Another says she had to ride to a different ice cream restaurant with a backpack. They gave many examples of drug deliveries.

So, where are those children? Andrea thinks.

The children could draw maps of their usual route, because they always took the same ones. The older children told their stories of making the products in a kitchen basement. From the description of the ingredients, it seems it wasn't only cocaine that they were making; crystal meth may have been a frequent product of their hard work. Older children were there to help and teach the younger ones. The stories are long and full of details. Andrea is pleased that she collected so much evidence on video. By lunchtime, Andrea had done enough for one day so decides to leave it there and find some lunch for herself and Harry.

Arriving back at their quarters, Muriel is busy cooking as they have been given groceries from Julia. She is cooking some soup, sausages, and frozen fries. They are welcome to eat in the officer's mess every day but there is a dress code, smart casual, and Muriel enjoys her army tracksuit pants too much. They are still slightly hungover from the night before.

Sitting around the table eating lunch the team talk about the next steps. They have to discuss where Andrea should go with the evidence. How long can they hold Caroline before someone in the FBI notices. Do the FBI know she is here and whether Andrea can be arrested or sued for false imprisonment if they can't get something on Caroline? These are all questions they asked eachother.

All of this is mulled over whilst tucking into Muriel's cooking.

'We need to ask the children about Caroline. Otherwise, we need to let her go,' says Muriel.

'They mention an "Aunty Caroline" who brought them sweets. So, let's take a photo of her and see if the children recognise her,' suggests Andrea.

'That could be traumatising,' says Harry.

'These kids have been groomed. They really think the ice cream restaurant people are good and they like the headmaster.'

'So, they might look at her pictures and say "That's Aunty Caroline".'

'Yes, they might,' says Arnold.

'Has anyone talked to the bitch today?' Muriel asks.

'No. I'm letting her stew,' says Andrea.

Andrea wonders how wide she should cast the net. To put her mind at rest, she wants to eliminate as many people as possible. She gets Muriel's computer out of the car and starts searching for images of prominent people.

Could the mayor be involved? What about the Chief of Police, Natalie's boss? What does he look like? And Detective Cameron. And finally, Max? All these possibilities run through her head.

After lunch, Andrea goes back with Harry to the ward area with a bad feeling in her stomach and questions keep mulling around in her head. *If all of these people are involved, how big is this? How far does it go? Were the children also trafficked? Were any of them killed on purpose, beside the recent overdosing at the barn?*

Andrea has photos printed of Caroline and various other people. As she approaches the children to ask them if they recognise any of the people in the photos, her heart is in her throat.

Luckily, no one recognises the Chief of Police. But that doesn't mean he isn't involved or had turned a blind eye whilst taking revenue. They all recognise Natalie's boss though, Police Captain Mike Harrow. They say he is a nice man and that he came into the restaurant a lot to taste what they were making. Then the last photo she shows them is of Max.

'Oh, yes. Yes, I've seen him,' one of them says.

Andrea's heart sinks. If she can't trust Max, where can she go?

'He was here. He came in and asked us if we were feeling better.'

'Oh, thank God.'

'He told us you were a nice lady,' one of them says.

'Oh. So, you hadn't seen him before coming here?'

'No,' they all say.

Andrea is relieved.

'Will we be going home soon?' one of the girls asks. 'I have things to make in the restaurant. I haven't finished yet.'

'Yes, when do we go home?' another one asks.

'We're feeling much better,' a boy says. Andrea still can't remember all of their names.

How is Andrea to answer that? She wants to take them to their real parents. Their ice cream foster dad is dead and she has locked up their ice cream foster mother. She isn't going to be popular.

They gather around her in anticipation of her answer.

'Well… do you remember the other homes you had? Before moving to live with the people at the ice cream restaurant?'

'Yeah, but they said we couldn't live there any more because we had to work,' one child explains.

'I think they want you back,' Andrea says.

The children look shocked.

'And we are going to look for those parents.'

'Really? That's not what we were told,' says another child.

'Can we have some sweets?'

'They are not sweets that you have been given,' Andrea explains.

'Yes, they were and they made us feel good.'

'It was great!' another says.

'No, they were illegal drugs,' Andrea says, in her "mother" voice.

'No, they were sweets.'

'No, they were illegal drugs and the ice cream restaurant owners should not have kept you away from your parents.'

'Are you saying we were kidnapped?' asks one of the older children.

'Rather just kept for too long,' Andrea lies. 'And your parents need to be contacted.'

'Really?'

'Yes, we need to find your parents. Do any of you remember where you lived? And your last names?'

Some of the children can remember their last name, but other younger ones cannot. Harry thinks there must be a school register that he can hack into and just search for their first names, then the police reports on missing children, and try to match them up.

'Are you happy here though for the moment?'

'Yes,' some of them say. But some of them look sad.

'But we have nothing to do or make. We usually make powders and pack sweets into bags.'

'I could have some crafts and things brought here and you can make things.'

Some of the children seem excited by that.

Andrea tries to hold back the tears. She can't believe the amount of energy they have considering the near-poisoning just yesterday. Harry looks at her with pride with how she has dealt with the situation and explained everything without distressing them too much.

Andrea goes to talk to Max to give him an update on the children and Harry heads back to their quarters. Julia tells her to go straight in and gives her a smile as she saw them dancing slowly the night before.

Entering his office, he looks up from his desk, looking slightly nervous.

'Afternoon, Max,' she says.

'Afternoon, Andrea.'

'I just wanted you to know that I have been successful in gathering the evidence and I'm also eliminating suspects.'

'Oh.'

'And I'm not sure how long I can hold hostages in this country without talking to the police.'

'It's a grey area where the military are concerned. You need to resolve this swiftly to protect yourself really. Strictly speaking, you could be arrested for false imprisonment. You have no jurisdiction here. But we do work with MI5'

'Jesus.'

'But you're onto something and that's where we can help. The ice cream lady attempted to murder the children and as did

Caroline Hardy. So, you're protecting US children at the moment.'

'I think the Chief of Police is clean... but Natalie's boss, Captain Harrow... the children recognised a photo of him and said he used to test the product.'

'Bloody hell,' he says.

She looks at him and he still looks handsome in her eyes, even with a slight hangover.

'I suggest you go to the Chief of Police, or I can call him to come here. That would be safer for you.'

'When could you organise that?'

'Well, your hostages should really have legal representation. Tomorrow morning would probably be a good time to let the police in on the good news, children rescued from slavery, and then the bad news... hostages taken and a dead person back at the farm. You'll look bad if you take too long and it could work against you.'

'Yes. Thanks. I'll get onto it. I'll go back and start questioning the hostages.'

'Andrea. Would you like me to help with the interviews? I've done it before.'

'That might be a good idea.'

'I'm sure you can handle yourself and they won't get the better of you. But there are certain skills: getting them to trust you, offering them something in return...'

'Okay... yes please,' she says.

'Get the camera and I'll have an officer bring Caroline to an interrogation room beside the cells. I will meet you there.'

'Okay.'

Max and Andrea meet outside an interview room where Caroline Hardy was brought by a guard. They enter with the video camera that Andrea has brought but also a free-standing camera was there in the room. Andrea wanted to use both. She wasn't taking any chances. They sit down, looking at Caroline who looks like a cat with her tail caught between her legs. She's nervous and angry at the same time. Max starts talking to her first, but they don't put the cameras on just yet.

'Ms Hardy. I trust you are being well looked after?'

'What the hell is this? Am I under arrest?' Caroline yells.

'Not technically, but it is highly likely that you came to this property to harm children that are in my care. So, I am detaining you.'

'You can't do that.'

'Well, we will see about that. And as no one knows you are here... no one is coming to get you, are they?' Max threatens.

Caroline said nothing.

'What are you looking at?' Caroline says to Andrea.

'A sad, sad woman,' Andrea replies.

'Fuck off,' Caroline snaps back at her.

'You know you're not that clever, Caroline. You could have just said I was some mad woman who had assaulted you and planted a compact full of cocaine. But you haven't even thought of that!'

'That's what I will say when I get out of here.'

'So, you admit it's cocaine?

Caroline says nothing.

'What do you mean when? Don't you mean if?' Max says. 'You're a child killer. You don't deserve a trial.'

Andrea looks at him.

'I haven't killed any children.'

'What about the one found drowned with a backpack full of cocaine?' Andrea questions.

'That's got nothing to do with me. She must have been riding along near the river and lost her balance or something.'

'She shouldn't have been near the river. She should have

been at school!' Andrea says.

'Fuck off. The kids love me. I'm like family. Their parents knew where they were. They didn't have good parents. They wanted to stay with Mr and Mrs...' Then Caroline stops and doesn't say their last name.

'You're disgusting,' Andrea says, hoping Caroline will continue to talk, when she could have just said "No comment."

'Fuck off,' Caroline barks.

Max takes over. 'Let me put this to you as plainly as I can, Ms Hardy. The children have identified you from a photo. You are not technically arrested... no paperwork has been filed... the police haven't been called... and you could stay here forever... no one will ever know,' Max says with a serious face.

Caroline looks shocked. And Andrea tries to pretend that she knew he was going to say that.

'So, start talking because you're not going anywhere. We want names, dates, volumes of drug, types of drugs, children's names and surnames would be very useful, and dates that they were encouraged to leave their parents,' he stresses.

Andrea pipes up and says, 'I want the names of other operations in other restaurants, schools, the headmaster's routine schedule of delivering drugs, the tunnels used. I want a map drawn and every bloody thing you know about this evil operation,' demands Andrea.

Caroline says nothing. She thinks that if the children were under the influence of drugs when they identified her from a photo, she could have that evidence thrown out of court. But she worries that the army could "make her disappear".

'We have recorded stories from the children, the number of times you visited their drug kitchen, the things you used to give them. The number of years that they knew you. You knew their parents would want them back and you did nothing. And who were the people who came to our house to kill my family a few days ago,' Andrea yells.

Caroline says nothing.

'You are looking at charges: kidnapping, perverting the course of justice, drug distribution and trafficking, a felony, and the sentencing will be affected by the fact that you used children. There's the murder charge for the girl who drowned,' Max says.

'I said I had nothing to do with that. I was nowhere near her.'

'That's the only thing you say you have nothing to do with?' Andrea questions.

Caroline doesn't answer.

'We'll leave you to think about it,' Max says.

'You're bluffing. You wouldn't detain a US citizen.'

'You're a domestic terrorist. I am trained to kill to protect US citizens. Since coming back from my last tour in Iraq, I've blurred the lines a little,' he says and then smiles at her as he leaves the room. Andrea goes with him and pretends she's on board with the whole "let's kill Caroline" routine.

When they get far enough down the hall away from the interview room, Andrea questions Max.

'Are you kidding about that?'

'Ummmm... well... wouldn't the world be better off if...'

'Jesus!'

'Andrea, you have to understand that army officers decide who lives and who dies.'

'What are you talking about? We need her evidence. I think there are more drug kitchens.'

'I'm joking.' He laughs. 'But I got her worried, didn't I? I find if you start an interview with "No one knows you are here," they start to blab.'

'Yes,' Andrea says, rolling her eyes. 'But what about the whole *gaining their trust routine.*'

'Oh, I never use that. Come on, let's give her the evening to think about it. Would you like to eat dinner at my place tonight? My quarters are four houses down from yours.'

'Oh,' Andrea says, thinking it might be a date. 'Ummm… well…'

'Look. I'll make enough for two and it's up to you. Decide later. If I see you, I see you.'

'Okay. Thanks,' she says smiling.

'Caroline might confess tonight, or in the morning. But if not, we should inform the police by lunchtime tomorrow.'

'Okay.'

'Okay, see you later maybe.'

Andrea smiles and thinks of how manly he was when he took charge of the interview and threatened to kill Caroline.

Walking back to her barracks, Andrea thinks of the girls, and Luke, and Greg, in that order. She feels guilty for enjoying a break from the girls. *Is that bad?* she thinks to herself. Her life has definitely been turned upside down. Her new house will not be a "safe haven" any longer. When this is all over, where will she live? Where will the kids go to school? Will she finally have quality time with Harry? These are all the things that weigh heavily on her.

She enters her house quarters and finds Harry talking to Muriel and Arnold about the good old days as spies for a special division of the FBI. They are talking about being undercover and working in places like Budapest and Moscow, to name just a few. It seems like they were very fond of each other back then. Andrea sits down to listen and can see that Harry is fascinated. He hangs on their every word. So maybe Andrea has done him a favour by bringing him into this exciting new life… At least that's one way of looking at it.

'Has the bitch started talking?' Muriel says, referring to

Caroline.

'No. Just swearing at us a lot,' Andrea replies.

'I always suspected her,' Muriel lies.

'There's nothing worse than a mole in the agency. It threatens the security of the country,' says Arnold.

'Yes. She could be up to all sorts,' adds Andrea.

'Like what?' asks Harry.

'Well, selling information, secrets,' Arnold explains.

'What secrets?' Harry asks.

'Well, they are secrets, Harry… but things like weapons… the country's emergency planning.'

'I'm exhausted mentally. Are you planning on cooking tonight, Muriel?' asks Andrea.

'I am. Julia gave me some lovely chickens and thought I would roast both of them and then we'll have enough for sandwiches tomorrow if we can't face the officers' mess.'

'Sounds good,' says Arnold.

'I might have dinner with Max.'

'Okay, you go to the mess. Whatever suits you,' Arnold says.

'No. I mean he's cooking for me…' Andrea divulges.

'Oh dear,' says Muriel, slightly shocked, even though she saw them slow dancing the night before.

'We will be okay here, Andrea, go and have fun,' Arnold says, as if he is her father or something.

'Yes. We'll be fine,' says Harry.

'Okay, I didn't want to be rude,' Andrea explains.

'Andrea… Mum… have fun. You only live once,' Harry encourages.

'Thank God… I couldn't go through all of this again,' she jests. 'Tomorrow, Harry, can you see if you can make a spreadsheet of these things for me, after hacking the various departments?'

'Okay,' he says eagerly.

'Date of death of new-borns in Spring Town hospitals in the past ten years. Another column for "Unmarried Mother". Write yes or no. A column for date of adoption, parent's name, address, date of purchase of house in Spring Town, get from whatever the Land Registry is here. Then in a separate spreadsheet, number of missing children in past ten years in Spring Town compared to other suburbs of Philadelphia. How many children at Oakville are adopted? To get this, match the parents' names from the other spreadsheet. That won't be on the Internet, but you could hack the school computers.'

'Cool. I'm on it.'

CHAPTER 16

The Dinner

Andrea decides to shower and get ready for her 'date'. *It must be a date*, she thinks to herself. He doesn't have a wedding ring on. They *had* kissed. Now he wants to cook for her. *It is a date!* she decides.

Oh, what to wear, she thinks. The track pants seem kinda sexy, and maybe an army man's T-shirt or something. *Oh God. How drab.* Just then Julia pops in to offer Andrea another dress for the occasion. *Thank God*, Andrea thinks.

'Hi, Andrea. This might fit you. It's just a wraparound (dress) and some flat shoes. You look like my size so when Max said he was cooking for you, I wondered what you would wear. He tends to dress up for everything. Sorry if I'm interfering.'

'Oh, that's a lovely dress. Thank you.'

'No problem. Have a nice evening.'

Andrea feels excited and anxious at the same time. She tries not to show it whilst shutting the door as Julia leaves. She hasn't been on a date since she met Greg. Having got all dressed up, with the little makeup she had in her handbag, Andrea says goodbye to the others and walks down the path to the last house on the row of detached quarters. Several yards from this house, she can already smell the cooking and a fire burning. Her pulse quickens and her tinnitus gets louder. *Am I doing the right thing?* she questions herself. Could this be leading her into a situation where she would have to leave Greg. *Would Greg care?* she wonders.

Walking up the steps to the house, two barking Labradors rush out from behind the screen door. Max rushes out behind them.

'Sorry. Sorry. They are friendly really,' Max explains. 'He's Guns and this one's Roses.'

'Oh really?' she says sarcastically with a smile on her face. She looks at him in his smart clothes. Immaculately ironed canvas trousers, shirt with a stiff collar and lovely tan lace-up shoes. His black and silver hair has been washed and combed back. She can smell the shampoo as he leans down in front of her to grab the dogs by their collars. She can smell another aroma from his face as he kisses her on the cheek. Andrea goes for the other cheek to kiss too, as they do in the UK, but it's not an American greeting so it gets a bit awkward.

'Sorry,' she says. 'We do both cheeks in the UK.'

'Oh yes. I had forgotten.' He leads her into the house.

'Lovely dress.'

'Thank you. It's Julia's,' she says.

He just smiles.

Handing her a glass of red wine, he rushes back to attend to the cooking. She surveys the lounge room which is full of memorabilia from different countries. He looks at her as she walks around the room. Her shoulder-length hair and hourglass figure is mesmerising to him. She turns around to catch him looking at her, so he quickly attends to the dinner.

There are candles on the table and the settings look like they have been measured to be equally spaced apart with a ruler. *Is this why he's not married? Is he this anal about place settings?* she wonders. *Did he drive a previous wife mad by getting the ruler out each time she wanted the table set? Is his wardrobe military-like? Is he obsessive compulsive? Does he file his socks in colour order?* She has to find out.

Andrea asks to freshen up after the long walk, from four houses away, just so she can look into the bathroom cabinet, and maybe his wardrobe. If he is obsessive compulsive, she will not bother kissing him again, she thinks. No point in having a fling with someone who tears your clothes off then makes you wait while he folds them neatly.

After gaining permission to use the facilities, she walks down to the bathroom. With a fast-beating heart, she opens the cabinet above the sink. It's full of medicine! *Oh no*, she thinks. He's either a druggy or a pusher or completely mad and having to take huge quantities of meds each day to appear sane. *What the hell,* she thinks.

She reaches in to look at the names of the drugs on the bottles and notices they are not prescribed for him. They are for a "Miranda Findlay." *His wife?* she thinks. She must still live here. They have all sorts of drug names that are hard to pronounce and many different ones, all for this Miranda person? She is determined to weave questions about this into the evening's discussion.

Next is the wardrobe. *Is he too tidy?* She can hear him whistling whilst cooking, so she sneaks down the corridor and quickly opens the wardrobe. To her fright, there are ladies' clothes in there. *Does a woman live here or is he a cross dresser?* she wonders. *Or has he had a sex change?* She thinks for a minute that he is too good looking to be a man. *Maybe he's a woman?*

'Andrea,' he then yells. 'Stop snooping around and come for dinner.'

God. Nothing gets past him, she thinks.

She doesn't know how to look innocent, walking back into

the room.

Hesmiles at her.

'Come sit,' he says placing a plate of lovely beef bourguignon in front of her.

'Is this to your liking?'

'I'm vegetarian.'

His face crumbles.

'Just kidding. I needed to get you back for the whole *let's kill Caroline* thing.'

He laughs.

'It looks lovely. I really do appreciate how well we have been looked after. I think if we had put the children into several different hospitals, and stayed in a hotel ourselves to hide, we might all be dead by now.'

'That's a good start to the evening conversation,' he jokes. 'Let's not underestimate the fact that you were travelling with two highly trained killers yourself.'

'Yes, I guess they do make me feel safe, Muriel and Arnold.'

'But I'm glad you're here,' he says, looking at her with misty eyes. She doesn't know what to say so she changes the subject.

'Have you been told anything about the case?'

'Oh, they had to tell me the main bits before I granted permission for you to stay here. I don't go along with all that security clearance stuff, I demanded to know.'

'I see.' Then she starts her inquisition. 'Umm... can I ask about the pills in the cupboard? Sorry. I opened it by mistake.'

'Yes. They are my late wife's.'

'Oh, sorry!'

'It's okay. It's silly really. She passed away five years ago from cancer and the pills were so expensive. I kept them in case anyone else might want them. But then just kept them because they remind me of her. I kept her lovely dresses. The ones she used to dance in at all the army balls.'

Andrea was starting to feel slightly uncomfortable.

'She was a young woman, only forty-nine.'

'I'm sorry to hear that.'

'The dresses still smell like her,' he explains, then wishing he hadn't sounded so pathetic.

Andrea tries to hide the fact that this was all getting a bit weird. She imagined him going to bed holding a dress every night. *Maybe he has a blow-up doll too… and he dresses it in a different ball dress every night and they waltz around the lounge room?* Her mind went wild with possibilities.

'Mmmm,' Andrea says, not knowing what else to say.

'Is it wrong, Andrea? Do we have to forget about people? If it makes us happy to remember them… why can't we just remember them?' he asks.

'I think it's nice to keep things and be happy rather than being sad,' Andrea says as she almost convinces herself of that, trying to make him feel as if he wasn't creeping her out.

'Tell me more about yourself, Andrea. How did you get into MI5?'

'They recruit graduates straight from uni. They sent a letter to invite you to an assessment. Not to everyone, just the top three per cent. I thought it might be interesting. I was an analyst not an agent.'

'Oh.' That's one thing he didn't know.

'Yes, this is my first field assignment.'

'Really?'

She doesn't want to say that she wasn't aware she was on assignment. She feels silly enough by being duped.

'I hear you have a family?'

'Yes, two girls and my husband, and Harry was adopted out when I was very young. We've only just been reunited.'

'Really?'

'Yes. I think when you're young you are selfish. I told myself that someone else can take better care of my baby. But it's a lie that you tell yourself. I gave him to two strangers. Where's the logic in that?'

'Don't beat yourself up. We all try to do what's right at the time. You have found him now and that's what matters.'

'Yes, I suppose,' Andrea says, trying not to get emotional. 'Do you have children?'

'Yes. I have two boys.'

'Are they like you? Are they in the army?'

'Oh, like me? Ummm, no. I think when my wife died, they changed. They get casual jobs and do a lot of gardening for other people, like putting ponds in and making water features. They like that sort of thing.'

'Oh. Well, that's good. The outdoor life,'

'I just want them to be happy,' he says.

There's an awkward moment where Andrea doesn't know what to say.

'How do you like the meat?' he asks.

'Oh, lovely, thank you.'

'I meant to put some music on. Do you like ELO?'

'God yes. That's a relief, I thought you were going to put on some heavy metal music for a minute there.'

'You're not a fan?'

'I have to be in the mood.' Andrea thinks that heavy metal music on top of dresses and medications of his dead wife would add up to "psycho!"

They finish their main meals, which Andrea found delicious

and move on to a chocolate fondant pudding. He loosens up a bit and starts telling her about his life before getting married, probably as a way of avoiding discussions about his wife. He eats carefully, not wanting to make a mess. Anyone would think he was British, apart from the accent.

'Have you been to the continent much? I think Rome is my favourite city in Europe. Do you have a favourite?' he asks.

Wow, Andrea thinks. It's her favourite too, but she doesn't want to sound corny. She doesn't want to ask him when he last visited. It was probably with his wife.

'Ummm, Barcelona.' She changes the subject. 'Do you have a home outside the base?' As she says it, she knows what he's going to say… *yes, a house full of my dead wife's things.*

'No. I sold up. The boys have a lot of the furniture. I gave them their share of the inheritance money and they have bought their own houses.'

'Oh great!' She is now worried that she sounds too eager. She's attracted to him even though he's a bit weird. He continues talking about how he's 'free as a bird' and has whittled down his possessions to what she sees around the lounge room. But she stops listening and just watches his mouth move as he talks and wonders if she will kiss him again that evening.

'What do you think, Andrea?' He wakes her up from her daydream.

'Oh, sorry, I was miles away.'

He looks disappointed and senses that he might be boring her.

'So, Caroline hasn't said she will confess yet?' she asks.

'No. Let's call the police in the morning. We have to, otherwise you'll be charged with kidnapping.' He laughs.

'And you? Will you be in trouble?'

'Well, *you* assaulted her,' he jokes. 'I could deny all

knowledge,' he says jokingly.

She rolls her eyes at him.

'It's a sad day when children are being treated this way. And you'd think they are safe at school, from drug dealers,' he says.

'I wonder if the headmaster has done a runner,' she adds.

'Why?'

'Well, Mr and Mrs whoever went to the school before travelling to the barn,' she explains.

'I'm thinking the FBI would be a better call. Arnold did murder Mr Ice Cream Man,' he advises.

'Yes, there's that. And the body needs to be recovered.'

'Police can be quite dogmatic and they will probably arrest him first and ask questions later.'

'Okay. So… who in the FBI?'

'I will call someone… this can all be done very discreetly.'

'Oh, thank you. What a mess I'm in,' she sighs.

'Well people who help people are often in a mess because they don't just walk away.'

'I guess.'

'It's great what you've done, Andrea. You should be very proud of yourself.'

'Thank you.'

'Really, Andrea. Let's make a toast…' He was on his third glass.

She holds up her red wine.

'To the most intelligent, attractive, witty and feisty agent I know!'

'I'm probably the only one.'

'You're the only female agent that I know, apart from Caroline, and she's unattractive.' They both laugh and drink up.

After the dishes are cleared, he puts some more wood on the fire. They sit on the sofa and talk. Every now and then, she's not sure if she is attracted to him. One minute she is. Then she's not. Then she is...

'So, when do you plan to retire?' she asks him.

'Oh, I don't ever want to stop working, but I might change my job.'

'Oh?'

'Well, I'd like to continue helping people. I like the physical aspect of the job. We have to maintain our fitness, our discipline here. It keeps me focused, especially after...' and he doesn't say it.

'It must have been horrible for you.'

'Well, yes, and you become the person that no one wants to be around because you're so sad. Then you have no company. People can't wait to get away from you because they run out of things to say and ways of trying to cheer you up. You're probably trying to get away from me now. I bet you're planning your escape,' he says jokingly.

With that, Andrea leans forward to gently kiss him on the lips. She feels so sorry for this poor gorgeous man that she instantly wants to heal him. He kisses her back and he can't read whether Andrea wants to take it further. It's just as well he doesn't try because she is still confused about it all, being married and everything.

'Sorry, Andrea, but I have to ask,' he says pulling away from her. 'Your husband? How are things?'

'Oh. Ummm.' Andrea is shocked to be put on the spot and feels she has to justify why she was kissing him.

'He's... ummmmm... well... I just think he's often hard to reach emotionally and physically. I feel like I'm lonely... but I'm married... so how can I be lonely?'

'Oh.'

'Yes. I can be in the same room as him and he doesn't notice me. I can be talking to him, and he doesn't look at me. After having the girls though, it's too late to leave. I just made the best of it.'

'God, that's so sad.'

'Yeah, I guess. I think the key to happiness is to lower your expectations!'

They both laugh.

'Oh, Andrea, that is a horribly sad outlook on life,' he says while she's still laughing.

'Yeah, but it's true.'

'I guess.'

'Look. Take you for example. Your wife died… but you're happy because you're making the best of it… and you're okay.'

'Am I happy though?'

'Yes, I think you are happy because you have the army, and they are your friends. You have the structure… you have—'

He stops her talking by kissing her and they lie down on the sofa, kissing.

By three a.m. Andrea wakes up on the sofa. She wonders for a second if they have had sex but then realises they haven't as all her clothes are intact. Max is sleeping on the floor next to her. She wakes him and asks if he will walk her home.

'Yes, if you want to go home.'

'I just think I should be there when Harry wakes up. I don't want him to worry.'

'He's with two trained killers.'

'Yes… I know… but…'

He stands up with his clothes looking like they are still perfectly ironed. She straightens her dress and hair and puts her shoes on.

'It was a lovely evening,' she says.

'Thank you for your company.'

'Thank *you.*'

They walk back to her house. He holds her hand for the last part of the walk and then she kisses him on the cheek and goes inside. He walks away slightly heartbroken... wondering why the kiss was on the cheek and not the lips.

Women can be so fickle! I should have hidden the dresses, he thinks.

As he walks away, Andrea wonders if he's going to go home to sleep with his wife's dresses.

CHAPTER 17

The FBI

It's the morning of the day they have dreaded. Max makes the call to his friend in the FBI, George, and explains everything.

'I have one of your agents here, a Ms Caroline Hardy.'

'Oh yes.'

'I had to detain her.'

'What? Why? She was working on the missing children case, undercover.'

'That's just it, George. She came here to kill them.'

'What!'

'Yes, I have eleven children here and a lady who worked in the ice cream restaurant and Caroline Hardy.'

'When did this happen?'

'It's a long story. Can you come here to discuss it and don't bring a squad of black SUVs. We need to talk.'

'Okay, Max, I'll be there within the hour.'

George arrives and has only two agents with him, wearing their FBI jackets. The three of them enter Max's office and sit down.

'We have evidence, George, that Agent Hardy knew the missing children and didn't tell anyone where they were. She was using them to make drugs in one of the ice cream restaurants owned by a lady we have in custody and another man who... um... was killed when they rescued the children.'

'Who led the investigation?'

'An agent from MI5, living here…' Max didn't know how to describe Andrea's connection.

'Great, so why no police?'

'Captain Harrow is involved. A local Chief,'

'Shit. Really?'

'Yes. That's why we couldn't trust him or take the kids to a regular hospital.'

'Jesus.'

'Yes, he may have tried to clean up the operation.'

'I don't believe it. Caroline wouldn't hurt children either.'

'Well, let me show you something,' he says, turning his computer around so George and the two agents can see it.

'Here is the MI5 agent, Andrea Mitchell, collecting Caroline from the room where she's been held. They are now walking towards where the children have been recovering. Now, they were shown her picture yesterday and they recognised her, saying she bought them sweets and visited them regularly in the drug kitchen… now watch.'

Caroline seems reluctant to walk into the room when she sees the sign 'Hospital Ward'. Andrea forces her to walk by pushing her from behind. Caroline walks in and the children start calling out her name, 'Caroline! Caroline! Do you have sweets? Sweets. Sweets,' they yell.

'Here are the sweets, George.' Max hands George Caroline's handbag full of sweets. 'I haven't got them analysed yet, but the children said they make them feel good and they work for these sweets.'

They continue to watch the video. Caroline looks very uncomfortable as the children know who she is. They get out of their beds and gather around her.

'She would visit them in the drug kitchen and get them addicted to sweets or drugs… whatever they are. We have video testimony of each child.'

'Bloody hell. She knew all along where they were?'

'Yes.'

'I can't believe it. Well, I have to take her in,' George says.

Andrea joins them and starts debriefing George from the beginning, starting with the dead body in the pool. Then the weird mothers and the after-school club, the girl who was found drowned with a backpack full of cocaine. She went on to explain her consultancy work with Natalie Bellino (which is why she didn't alert the police), the tunnels and the after-school club, the headmaster, the ice cream restaurant carnage, Luke living in her loft, and that Caroline knew he was there. She continues with the events of the cartel coming to warn her off and the ex-agents that are helping her, finding the children in the barn and finally, a dead man lying in the long grass back at the barn.

'Wow. You've been busy, Agent Mitchell.'

'We've been trying to find out why children seem to "disappear" in Spring Town. It's as if everyone got used to it. It was a closed secret of some sort. The school mums didn't really talk about it,' Andrea explains.

'Right.'

'And there's more,' Andrea says.

'What do you mean?'

'Babies are taken from unmarried mothers and "given" to married couples. I'll have the data to prove it soon. The unmarried mothers are told that their babies have died. The adoption records are all weird. My son's looking into it.'

'Yes, there's an investigation into the adoption agency at the moment being conducted… oh… by Caroline.' George says.

'Spring Town is a mess and I think this drug trafficking

extends to the UK because my boss sent me here, specifically here,' Andrea says.

George is very grateful, and they decide to give the children a few more days in the ward for fear of distressing them further. He planned to get social workers to visit and try to track down the parents. He said he would bring clothes and games for them to play.

Muriel, Arnold and Harry were all told to give statements. The interviewers were very thorough, every detail was covered. Arnold was grilled the most because he had killed Mr What's-his-name. Muriel had killed two members of a cartel at Andrea's house but that was cleaned up by Caroline, so she simply said she was under Caroline's orders to kill them. George brushed over the fact thatno one had told him at the bureau what was going on with these 'clean-ups,' which involve pretending nothing has happened... no body... no murder.

After many intense hours of questioning, the FBI finally leaves. As George turns around to leave the office though, he has a few words of wisdom for Andrea.

'Where will you go now?' he says.

'Sorry? What?' She says.

'Well, the cartel know your name and address and they will realise that two of their members haven't returned home, so...'

'So...?'

'So, you will definitely be on their "Hit List".' He explains.

'Oh, Jesus!'

'So, we can give you all a new identity. You can join your family in the safe house.'

'Maybe I should just go back to England.'

'What?' Max says, in a surprised voice.

'It's an option!' George explains.

'Jesus.' Andrea says with a sigh.

Max is listening to all of this, and his heart sinks when he hears the word "England".

George leaves and Andrea flops down into a sofa in Max's office while he pours her a Bourbon.

'Well… that went well… they believed you and they are taking Caroline and Mrs What's-her-name for questioning. You had better stay here to be safe until you figure out your next move.'

'Jesus. My life is over. I'll never be free to roam the shopping malls again without looking over my shoulder.'

'Ummmm… yes… you're right,' Max says, feeling happy that she needs his protection.

'Thank you,' she says to Max as she gets up to leave. She speaks to him in a in a more professional tone, as if she has only just met him.

Whilst walking back to her house, she remembers that she must have fallen asleep during the kissing on the sofa. *How embarrassing*, she thinks. *He must be a boring kisser*!

Back at the house, Andrea walks in to find Muriel and Arnold having some wine and snacking on cheese. Harry has found ice cream in the little freezer, so he's happy.

'So…' Andrea says, 'how do you all think it went? How were your interviews?'

'Fine,' says Muriel. 'The usual.'

Andrea doesn't know what *the usual* is…

'It was straightforward. We won't be charged with anything.'

Jesus, Andrea thinks. *How can they be so calm?*

'George said I would be in danger now because of the cartel.'

'That's right,' says Arnold. 'And so is your family.'

'You need to think of where to live,' adds Muriel.

For some reason, they didn't worry about their own safety.

'I'm sorry, Harry,' she says to him.

'Hey. I'm having a ball. In the last few days, I've met my biological mum… a secret agent. So secret that even she didn't know she was one… and I've found two sisters… got to work with FBI agents… witnessed a few murders… and got to live in an army base.'

Andrea smiles at him.

'I feel safe with you, Andrea… Mum… even though it's dangerous.'

'Well, the FBI agent thought that England might be an option, rather than getting new identities and living here.'

'Great. Let's go!' he says enthusiastically.

'I'll need to speak to the girls.'

'And Greg? Will he be happy?' harry asks.

'That's a conversation I will have with him. You saw how furious he was when he drove off from Muriel's house.'

'Yeah.'

'He just wanted to come back here and lead a quiet, peaceful life.'

'Jeez. Wait until he finds out that he might have to leave.'

'I think this will be a deal breaker,' Andrea says, looking sad.

Arnold and Muriel look over at Andrea and genuinely feel sorry for her. She has saved the children from a life of drugs and potential death, but now has so many problems herself.

'I'm not being melodramatic… but basically… I'll never be safe again… always looking over my shoulder.'

'Come on, Andrea, it's not that bad,' says Arnold. 'We've

gotten used to it over the years.'

'Yes. At least you know *who* is after you. And if you leave the country, they won't bother going over there to find you,' says Muriel.

'They just want you out of their way,' says Arnold.

'Who though? We don't know who,' Andrea asks.

'Well, their car was outside your house. The FBI will know who they are.'

'There will be arrests, Andrea. You can count on it,' Muriel assures.

Andrea tries to stop sounding so negative in front of Harry.

'I'm so sorry, Harry. I feel as if this is the only place that we are safe.'

'It's okay, Mum. It's fine... How long will we be here?'

'Just a few more days during the initial investigation and until we decide where to go. We'll need to be contactable to give evidence, but we can always do that by a video link.'

'I need to know when it's safe to see the girls... to get our stuff from the house... passports and stuff.'

'Let's take each day at a time, Andrea,' says Muriel.

'Yes, you are safe here. The girls will be safe, and you have done a good thing... the children are safe too,' says Arnold.

'It's okay. I'll pull myself together.'

Harry looks on and is worried about her, more than his own safety.

'You know, I've been thinking, Caroline probably killed the teacher at the school. She got updates from Natalie so knew about the undercover work,' Andrea says.

'Then she tried to kill Natalie when she got too close,' Arnold says.

'Yes probably,' adds Muriel.

Andrea decides to start cooking some pancakes to go with

Harry's 'ice cream lunch' and to avoid any more discussion about the future… or the recent past. Their fridge and pantry had been stocked full by Julia. Harry jumps up to help her. They seem to both want to do something normal, something mundane, like a normal mother and son. Arnold and Muriel get some playing cards out to play rummy.

'Mmmm,' says Harry. 'I think I like being here.'

Andrea looks over at him lovingly.

'How was your date last night?' asks Muriel.

'Oh, it was fine. We are just friends.'

'Riiiiight,' Muriel replies.

'Why do you say it like that?' she asks.

'Welllll. He seems to like you,' Muriel says.

'I guess.'

'How are things with Greg?' Arnold asks.

'Oh, I don't know.'

'What is he really like?' Harry asks.

'Well. He can't help it but… he's… aaa… nnn'

'Nerd?' he jokes.

'He's a narcissist.'

'Oh… ummm… what's that?' asks Muriel.

'Well, it is quite common… really.'

'Oh?'

'Yes. At uni I learned about personality disorders. A person can become a narcissist if they grow up with very little love or self-esteem,' explains Andrea. 'They can't help it really. As adults, they are only concerned with their own welfare. They rarely tell the truth and are only happy when they are talking about themselves and getting attention. When I get attention from other people, he doesn't like it.'

'What attracted you to him then if it wasn't his personality?'

Muriel jests.

'He was very charming. Narcissists have this charm which draws people in. He was really quiet nice and doted on me before we got married.'

'What about after you got married?' Harry asks.

'Well, he got jealous of the girls. That's because the attention wasn't on him. And he didn't like being in England because he was regarded as a foreigner, less status, I guess. He couldn't wait to come back to the US. I know he won't want to leave.'

'You've got some big decisions to make then,' Muriel says loudly, in an headmistress tone.

'Yes.'

'How do you feel about Max?' Harry asks.

'He's lovely really, as a person. I don't know if I feel anything for him. I've only just met him. Anyway, he's still grieving for his dead wife.'

'Really?'

'Yes. But it's nice to have someone look at me finally. Greg doesn't look at me... you know... and he doesn't talk to me either'

'I see,' says Arnold.

They carry on cooking and later sit around eating and drinking coffee spiked with alcohol, laughing and telling stories. They make a good team, the four of them. Andrea feels like she is still working even though the hostages have been handed over to the FBI. Her mind stays on the case as she wonders how long Mr and Mrs What's-their-names operation has been running.

In the evening, Andrea decides to go to visit Max to see if he's still awake and to see if he has heard anything. Knocking on his door, she's worried that he might answer it dressed in his wife's clothes, an image she just can't get out of her head since seeing the dresses.

'Andrea. Hi. I've had work to do so haven't been able to cook your dinner or anything.'

'Oh, I'm just here for a chat. But if you're busy…' she says as she turns to leave.

'No. Come in, come in. How can I help?'

'I was about to go to bed early, but I didn't think I would sleep,' Andrea says.

'Yes. It's been a difficult few days for you,' Max replies.

'Mmm,' Andrea agrees.

'Have you all eaten over there?' He asks.

'Yes. Yes. We had one normal evening finally. Harry deserves that much.'

'Great. Would you like some wine?'

'Ummm, well, I guess. I just wondered if you knew anything more? Seeing as you know George.'

'Well, yes, George and I go back to when he was in the army.'

'Oh, was he?'

'Yes. Ummm, he mentioned that Caroline confessed.'

'Really!' Andrea is delighted.

'Yes, well, the children made such a positive identification. They knew her name and they recognised her. He's trying to get her to confess to some murders.'

'God. That's progress!'

'Oh, the teacher found dead at the school. Caroline did that.'

'Oh dear.'

'Yes, and I'm afraid Natalie Bellino, the woman you were working for… is very sick due to the poison. But she will pull through.'

'Oh my God,' Andrea says as her eyes fill up.

'But to cheer you up… Caroline shot the headmaster, Mr Smith before coming here.'

'He's dead?'

'Yes, it seems she was picking off the witnesses one by one.'

'JESUS. WHAT NEXT?'

'Yes. What next? I have wine.'

'Can we sit in front of the fire for a bit?' she asks.

'Yes sure.' He walks over to her, and they sit on the rug. He puts an arm around her and lets her rest her head onto his shoulder. She remembers how Natalie had asked her to work on the case.. *Poor Natalie,* she thinks.

They stare at the fire as if it will give them answers. Eventually, they fall asleep on the rug.

CHAPTER 18

The Arrests

Max is up for work early in the morning and left Andrea asleep on his sofa where he had put her in the early hours. He pops in to tell Muriel that she is asleep in his house and that she is okay. He tells her that Natalie is very ill from poisoning and that they think Caroline did it. He explains how Caroline must have shot the headmaster on her way to the army base yesterday. Max then looks in to check on the children who are all sitting up in bed eating their cereal and fruit juice. Walking down the corridor to his office he goes past the communal room where officers watch TV and hears a news broadcast.

We have reports that eleven children who were feared to have run away from the suburb of Spring Town have now been found. Parents will be contacted by the police. No more details have been released. We have been told that the children are healthy and being cared for.

Jesus, thinks Max. *Are they going to stage the reunions here?*

Max is notified that the social workers will turn up at the main entrance and are buzzed in after the usual search for weapons. *Just another normal day in the army,* he thinks.

Andrea wakes up and wanders back to her house where Muriel is up making a Full English for Arnold and Harry, even though Harry is still in bed.

'Morning, Andrea,' Muriel says. Andrea can't believe Muriel is still being nice to her. 'Have you seen the news?'

'No.'

'They are contacting parents who reported missing children,' Muriel asks.

'Really?'

'Yes, it's all over the news… *eleven children found etc. etc.'*

'God. And Max said last night that Caroline had confessed and… the headmaster is dead… and Natalie…'

'We know, dear. He popped in to tell us this morning. Poor Natalie.'

Andrea takes some breakfast to Harry and sits the tray on his bedside table as he wakes up. She goes back to sit down to eat with Muriel and Arnold.

'I might as well go home now,' says Muriel.

'Really!' Andrea says. 'Is it safe?'

'Well, if Caroline has confessed and we're not going to be accused of anything. I could pop off and water my garden. I have things to do now that the drama is all over.'

'I guess. Do you have to increase your security on the house?' Andrea says in a sombre tone.

'Not really. I might buy another few guns.'

'Me too,' says Arnold. 'Caroline has confessed. The cartel probably don't know where I live. My house is like a fortress anyway.'

Andrea gets a flashback to when he shot the man at the farm. She suddenly feels vulnerable at the thought of them leaving her, even though she is in the middle of an army base with trained killers to protect her.

'That's a shame,' says Andrea, suddenly feeling like her new family is breaking up.

'Is the adventure over?' Harry says, as he walks into the room.

'I'm afraid so, Harry. But we've enjoyed working with you.'

'Oh, it wasn't work.'

'Well, we enjoyed meeting you, Harry.'

'Yes. Likewise.'

Andrea felt sad. It was like being in a movie for the past few days. Meeting a dashing major general and saving the children. *Couldn't it just go on?* she thought.

'Muriel, how do I get hold of Greg and the girls?'

'Oh, umm, speak to the FBI and get put through on a secure line.'

'Oh okay.'

'Sorry but Caroline didn't want me to tell you that before. I thought she was a bit strange, looking back on it.'

'I'll do that today,' Andrea says.

Andrea has a shower and dresses in another pair of gym pants and T-shirt then makes her way over to Max's office. On her way there, she knows that her routine of being able to see him whenever she likes will change once she leaves the base. What if she leaves the country? Will she ever see him again? *First things first*, she thinks. She has to go to her house and get her belongings and passports.

Entering Max's office She notices that he is looking at her differently and she felt flushed. Greg hadn't looked at her that way in years.

'Morning. Can I borrow some protection?' she asks.

'Morning. What do you mean specifically... a gun?'

'No some officers. I need to get things from my house and I'm too frightened to go there on my own.'

'I'll have two officers take you there. Just say when.'

'Thank you. It's all over the news.'

'Indeed. You'll be famous.'

'Oh, I want to remain anonymous.'

'Oh, I mean you'll be famous amongst the FBI crowd. They'll probably offer you a job.'

'I don't know about that, Max. I think I need to leave the country. Get the girls and go back to England.'

'Really? And Greg?'

'He'll never come with us back there.'

'Oh…'

'Yes.'

'Oh, I forgot. They may have found your Luke's real identity.'

'Really? Who is he?'

'He's Samuel Hanson, eleven years old and went to the same school. So, they are trying to find the parents.'

'God. Imagine that. Having a child missing.'

'Yes, I can't imagine.'

There's an awkward silence.

'Andrea, I hope I'm not being too forward by saying that I'll miss you if you go to England?'

'Max, we don't even know each other.'

'You're right.'

'I think I need to leave the country. Everything points towards that decision.'

'I understand,' he says looking sad. 'The officers at the front desk will organise your security. I'll tell them it's authorised.'

Andrea leaves his office and goes to the front desk. She tells the others what she's doing, and Harry insists on going with her. She explains to Harry that they must stay at the base until all the children have been reunited with their families. So, they are just going home to get supplies and then will come back to the base for a bit longer.

Sitting in the back of an army SUV, Andrea looks out the window as they drive along the highway. She tells herself that the scenery is boring just to get her mind ready to go back to England. Driving into Spring Town it looks eerie for the first time. She originally thought it was lovely, but so much has happened. This was the town where children were vulnerable and preyed upon. They were extremely unlucky. Unlucky to be living there and going to that school. Unlucky that their original mothers were unmarried and so they were adopted out. It was a cruel town, and everyone was in on it.

Pulling up in the drive, Andrea waits until the army officers go in and check her premises first. They then 'cover' Andrea while she and Harry get out of the car and go inside the house, which wasunlocked!

Andrea starts crying as silently as she can without the Harry seeing her tears. It's the glimpse of normality that is no more and has tipped her over the edge.

'Mum… don't get upset.'

'Why can't my life be normal?'

'Normal is boring, Mum… you know that… you wanted to help people. You didn't like real estate.'

'I guess.'

'Let's get the things we need, Mum… come on… computers…'

'No, not computers.'

'Oh yeah… you're right… umm passports, clothes, and chocolate. There's not enough chocolate in the army base,' he says, laughing.

She laughs and looks at him for a moment.

They walk around slowly, gathering their belongings. Andrea finds the keys and locks the house up.

Driving out of the drive, she cries again. The officers notice this time.

'All okay, ma'am?'

'Yes,' she says whilst wiping her eyes.

Harry reaches down and holds her hand. 'It's going to be okay,' he says.

'I know. I know, Harry. Thanks. Sorry. Just feeling a bit emotional.'

'It's natural.'

'Yeah.'

They look over at Muriel's house and then at each other, remembering how she sheltered them.

They drive down the road and Andrea reminiscences about the first time they saw that house and the lovely suburb of Spring Town. She can still remember the feeling of a *new start*, and the anticipation and excitement of living in the US. Harry looks over at her and knows what she is thinking.

They are only a few blocks away when they hear a large bang. The officers are shocked and the car swerves. Andrea thinks they have a flat tire but then quickly realises that their car has been shot at. The army officers yell at them to get down. Harry and Andrea dive down as low as they can. The shots seem to be coming from behind the car.

'GET DOWN,' the officers yell.

'It must be the cartel,' Andrea says. 'They must have been waiting for me to return to the house.'

'Get down, ma'am.'

'What's happening?' Harry asks from low down in the back seat of the car.

Another shot doesn't penetrate the windows as they are bullet proof.

'Bullet proof windows,' Andrea says to Harry.

'Thank Christ,' he says, covering his ears.

'How close are they?'

'Not too close. I want you guys to get out of the car and hide,' one of the officers says.

'WHAT?' Harry shouts.

'It's better, Harry,' says Andrea, knowing what the officers probably have planned.

Another shot is fired.

'SHIT,' yells Harry.

The officer sitting in the front calls the police and they prepare an ambush on Highway 95.

'Jesus.'

'Find somewhere to let us out,' Andrea orders.

'Yes, ma'am.'

'Is that a good idea?' says Harry.

'Yes. Harry, let them do this. It's safer.'

'Will we be safe though?'

'Yes. I promise.'

The officer loses the car chasing them for a few seconds and turns down a back street.

'Get ready to exit the vehicle and take cover,' the officer instructs.

'Yes. We're ready,' Andrea says confidently.

'Are we?' wonders Harry.

'It's okay. You exit that way and hide behind that dumpster and I exit this way.'

The car stops so they can get out. Harry dives out the right-hand side of the car and Andrea dives out the left-hand side, they both hide behind various dumpsters. Their vehicle hardly stops for them to get out and then it speeds up again to look like it hasn't stopped at all, to give the impression to the cartel that the targets are still in the car. As the car speeds off, Andrea yells out to the officers.

'Don't kill them.' She wants more arrests made. She doesn't think the job is finished. *There must be more people involved,* she thinks.

Harry stays low behind a dumpster and waits for Andrea's signal.

'Harry,' she whispers.

'Yep,' he says, slightly annoyed.

'Let's go.'

'Go where?'

'To a hotel. I need to rest.'

'What!'

She walks over to him because he is too scared to come out from behind the dumpster.

'Come on. They've gone. And the police will block the highway.'

'They must have been waiting for us,' he says, still annoyed.

'Yes, so we can't go back there.'

They walk down the lane and flag down a taxi. Driving up to Downtown Philly, Harry is visually shaken. She puts her arm around him. They get dropped in the middle of a busy street and pay with cash that Andrea had taken from the house. The girls had always insisted that Andrea keep an emergency roll of cash, next to the passports at the back of her cupboard. She didn't count it but knew it was at least a few thousand dollars. They would say *"You never know what could happen, Mum"*. She smiles as she thinks of them.

They walk down the street and into the first big conference hotel they can find. Harry thinks they are checking into a room to rest, but she explains that they will need to see ID for that and she wants to be anonymous. Instead, she wants to go to the spa.

'So, what are we doing here?' Harry asks.

'I need a massage.'

'Seriously. That's your priority?'

'Yes. We need to hide. What better place to hide than in a spa?'

'Okay,' he says sarcastically.

'Harry, I know this is not great, but I think you will be safe if we leave here.'

'What do you mean?'

'Well, we leave Philadelphia. We go to the airport. You have your passport, right?'

'Yes.'

'Well, let's just go, after my massage. And can we get your hair cut here too?'

'My hair, that's what you're worried about?'

'We need to look different. Let's change our look and get out of America.'

'What about the girls? And Greg?'

'They can join us when it's safe. But until then, we can't go to their safe house because someone might following us. We can't live in the army base forever; we can't live in Spring Town.'

'Yeah, I guess,' Harry says quietly, as if he's disappointed.

'Unless you want to go home to Canada?'

'NO!' he says.

'Are you sure? In that case, I think England will be our best bet.'

'Yeah. Sorry, I'm a bit irritable. I'm not used to people shooting at me.'

'Yes, I know. You're used to being the one who shoots the gun,' she jokes.

He laughs and succumbs to the spa options.

They have their massages in the lovely five star conference centre. Andrea asks for some stationery from the concierge and they put the passports of Greg, Alice, and Sophie, with a letter to Max in an envelope. She shows the concierge her old MI5 business card and asks him to promise to have the envelope hand delivered to Major General Max Findlay at the army base in Delta.

They go to the hair salon part of the hotel and Harry agrees to have his shoulder-length hair cut and gets a *Number one* at the sides. Andrea gets her hair dyed red. They leave the hotel and hail down a taxi. Driving to the airport, Andrea feels guilty but is sure she is doing the right thing. Worried that someone could be following her, she keeps looking out of the back of the taxi and the drive seems to take an hour even though they arrive in forty minutes. Harry is nervous getting out of the taxi and also when lining up for baggage check in.

'We have no baggage,' Harry says. 'We look like terrorists.'

'It's okay. Stay calm.'

There are only business class seats available and her heart sinks as she thinks of the expense. But luckily the roll of cash in her pocket extends to cover the flights.

They head to the bar in the business lounge to calm Harry down.

'Are you okay?' she says, handing Harry a gin and tonic.

'Yeah but. I think it's just all weird.'

'It will be weird.'

'Are you okay about leaving everything behind?' Harry asks.

'I just want to keep everyone safe. We can't risk going to the safe house to be with the others. I think the only way I can keep them safe is to stay away from them just now.'

'Yeah, I guess. And Max… he thinks you've just gone out to get some clothes from the house.'

'I wrote him a letter.'

'Oh.'

After four hours theovernight flight to the UK is boarding, and they find their comfortable business class seats. For some reason there are a lot of military on the flight, which is a new thing since terrorism became worse. Harry falls asleep straight away, but Andrea is enjoying a full five-course meal as soon as they get into the air. She is finally relaxed.

'*Catch me now*,' she says under her breath as she tucks into her lamb shank and glass of red wine.

Back at the base, Max is updated about the ambush on Highway 95 involving two of his officers and the Philadelphia police. Two men were in a gun fight with the police which resulted in the cartel guys running out of ammo and being arrested. He asks about Andrea and is told that she was dropped off in a lane to keep her safe. His heart sinks. He waits by the phone for the next twenty-four hours until finally, the following day, a letter is dropped at the main gate for him. It's a Parkview Conference Centre envelope, and he opens it with haste, hoping it's from her.

Dear Max,

By the time you get this letter I will be far away. I realised when I went home that it wasn't safe for me in the US. I had my son with me and the cartel wanted to kill us. I have to lay low. Please hold onto these passports for my children and husband. I'll write again when I can.

I'm sorry for not saying goodbye,
Love,
Andrea X

Max falls back in his seat. He is devastated. Just when he was starting to enjoy life, again he falls back into sadness again. He can't cope with things going wrong again, not without some warning. When his wife died it was sudden. Her cancer was too far gone and they had little time to prepare, just six weeks. She had avoided doctors all her life and hid her symptoms. That didn't help with the grieving.

Max walks back to his house even though it is not time to clock-off. He pours himself a large glass of Bourbon and lies down on his bed, bringing the bottle with him. He feels slightly guilty as it's work hours. But also, knew that he should have contacted the police or the FBI earlier, but he wanted more time with Andrea. He wanted her to stay for as long as possible. But now she's gone and he doesn't know where she is or whether she will ever come back.

CHAPTER 19

The Escape

Andrea and Harry arrive at Heathrow London Airport at three p.m. the next day. They get a taxi to go straight to MI5 in the city because Andrea wants to confront her old boss, Patrick. She is going to ask for a different name and new credit cards so she can live undetected by anyone who might be looking for her in the UK. Driving around London, Harry seems to have cheered up. The MI5 building is in the centre of London, and they drive past Buckingham Palace to get there. The taxi drops them off outside and they enter the building on the Thames River. She doesn't have her original ID badge, just a another business card. The security guard calls upstairs and speaks to Patrick. He comes down to meet her at the security desk.

'Heeelllloooo, Andrea.'

'Hi, Patrick,' she says angrily.

'You don't seem happy to see me.'

'Well. It's been a shit show.'

'Yes, indeed but you've been amazing. There's been lots of arrests in the past twenty-four hours.'

'Really?'

'Let's talk upstairs,' he says.

They get into the lift.

'Sorry, this is my son. Harry.'

'Yes, I know. Nice to meet you.'

Andrea rolls her eyes. Once again, people know everything about her.

Harry is amazed by the architecture of the building and the time it takes to get to one of the top floors.

They enter Patrick's office, having walked past some of her old colleagues, who don't recognise her with her red hair and look at her oddly.

'Have a seat and I'll get you up to speed on the case,' he says as if she is still working on it.

He updates her whilst handing her and Harry some Bourbon on the rocks and gives her details of the number of stings involving cartels that they have raided. There have been other restaurants who were using their kitchens in the evening to make drugs, some other children were rescued and some of the ones from the army base are going to be reunited with their families this week. Then there's the fake adoptions. He goes on but Andrea zones out. Sometimes she's interested and sometimes she's not. She feels she has done her part and now wants a nice quiet easy life. She wants 'out'.

'Now, we can set you up with an office and you can work from here on some similar cases. We're not sure if this thing has spilled across the water.'

'Can I just stop you there? I am finished. I don't want this sort of life. I've just escaped the cartel,' she says, trying to compose herself.

'Yes, and very skilfully too, if I may say so.'

'NO,' she yells. 'You put me in a dangerous suburb. You put my children in danger and now I want out!' she yells.

'Oh well.'

'I want a new identity, and safe house, for me, Harry and my kids…'

'Well, Andrea, you're very good at what you do.'

'Or I'll sue.'

Patrick looks shocked.

They argue a bit more and then he gives up and tells her of a safe house in Cornwall, on the west coast of England. He arranges for her to have an MI5 car and says he will get new ID and passports.

She finally relaxes. Harry has nodded off on the sofa in Patrick's office and she wakes him up and says they have a car and house to go to.

'Cool,' he says, in a better mood now.

'I need a gun if I'm even going to consider your offer,' she says to Patrick.

'Arh... I'm not so sure.'

'I'm on the payroll. I'm at risk.'

'Okay. Okay. Go to the staff restaurant downstairs. In about an hour I should have everything you need. I'll come and get you.'

Andrea takes Harry to the office restuarant, and he is in heaven... food everywhere.

'This is great!' he says. 'Is it all free?'

'Not really because you have to risk your life to eat here.'

'I see what you mean.'

Harry is starving as he slept through dinner on the plane. He tucks into some spaghetti Bolognese and garlic bread. Andrea starts to think about the girls. She was busy before and felt guilty about not missing them. But now... being back in London, she realises how far away they now are.

'When do you think the others can come over?' Harry asks.

'You've just read my mind,' Andrea says.

'I could tell you were thinking about them. You looked sad.'

'Mmmmm. Well, they didn't ask for this either.'

He smiles as he tucks into his pasta.

'Where do you think they'll send us to be safe?'

'Cornwall,' she says.

'Great. It's famous. isn't it...? For something...'

'Lots of great things... beaches, clotted cream, pasties, which are like a pie, and ice cream,' she says.

'Sounds like my kinda place.'

'Yes. It's beautiful down there. The scenery is amazing.'

'Did you live there before?'

'No, we lived in North London, but took holidays in Cornwall.'

'And where do your parents live?'

'Oh, Buckinghamshire. I don't want them to know that I'm back. Not yet.'

Patrick find them in the canteen. He has a package in his hands of new passports, credit cards under a different name and some cash.

'What name have you given me?' she says opening the package.

'Olivia Marshall! I guess that's okay,' she says.

'And what's my new name?' Harry asks in an excited voice.

'Stephen... Carpenter... sounds a bit common,' she says to Patrick.

'Look I had to work fast. Here's the keys, and the address for the cottage is inside. My mother actually lives close by so she will settle you in, if there are any issues with hot water or electricity there's her number.'

'Okay. Thanks. And the guns?'

Patrick reaches into his overcoat and pulls out two small handguns.

'Oh, I get one too.'

'Well, you might as well. But let Andrea be in charge of

them.'

'Cool,' Harry says as Andrea puts both guns into her backpack.

'Well… we'll be off then,' says Andrea.

They jump into a shiny black SUV and drive out of the carpark, heading for the M3 motorway.

She doesn't bother to look at the address in the package.

'Doesn't this thing work?' Harry says, trying to turn the sat nav on.

'No, they usually dismantle it.'

'Great. I guess we must go "old school"… with a map of some sort.'

'Yes, we can buy one from a petrol station if there's not one in the boot.'

Harry starts navigating with the map he finds on the back seat, but Andrea doesn't really need his help. She's just trying to take his mind off things. Within a few hours they have passed Salisbury and it is plain sailing from then onwards. Andrea has a feeling she knows where the safe house is anyway. Patrick's mother lives on a farm in between Devon and Cornwall, so she heads in that direction then stops at a petrol station. She fills up the car and buys some bread and canned soup, anything that looks nutritious, from the shelves inside. Jumping back into the car, she notices that Harry is still sleeping, so no chance of light conversation there.

She wonders what could she have done differently. Could she have prevented this from happening? Why did she get involved in the problems in Spring Town? Why didn't she just move? What are normal people doing today… shopping at Selfridges, lunch in Covent Garden?

The cottage is on a farm and, as she had guessed, Patrick's mother has left a note for them, telling them to come up to the house for late supper when they arrive. Andrea's not sure how to break that news to Harry who is still yawning as he enters the lovely stone cottage and nearly bumps his head on an overhead beam.

'We have an invitation for dinner at the main house. Do you want to go?'

'Aren't you tired?' he says.

'Yes, I guess so. I'll go up there and let her know we're not coming.'

Andrea has a quick look around the cottage, claims one of the rooms, and then looks outside to see where the main house is. It's on top of a hill so it is easy to spot. She tells Harry to have some soup and that she'll be back shortly.

The full extent of the house is revealed as she walks towards it. Over each small hill, more "wings" of the house are visible. It must be a half-mile walk, but Andrea is thankful to be out of the car. It is a Georgian house with extra bits added. Very grand. She imagines Patrick growing up here and how he was probably spoilt rotten.

'That's why he thinks he can play with people's lives and send them to dangerous places,' she says out loud.

Arriving at the front of the house, a man opens the door before she has a chance to knock.

'Ms Marshall,' he addresses her with her new name. 'We've been expecting you. I'm Reginald, the Estate Manager.' He leads her into a large reception area.

'Can I take your, ummmm... hoodie?'

'No... well... I'm actually not staying for supper. But thank you. I really need to rest. I just wanted to meet Mrs Stewart and thank her.'

'Of course, you must be exhausted,' he says. 'I have stocked the larder in the cottage with wine and there is a shot gun under the stairs if you should need it.'

'Thank you.'

'You can't be too careful,' he says, as if he knows something. 'There are foxes everywhere on this land.'

'Oh. Thank you.' She's not sure what he really means, whether he knows what Patrick does for a living or not. She wonders if the gun is to kill foxes or for humans.

'Olivia,' someone says from behind the man.

'Hello, Mrs Stewart, I'm afraid I'm in no fit state for supper. It's been a long journey and a difficult few days. Thank you so much for letting me stay here.'

'Not at all. Call me Veronique. And you've met Reginald... All of Patrick's friends arrive here saying that they are exhausted. I'm never sure if they are jet lagged or overworked, or both!'

Andrea just smiles, not knowing if she knows what Patrick does for a living either.

'Well, let us know if you need anything. There is a computer with Internet in the library if you need to work. There's no Wi-Fi in the cottage I'm afraid,' she says. 'And your son... is he with you?'

'Oh, yes. Stephen.'

'He may like to do some clay pigeon shooting with Reginald some time?'

'Lovely. That sounds lovely,' Andrea says as if she is back where people talk about normal things, like country sports and not drug trafficking.

'Okay well. We'll say goodnight. If you need to call us, you just pick up the phone and dial 123. Patrick had it installed for guests.'

'Thank you.'

'You're welcome, goodnight.'

'Goodnight.'

Andrea walks back to the cottage feeling relieved. In twenty-four hours, she's managed to avoid bullets from a drug cartel and a supper with two strangers. She's now desperate for a hot shower and a tin of soup.

The scenery is lovely in Cornwall, and she takes it all in on the walk back, which seems to take longer than the journey to the house. The grass is long and she whooshes through it in her army pants. It makes her think of her few days in the army, wearing other people's clothes, and she thinks of Max and how handsome he is. She wonders if he has got the letter yet and what his reaction will be. It has been years since a man looked at her. She knew she would miss him and now feels sad returning to the cottage.

Harry seems to be up and awake. He's cooking an omelette from some eggs he found in the fridge.

She starts to worry that they will be on different time clocks. He'll be awake, making noise in the cottage, while she's trying to sleep. Andrea says goodnight and goes to find the shower. Harry has plans of his own and intends to stay up all night keeping watch.

CHAPTER 20

The New Life

Andrea and Harry enjoy lying low in their new location. They're not in the mood for socialising and are enjoying doing nothing. One morning there's a knock on the door and a letter is put through the post hole. It's a letter from London so Andrea hastily opens it. There is another envelope inside which says, 'Please forward to Olivia Marshall'. She opens it and doesn't recognise the handwriting. She flicks through the several pages to see that it is from Max. Her heart starts to beat quickly and then she panics. He tracked her down so swiftly that he resembles some sort of desperate stalker. She reads the letter.

Dear Andrea,

I hope you don't mind me writing to you. I have so much to tell you and wanted to keep you updated. George checked the flights and so I have a clue as to where you've gone. I thought that if I write to you at MI5, they will be kind enough to pass this letter on to you, being British and all that!

George said you hadn't been in touch with your family, so he has given me an update for you. The girls are ok being home schooled by someone from the FBI. They are not allowed Internet access for a while longer. Greg has been hostile to the FBI liaison staff because he wanted his phone and they refused. The boy who was with them, Luke, or Samual, has been reunited with his family. There is apparently a rabbit that is keeping the girls occupied.

Apart from that, there were more arrests. The two men that you and my officers lured into a trap had mobile phones on them that proved very useful as evidence of contacts and could place them at certain properties on certain dates. Caroline has been charged with the murders of the headmaster, the teacher/cop who died in the pool, and of the attempted murder of Natalie Bellino, who is now doing much better.

There is more news about the adoption agency. It has been taken over by the FBI for the time being. There is a long list of women who thought their babies had died who are now being told that they are alive, but they can't see them for the time being, as they have been adopted... it's complicated.

This must sound very morbid even though it's good news. I hope everything is good with you and that you now feel safe. I think the FBI want your family to stay put for the time being until they are sure they have arrested everyone.

I also just wanted to say that I really enjoyed your company. It was great to meet you. You are an amazing woman and I wish you every success in the future. I hope it all works out for you Andrea, I really do.

All the best,
Max X

Jesus. He's slightly devastated, she thinks. She holds the paper up to her lips and smells it, remembering the times they spent together, eating his lovely cooking. She wasn't used to a man taking her seriously. Greg had always thought that all her opinions and ideas were ridiculous. He made her feel that she wouldn't be able to work in a 'higher' position at MI5 because she had so many wild thoughts! He's probably hating all the credit she has had since the arrests. His life has been put on hold because of something she uncovered, and she has the FBI working on it day and night. *He must hate that,* she thinks. She decides to write back to Max via the MI5 post, to avoid being traced.

Dear Max,

Thank you for the letter. I <u>was</u> wondering how everyone was. I am so grateful to you and the army for taking such good care of us. I felt like I was in limbo there and it was a nice place to be for a while.

I guess I must think about what to do with my life now and where to stay. I think the USA is not for me and neither is fieldwork.

I enjoyed your company and your cooking. It was nice to have a friend when I needed one.

Look after yourself

Love

Andrea X

A few weeks go by of just normal boring life in Cornwall and Andrea loves it. She's finally getting to know Harry and they have endless days to spend with each other without having to draw a weapon. They go into the town to get groceries regularly and enjoy chatting to the locals. Harry tries his hand at clay pigeon shooting, which he excels in, and Andrea often sits in the garden of the cottage and reads. She's wondering how long she will lie low and what she will do in the future for money. One day, Patrick's mother comes down to visit her with a message from Patrick.

'Helloooo, Olivia,' she says. Andrea still can't get used to the name. 'I have a message for you from Patrick. He's wondering about the job offer and whether you have considered it.'

'Oh, umm, not really. I think ummm...'

'Take your time, dear. Don't let him rush you. You are welcome here. Stay as long as you like and decide what you want to do. Women have more options these days. It wasn't like that in my day.'

'Thank you, Veronique. Would you like some tea?'

'Well, yes, if I'm not disturbing you?'

'No, not at all.'

Veronique sits down at the small round kitchen table and looks around to see if everything is as she left it.

'Is Earl Grey okay?'

'Yes, lovely.'

'I've just been enjoying being here so much, Veronique, that I've forgotten that it's not real life.'

'Go on,' she says.

'Well. My other children are elsewhere, and I can't join them yet until I know that we will all be safe,' Andrea says, trying to gauge how much Veronique knows.

'Andrea... oh... Olivia... oh fuck,' Veronique says, then looks embarrassed at Andrea.

'Oh, so you know?'

'Yes. I've hosted many a fugitive in my time. Patrick only sends me the ones that he thinks I will get on with. Since my husband died, it's just me and the gardener, odd-jobs man...Im not sure what to call him.. I don't really like having staff because you can't really trust anyone. It took me years to trust Reginald'

'Quite right,' Andrea says.

'How do you know if you look at an advert in "The Lady" that the au pair looking for a job is not going to slit your throat and bury you in the back garden?'

Andrea giggles.

'I always thought it was weird how people would employ just any old stranger to be a nanny.'

'To look after their prized possessions,' Andrea says.

'Yes, quite. We kept Patrick at home here. He didn't go to boarding school. He went to the local comprehensive school and I looked after him myself.'

'Really?'

'Yes, you would never know. The things they teach them at boarding school, how to behave, which fork to use, how to speak, we taught him that. It also saved us a lot of money.'

Andrea smiles at her.

'So, you have two girls, I hear.'

Andrea is wondering what else she knows. 'Yes, they are in the US with their father. They can't come here until some more people have been arrested.'

'Really? That must be worrying for you. It does sound fascinating though, your work. Patrick gives me snippets, but he's not supposed to tell me anything.' She gulps down her tea as if a hurry. 'I worked for the government during the war. That's how I met my husband. I guess Patrick has it in his blood, you know... secret service... Oh fuck, I forgot, Reginald is giving me a lift to town. Do you want anything?'

'No. Thank you.'

'What about a watercolour set?'

'Pardon?'

'Everyone paints here. Do you want to have a go? It's really relaxing. Or some books to read.'

'Ummmmm.'

'Watercolours it is then,' Veronique decides, as she gets up from her chair and rushes out the door.

Harry wakes up when he hears gun shots going off from a distance.

'Tell me it's shooting season and not a drug cartel,' he says.

'It's just shot guns, Harry. Go back to sleep if you like.'

'You know I never thought I'd say this but I'm kinda getting sick of doing nothing,' Harry moans.

'Really?'

'Well, when I used to do nothing, I always had a computer to search or play games on. You know… not just nothing…'

'I'll have a think. Veronique is buying me some watercolours.'

'Can you paint?

'I used to, years ago, at school,' Andrea replies.

'Ummm, well, can she come up with a hobby for me?'

'After she comes back from town, why don't you ask her if there is any work to be done around the house or on the land?'

'Oh… umm…'

'Come on, Harry. It will be good for you and Reginald seems nice. I think he could teach you some general DIY stuff.'

'Great. Speaking of guns and old people, I wonder how Muriel and Arnold are doing?'

'Yes, I hope they are okay.'

'They were sooooo interesting,' he says.

'Yes, there have been some arrests apparently. I got an update from Max.'

'Great. So, we'll be showing our faces a bit more.'

'Soon,' she says.

'I bet Arnold moved into Muriel's house.'

'Yes,'

'They've probably been hard at it ever since.' Harry says, laughing.

The next two weeks are filled with Andrea trying to capture the Stewarts' estate in watercolours and Harry learning to chop wood, mend fences, and cut grass. Andrea is out the front of the main house one day with her watercolour kit when a car pulls up. Apprehensive, she pulls her shawl over her head as if to appear like an old lady.

'Andrea,' a voice says. It's Patrick stepping out of his sporty Jaguar.

'Oh... Hi... I'm just,' Andrea says, feeling embarrassed that she's trying to paint.

'She does that to everyone, forces watercolours on them. No need to explain. How are you?'

'Oh, much more relaxed,' she says remembering how she threatened to sue him if he didn't give her a gun.

'How are they treating you otherwise?'

'Oh, it's lovely here... and your mother has been so nice.'

'Yes, I'm sure. She's usually trying to marry me off to any woman living in the cottage. But as you're already married... I'm guessing she hasn't tried that on yet.'

'No.' Andrea looks a bit puzzled. She's not really interested in Patrick's love life. 'Are you here for the weekend?'

'Yes, but mainly to tell you in person that your family are on their way over.'

'Really?'

'Yes. They were escorted to the airport this morning so should be here by this evening.'

'Oh my God,' she says, putting her hands on her face. 'It's over. It's finally over,' she yells.

248

'Normality returns,' says Patrick, who is obviously lying.

Andrea sheds a tear.

'I must say I'm really sorry, Andrea,' he says, standing in front of her. 'But you'd always gone on about doing fieldwork. Then you wanted to leave, and I thought it's because I didn't give you a chance here. So, I gave you a chance over there. I thought you'd be pleased.'

'Well… I guess it was kinda nice being called Agent Mitchell for a while.'

'And you can be again…'

'Oh, no. I'd like to live down here in Cornwall and do some remote working for MI5. You know I would like data work or something.'

He looks disappointed but says, 'I'm sure that will be fine.'

She looks at him and realises that Patrick looks quite nice out of his suit. They walk past Harry chopping wood and go into the house to see Veronique.

'Come on, Harry, I've bought cakes,' Patrick says.

He drops the axe and rushes in behind them.

Sitting in the library having tea and cakes, Andrea thinks how she could easily live there. She would just have to divorce Greg and marry Patrick. Would she like that though? Would he be interested? *What does he look like with his clothes off?* she thinks. Then she realises that she must be getting desperate.

Andrea suddenly realises that she hasn't asked him about Greg. He says he is on his way over with the girls. *Greg won't want to stay in the UK,* she thinks. She shudders with the thought of the showdown that is bound to happen when Greg gets here. There's so much to prepare that she can't concentrate on the conversation. Veronique notices that the blood starts to drain from Andrea's face.

'Andrea, are you okay?'

'Yes, it's just been exhausting… the problems in the US, the escape to get here. I think I was running on adrenaline,' she explains.

'Andrea, when we went through the war here, people often became exhausted. Sometimes, there was no hope, no food, and bombs going off over our heads. As a child living in London, I was packed off and sent to live out here in Cornwall. When my mother came to collect me, she decided to stay. There was a happy ending. I grew up here and met Patrick's father and had a happy life.'

'I must sound very delicate.'

'Not at all, Andrea. What I am trying to say is that there are happy endings, and you have yours. You are here now, and your family will arrive, and you will make changes in your life.'

'Yes. Thank you,' she says humbly. 'I need to look to the future.'

'You are jetlagged though and I think Harry should walk you back to the cottage. Have a nap and you will be fresh for when your children arrive tonight at seven p.m.,' said Patrick.

Andrea is relieved. She gets flashes of bad things every now and then which seem to depress her mood, her bad marriage, the cartel chasing her and the children lying around nearly dead in the barn. It's all going around in her head from time to time and won't let her carry on with normal life.

They walk back to the cottage with Andrea leaning on Harry with her arm around his neck.

'I'm gonna be kinda jealous,' Harry moans.

'What do you mean?'

'Well, when the girls get here. I guess I'll be jealous of

them.'

'Why?'

'I've had you all to myself, haven't I?'

'Harry… that's silly.'

'Yeah, I know. I really want to see the girls, they're awesome.'

'Don't be jealous. You're a part of this family and they love you. I've tried to spread the love evenly.'

He laughs. 'Spread the love! That's a comment from the sixties.'

'I'm not that old.'

'They'll have so much to tell us. What they've been doing, what it's been like living under FBI protection,' Andrea says.

'I bet they loved it,' Harry says.

'Yes, but they probably gave them hell, playing jokes on them,' says Andrea. Then they both laugh.

Harry carries Andrea for the last bit of the walk. As they enter the cottage, he lays her on the sofa to rest. Harry looks around the cottage for the two guns that Patrick gave them. He finds the shotgun under the cupboard stairs and sees the box of cartridges on a shelf.

'That could be useful,' he says out loud.

The cottage ceilings are so low that he has hit his head a few times since they arrived.

Feeling bored, he decides to pass the time with some shooting. He sneaks past Andrea with the shot gun and cartridges and walks away from the cottage so that the blasts will not wake her.

Walking down the road, he hides the shotgun in his coat and finds a neighbouring field to practise his shooting. *There should be no people in the sky*, he thinks to himself so it should be okay to shoot at birds. Finding a nice place in the grass, he lies on his back and looks up at the sky and sees birds flying past. He doesn't pick up his gun. He just lies there. There are people talking in the distance and laughing. Harry is curious and wants to find them. He gets up. Walking towards the noise, he sees tents. There are families eating and cooking on a barbeque and children playing. He watches them from a distance, hiding behind the trees. He sits there for ages, fascinated, people watching; it is one of his hobbies. He likes to watch the way people talk to each other, he decides who is in charge, who is dominant, who is frightened of the other. He sits there for ages but doesn't know how long, as he doesn't have his old mobile phone any more.

He decides to walk back, in case Andrea is worried and finds her in the kitchen boiling the kettle.

'Oh, hi,' Andrea says. 'You've been shooting,' she says nervously, hoping he hasn't shot someone's foot off.

'Not really.'

'What do you mean?'

'Well, I went shooting but didn't really want to kill birds. Does that make sense?'

'Yes.'

'There's been too much killing recently.'

'Yes, there has.'

'I might even go vegetarian!' Harry announces.

'There's no need to take drastic action.'

'I'm just kidding.'

As Harry and Andrea walk back up to the house just before seven p.m., they're wondering if the girls will arrive on time. Driving past them is an army car. It doesn't stop as it wouldn't be able to see them walking in the field. Her heart races. Andrea and Harry run to the house. As they get there, panting, they see the girls getting out of the army car. The driver walks up to the house and rings the doorbell.

The girls turn around as Andrea is calling their names as she is running. The driver turns around.

'Mum,' says Sophie.

'Mummy,' says Alice.

Andrea catches up to them at the front of the house. She is bent over trying to catch her breath. The girls run over to her. They hug and stay hugging for several minutes. Harry stands back and waits then joins in with a group hug.

Andrea feels someone looking at her and thinks that it must be Greg, in the car. He probably doesn't want to get out. She is waiting for him to say, 'I'll be in the hotel down the road,' as he used to when they went camping. She is too scared to look up but takes a big breath and looks towards the car to face him. He is not there, just an army official.

'Where is Dad?' she asks the girls.

'Oh, he got a taxi from the army base in Middlesex. He's going into London. It's fine, Mum. We nearly drove him mad,' says Sophie.

'Yeah, we flew in an army plane. It was great,' adds Alice, excitedly.

'Oh,' she says, puzzled but relieved.

'Where did he go in London?'

'He's going to stay with a friend and sent us down here with Max.'

'Max?' She looks up and the driver standing at the door, now talking to Patrick, is actually Max.

Her heart stops a beat. She smiles and walks over to them, with the girls still attached.

'Max!' she says, startled.

'Hello, Andrea.'

'Thank you. You didn't have to come all this way.'

'Well. I volunteered. I knew you would be missing them.'

'Oh yes.'

There's an awkward silence and then Veronique comes outside and ushers everyone in for supper. The girls see Harry and call over to him.

Max wants to talk to Andrea, but he cannot get past the girls.

They sit down at the long dining room table and Andrea can't take her eyes off the girls. They sit one each side of her and Harry sits opposite. He is happy to see the girls.

They are still holding each of her hands at the dinner table and are talking non-stop.

From the chit-chat between Patrick and Max at the table, it is clear that they know each other.

'Patrick and I go way back,' Max says.

'Where did you meet?' Andrea asks, with the girls holding her hands so tight she can barely concentrate.

'Oh, in the army,' Patrick replies.

Andrea can't remember Patrick saying anything about being in the army.

Max is looking particularly handsome as Andrea can just see him above the huge candelabra adorning the long antique table.

'Mum… the safe house was greeeeaaatt…' says Sophie.

'You're probably the only person who has uttered that sentence,' says Patrick.

'And, Mummm… you were like a legend among the FBI,' says Alice.

'Really?' Andrea says, trying not to smile.

'They kept saying Agent Mitchell this, Agent Mitchell that…'

'Did you really find all the children, Mum?' asks Sophie.

'Yes… in a barn.'

'And did Muriel kill any more people?'

'No.'

'Max said you stayed at the army barracks?'

'Yes.'

'How fun… Did you see any weapons?'

'Only ones pointed at us,' Harry pipes up. Andrea looks at him and mouths the words, *No. Don't.*

'There were loads of books to read at the Safe House and that kept Dad busy,' Alice says.

'Great.'

'Also, board games,' Sophie adds.

'We studied the FBI agents that stayed at the house with us,' explains Alice.

'What do you mean you studied them?'

'Yes, there was no Internet, so we had to amuse ourselves,' Sophie says.

'How dreadful,' Harry says.

'So, we devised a questionnaire,' says Alice.

'Yes, we had this theory that FBI agents all have to have similar personality traits.'

'But we were wrong.'

'Really?' says Harry.

'Yes, there are two types of FBI Agent personalities.'

'Yes. The nerd type which we called *Ubi Vermis Libre*, that's Latin for bookworm.'

'And the jock type which we called *Musculus,* Latin for muscles. But we found that none of them had played American football at college. The jocks were mostly track and field enthusiasts.'

'How much Latin do you girls know?' asks Harry, who is

getting slightly jealous.

'I know some important words to get by,' explains Sophie.

'Like what?' he asks again.

'Um… *Canis in calorem*, which means, the dog is on heat.'

'*Tu es mea vera mater, non*… You're not my real mother.'

'*Et purgata e me heri locus*… I cleaned my room yesterday.'

'*Ego postulo magis sinum pecuniam*… I need more pocket money.'

'What other languages do you girls know?'

'French and Spanish,' Sophie says.

The girls are in an excitable mood and keep talking over everyone. Andrea can't take it all in. The girls are home! Finally! She's hoping they will behave themselves at the dinner table. One of Veronique's dogs comes wandering in and the girls start acting up.

'Oh, how lovely… We need some pets, Mummy,' says Alice.

'Pets are basically prisoners though,' says Sophie.

'Oh God,' groans Andrea. 'Don't start, darling.'

'They are, and they don't know it, which is weird,' Alice says, and Veronique laughs.

'Think about it,' says Sophie. 'Dogs are on a lead. Their exercise and play time is scheduled. They are given the same plain food every day. They only mate or socialise when it's supervised.'

'And their babies are sold,' Alice says.

'Their liberties have been taken away, which is what happens when you go to prison,' adds Sophie.

'Cats are free though,' says Alice. 'But in a sort of open prison. They come and go. They could easily run away but they know their lives will be worse if they leave the open prison.'

Max chuckles and Patrick can see how similar the girls are to Andrea who always has an opinion and is not afraid to express it.

'I think cats adapt, become institutionalised,' Alice says, as the conversation continues.

'Birds know when they are in prison though, because the cage gives it away,' says Max, trying to join in.

The girls laugh.

'Do you think they sit there and wonder *why did I get life?*' says Harry, joining in. He's now remembering how much fun the girls can be.

'Fish figure it out, they keep hitting their heads on the glass tank,' says Patrick.

'They revolt and eat their cell mate,' says Veronique, as this has become the topic for dinner conversation.

'What about snakes?' Max says, as he has become fascinated by the girls after their long trip across the pond.

'They enjoy being captured because they are planning to one day eat their captor,' says Sophie.

'Yes,' Max says. 'I read about a snake that kept lying on its owner's bed and she thought it was being friendly. But apparently they do that to measure themselves up against their owner so they know when they will be big enough to swallow them wholeone day.'

'Ahhh.' The girls laugh out loud.

'What about mice?' Veronique says. 'Do they know they are prisoner when they are being kept as pets?'

'I think so,' says Alice, 'because they run and run on a wheel thing and never get anywhere. They know they have been duped.'

'What about rabbits?' asks Harry. The girls look over at him sadly.

'Sorry, Harry. We gave Thelma to an FBI agent who had children. We didn't want to put her through the flight and quarantine,' Sophie adds.

'She was becoming frightened, I think. I think she knew Dad

didn't like her,' explains Alice.

'Why didn't he like her?' asks Harry.

'Because she was shitting everywhere.'

'Alice!'

'Sorry. She was defecating everywhere. You hadn't toilet trained her.'

Harry looks confused as if he didn't know that was his responsibility or that it was even possible.

'One day, Daddy sat on a chair, and it had been defecated on,' explains Sophie.

'Yes, Thelma could have won a prize for defecation,' says Alice.

'Okay. Okay,' Andrea says as she tries to calm them down even though everyone is enjoying the conversation.

Max smiles at Andrea. Veronique smiles and mouths the word *lovely*. As if she thinks the girls are lovely.

'I think we should get some new pets though,' Andrea says, as if she's trying to tell them that they will be settling in the UK.

'Prisoners. Mummy. Prisoners,' says Sophie.

'Whatever. I think some dogs would be good.'

'We can name them Fred and Ginger after two of the FBI agents,' suggests Alice.

Andrea laughs.

'Are we safe now, Mummy?' asks Sophie.

'Yes, I think so. And we're together finally.'

'Yes, well, almost...,' says Sophie, referring to Greg who seems to have left them.

The girls decide that this is a good time to tell everyone about the attempted kidnapping back in Spring Town.

'Oh, Mummy, I didn't tell you that I had tested out my taser,'

Sophie says.

'WHAT!

'Well, ha man had hold of Alice and…'

'WHAT! WHEN?'

'When you saw us running down the road near the school that day.'

'What on earth?'

'He grabbed Alice.'

'Grabbed her?'

'Well, put a hand on her shoulder. So, I didn't want to take any chances and…'

'You tasered him? What happened?'

'He went' She demonstrates a person convulsing. 'And we ran off.'

Veronique finds the whole conversation riveting. Harry is trying not to laugh as Sophie keeps convulsing whenever Andrea is not looking her way.

'Why didn't you tell me?' Andrea asks.

'We were too pooped from the running,' says Sophie.

'And then it kinda became old news,' explains Alice.

'Where is the taser now? Actually, I don't want to know.'

Patrick pipes up to change the subject and says, 'If you girls ever want to work at MI5, give me a call.'

The girls giggle.

Andrea doesn't want to hear any more. It's all so surreal. One minute her life has changed upside down; the next minute, she's back in the UK in sleepy Cornwall and the girls are chatting away as usual. But she's glad she doesn't have to bother writing any more letters to Max because he is sitting there looking gorgeous and trying to catch her eye.

Max smiles at her across the table as if he knows what she's thinking.

'So, Max, you met my husband,' she says, with a gulp in her throat.

'Yes, we talked.'

'Talked? About what?' she asks, with a slight panic in her voice.

'Oh… things…'

Andrea suspects Max has said something about the fling they had which is why Greg has gone to London.

'He didn't want to come here to stay with your boss. He's still annoyed about the way you were kind of sent to Spring Town,' Max says.

Patrick sinks down in his chair.

'Well, that's all over now,' Andrea says.

Andrea is annoyed that Greg is in London, but glad at the same time. She didn't like hearing that from someone else. *Bloody Greg*, she thinks, making everything about him. Constantly wanting attention. *Well, he won't get it this time…* Andrea decides.

They finish their dinner, and the girls are told they can go and have a look around the big house.

Harry follows them to supervise, and the others take their drinks out on the veranda. After much small talk, Andrea is finally alone with Max so she can have a normal conversation.

'I'm stalking you,' he says in a joking way.

'Yes, I see. But thank you. Delivering my children to me in person. What can I say?'

'Your letter was a bit sterile. Considering we kissed and slept on the sofa together,' Max complains gently.

'Sterile?' she says just as Patrick returns to the veranda with brandy for them.

'Who's sterile?' Patrick says. 'I thought you had children, Max.'

They all laugh.

'Andrea. I think you should start using the Internet again. I'll set up accounts for you all. I think you are safe.'

'Oh. Thank you.' She looks at Patrick as if she is grateful and Max looks a bit jealous.

'How long will you stay here, Andrea?' Max asks.

'Oh, there's no rush,' Patrick jumps in.

'Do you have another secret assignment for her?' Max says sarcastically.

'No. She has decided to stay with us but avoid the fieldwork. I'm sure she will be very useful.'

'Can I work remotely then? Can I stay in Cornwall?'

'Of course,' Patrick confirms.

Max looks sad. Cornwall is a long way from Philadelphia.

Patrick can sense the chemistry in the air between Max and Andrea and decides to help his mother in the kitchen.

Andrea and Max look at each other not knowing what to say. He reaches down and holds her hand. She moves forward and rests her head on his chest.

'It is soooo good that you're here,' she says.

'Is it?' he asks.

'Yes.'

The evening ends when the girls fall asleep on the sofas in another room. Harry comes in to tell Veronique that they just collapsed and are fast asleep. Max drives into town where he is staying at a local hotel. Harry walks Andrea back to the cottage and they retire for the evening.

'You like him, don't you? You got on well at the army base?' Harry grins.

'Yes, we did get on well.'

'And where the hell is Greg? I'm sorry, but I don't like him,' Harry says.

'I'm starting to hate him. Is that too strong a word?' Andrea confesses.

'No.'

'He should have delivered the girls to me. Not just jump in a taxi the first chance he got.'

'Yeah. What an arse!'

'Do you think we should live down here, Harry? Is it too quiet for you? We could go house hunting? Andrea asks

'Cool. Yeah… anything away from the crazies.'

'Who are the crazies?

'City folk. I prefer the country.'

'You sound like you belong here,' she laughs.

'Yeah. It's kinda like Canada but the weather is better.'

'Jeez. I've never heard anyone say the weather is better in England.'

They retire for the evening.

In the morning, Andrea phones the big house to see if the girls are up. Veronique says she will entertain them if they wake up, so Harry and Andrea go straight down to the estate agents.

Looking through the estate agent's windows, she remembers doing that when she was younger. Now everyone uses the Internet, and they don't leave their house. She peers past a photo to see a man sitting inside that looks like Max.

'Shit,' she says.

'What?' Harry asks.

'Max is in there and I think he saw me staring at him.'

'Really?'

'Yes, really. Is he going to live here?'

'Would that be a bad thing?' Harry asks.

'He used to tell me that he was retiring and was looking for a place to settle down. He said the army reminded him too much

262

of his wife.' Andrea starts to panic.

Does that mean he wants a relationship? She thinks.

'Let's go before he spots us,' suggests Harry, as Andrea is starting to freak out. They walk down to the beach and sit on a bench. Harry goes to a van and buys bacon sandwiches, or "Bacon Butties" as he is told by the van guy.

'Harry, it's been lovely spending time together. I'll try to give you just as much time even though the girls are here now.'

'Oh, Andrea, don't worry so much. I'm stoked that the girls are here. We're going to have so much fun. They're so cool.'

'Yes.'

'I'm just glad we're here and we're all in one piece,' says Harry.

'Shit. There's Max. Here he comes.' Andrea says.

'Andrea... Harry... Lovely morning.'

'Yes. You're up early,' Andrea says nervously.

'It's the army training.'

'I meant to ask last night. How long are you staying?' she says, in a distant manner.

'Oh, I'm just doing some sightseeing and I have some business in London tomorrow too, then I'll catch an army plane early tomorrow evening.'

There's an awkward silence.

'Well, I'll see you later,' he says, as the conversation doesn't really take off. He decides to walk away.

'MAX,' Harry yells out, as if to help these love birds along. 'I saw you in the estate agent's. You going to retire here?' Harry yells.

'Oh, ummm, well. I might.'

'Yes, do,' Andrea says, then blushes.

'Well, the houses are lovely and it's so peaceful down here,' Max says awkwardly.

'It's something for you to think about then,' Andrea says, trying not to appear too eager.

'Yes,' he says trying not to smile too wide.

'You guys are hopeless. Do I have to do all your match-making for you?' Harry whispers.

Andrea blushes.

Max turns and walks away. She watches him and Harry watches her dazed expression. *He looks much younger in civilian clothes. He looks like a 'hot' Dad at a school sports day. The sort that all the mothers would be swooning over*, Andrea thinks.

Max wanders along the street and tries not to trip over the cobbles and eventually he is out of sight.

'This could be serious,' Andrea says.

'You're in love, Mum.'

'I don't even know him so that worries me. That I might just be in love with him because he has a uniform.'

'But he's a nice guy and you got to know him too,' Harry reassures.

'I'm not sure if he is slightly weird.'

'Well, that would be a change from being *totally* weird, like Greg.'

'Yeah, I guess.'

The next few weeks are difficult for Andrea. She is catching up with the girls, who prefer to sleep in the big bedroom in the main house, as there's no space in the cottage, and she has had tense phone conversations with Greg over the phone. She broached the subject of Greg maybe not living with them any more and the girls are fine about it. Sophie said he was throwing things around in the safe house back in the USA. They got a bit scared. That fuelled another argument between Andrea and Greg, and she demanded some money to buy a house down there. They need to sell their house in the USA but Greg plans to go back there to live, as he has managed to hold on to his job. With the financial side of things looking difficult, Patrick loans Andrea some money to put a deposit on a house in Cornwall. She knows she could get more if she sues him but doesn't want to start a war with the only family that they know down there.

After six weeks, they move out of the Veronique's place and into a lovely three bedroom detached with a large garden. It's not too close to the beach and shops, but walkable. The girls settle into the local school and make friends. Andrea stays home working on some data for Patrick. Harry is also given a similar job by Patrick, and he has given them both new laptops. Veronique drives her jeep down to meet them once a week for lunch and fills them in on the gossip in the town. Andrea goes to a book club one evening each week and the girls have joined a tennis club. Harry looks around for hobbies and gets to know some of the young locals one day who are scanning the beach with metal detectors. He brings back his treasures to show Andrea and describe how old each "artefact" is.

One night at book club, the organiser, Jan, goes to the door, says they have a new member that has come to join them. Max walks in! He doesn't see Andrea straight away but then does and tries to compose himself. He holds his hand out to her and says, 'Hi, I'm Max.'

She smiles and says, 'Hi, I'm Olivia.'

'What a lovely name,' he jests.

She blushes.

'Have you just moved here?' she asks.

'Yes. I'd been researching to find a place where there is very little crime and lots of lovely people to meet.'

'Yes. It's a good suburb… village… I mean…'

'Yes. That's what I hear.'

They watch each other whilst trying to take part in the book

265

club conversation. After it is over, she leaves swiftly only so he can follow her, and they can be alone. She hardly makes it down the path outside Jan's house before he grabs her and kisses her.

She kisses him back.

'Olivia. I hope you don't think I'm stalking you.'

'A little stalking can be a good thing. I feel sorry for people who have never been stalked,' she jokes.

They laugh and he walks her home.

Over the next few weeks, they see each other, and she often sleeps over, walking back to her cottage before the girls wake up for school. Harry catches her one morning.

'Is that the walk of shame?' he says, knowing where she had been because he was on babysitting duty.

'It is!' she says.

'Excellent,' Harry replies.

It had taken a long time, but Andrea had finally found contentment. She was no longer hoping to be somewhere else, or with someone else or in a different job. Everything was here, all her kids under one roof, her lovely Cornish life and home and her new man living down the road. There was nothing more that she wanted.